NIGHTMARE VISION

The figure had come floating slowly out of the fog, reaching for him, the mouth in the rotting face twisted into an ugly grin which exposed black stumps of teeth, the empty eye sockets glowing, seeking him out.

He had drawn back from it, kicking desperately for wakefulness like a drowning man kicking for the surface high above him.

A hand reached for him, drawing closer and closer.

I'm asleep, a voice told him, I'm asleep and I must wake up.

He had kicked violently, thrashing towards wakefulness, twisting his body away from the finger which descended towards his chest.

A dream. That was all it had been.

Wasn't it?

Then his eyes were drawn remorselessly around and up, towards the corner of the room to the left of his bed.

And it had been there.

Hovering near the ceiling. Watching him.

It had spoken then. In a voice that sounded like a dying man whispering.

"Next time you sleep you will be mine."

That was when he screamed.

W9-APT-910

THE UNHOLY

Michael Falconer Anderson

ST. MARTIN'S PRESS/NEW YORK

Library of Congress Catalog Card Number: 87-4412

ISBN: 0-312-90976-4

Printed in the United States of America

First St. Martin's Press mass market edition/April 1988

10 9 8 7 6 5 4 3 2 1

PROLOGUE

He saw it now as he waited at the bare kitchen table. Waited knowing that in ten minutes it would all be over. Knowing that then he would be able to sleep.

He saw it for a split second as he blinked. A horrible, cadaverous, putrid thing, its flesh hanging in jagged, rag-covered strips, its empty eye sockets glowing.

It seemed to grin at him in that instant as if to say: I'm still here. I'm still waiting for you to sleep. Then you're all mine. There is no escape. Eventually you have to sleep.

He slammed his right hand down on the table and glared at the two men playing cards at another table in the corner of the room.

Hans, tall and lean with an iron-grey crewcut, dropped his cards and half rose out of his chair. Joachim, a six-feet block of solid muscle, jerked his head around. They both stared at Kininsky.

'Idiots,' he bawled, his bloodshot eyes shifting from one to the other. 'Idiots. What am I paying you for? I might have been asleep and then. . . .'

His eyes dropped to the blank table surface.

'And then. . . .'

After a moment he heard the tread of shoes crossing the floor. He looked up and saw Hans lowering himself into a chair beside him.

'We won't let you sleep, Herr Kininsky. We *were* watching you.'

'I'm sorry,' Kininsky mumbled, 'I'm sorry.'

An apology. From Erwin Kininsky. From West Berlin's number one fixer, the man who feared nothing east or west of the wall, north or south of hell itself. Hans threw a glance across the room at Joachim, raised his eyebrows and shrugged. Joachim returned the shrug. What words could pass between them? How could they guess at what had caused this to happen to Erwin Kininsky? He had told them nothing. Only that they must keep him awake no matter what.

'My eyes must never close, no matter what the circumstances, day or night,' he had told them four days before. 'In a few days a man will come to my apartment for this box.' He nodded to the box then, a curt nod, almost a twitch. 'After that everything will be all right.'

Since then, Hans and Joachim had slept in shifts, one remaining at Kininsky's side at all times, shaking his shoulder if his head slumped forward or his eyes became glassy or if he showed any other sign, no matter how slight, of dozing off.

'It is five to three,' Hans said, touching Kininsky's shoulder. 'Your visitor will be here at three.'

Kininsky raised his eyes from the table and swayed in his chair. How beautiful sleep would be, how absolutely, wonderfully beautiful. But he couldn't . . . It would be waiting for him . . .

'Yes, yes, five to three,' he said like a man in a trance.

He stood up, gripped the table edge then turned awkwardly towards the door, heading for the bathroom.

On his way out of the room he passed the box which stood on top of a cupboard in the corner. It was metal, about a foot high and eight inches square at the base. A large padlock held the lid closed. It seemed to draw his eyes like a magnet but he fought off the powerful impulse to look at it.

He knew what had caused the nightmare which had engulfed his life. It was *that*. He had started referring to the contents of the box as *that* four days before when the *thing* had first come to him in his sleep. Even in his daydreaming he never allowed himself to think of the contents of the box. *That* was what had brought the nightmare. When *that* was gone the nightmare would be gone. Then he would be safe. Wouldn't he?

Hans followed him as he shuffled along the hall and turned into the bathroom. In the mirror above the sink he studied his face. It was as if he had aged ten years in four days. Hideous red veins trailed across his sunken eyeballs. The usually ruddy complexion of his face had been replaced by a deathly grey and the skin seemed to sag on the bones which supported it. The trenches under his eyes were almost black and the lines which ran out of them, usually fine, slender laughter-lines, had become harsh, deep slits.

He ran a hand over the thick, gingery stubble on his chin and thought about what it would be like to be clean-shaven. But he knew he dare not shave. His hands twitched and trembled too much for that and there was no electric shaver in the apartment.

Lethargically he squeezed a gob of toothpaste onto a toothbrush and began to clean his teeth. That helped a little. He replaced the toothbrush and half filled the sink with warm water.

It was as he bent over and began to splash water up into his face that he instinctively closed his eyes.

Instantly the *thing* was there again. The rotting half-human face with its empty glowing eye sockets was thrust close up to his.

He lurched backwards, snatched his eyes open and grabbed the sink to steady himself. He was trembling violently when Hans reached out and touched his arm.

'Are you all right, Herr Kininsky?' Hans asked.

Kininsky nodded.

All right? How could he be all right?

Staring into the water in the sink he recalled the first time it had come.

It had started as a dream in which thick fog was wafting from the mouth of an upward-sloping tunnel.

Then the figure had come floating slowly out of the fog, reaching for him, the mouth in the rotting face twisted into an ugly grin which exposed black stumps of teeth, the empty eye sockets glowing, seeking him out.

He had drawn back from it, kicking desperately for wakefulness like a drowning man kicking for the surface high above him.

A hand reached for him, drawing closer and closer.

I'm asleep, a voice told him, I'm asleep and I must wake up.

The hand drew closer, the grin widened.

I'm asleep and I must wake up. Quickly, quickly.

He had kicked violently, thrashing towards wakefulness, twisting his body away from the finger which descended towards his chest.

Then he was awake, his back pressed hard against the bed's headboard, his heart pounding, perspiration running down his face, chest and back. Ahead of him was the blue wall of his bedroom, the table with the Greek statue, the Renoir print hanging on the wall.

A dream. That was all it had been.

7

Yes, a dream.

Wasn't it?

Then his eyes were drawn remorselessly around and up, towards the corner of the room to the left of his bed.

And it had been there.

Hovering near the ceiling. Watching him.

It had spoken then. In a voice that sounded like a dying man whispering into a rusted, metallic drum.

'Next time you sleep you will be mine.'

That was when he had screamed.

Joachim shuffled the cards idly and studied the box. What could Kininsky have come up with this time, he wondered. At one time or another Kininsky had smuggled most things east or west over the border, including people, but what was it this time? Drugs? An incredibly valuable icon? He shook his head and tutted thoughtfully. Documents perhaps? Material which US Intelligence services would pay highly for? He nodded slowly, unconvinced.

That was when the box vibrated. The movement lasted only about a second but surprised Joachim. He shuffled the cards more slowly now. Then the box vibrated again and an odd fear began to tingle up his spine. He put the cards down, pushed a lock of hair back from his forehead and stood up.

What . . .

Then he heard Hans moving back into the living-room with Kininsky. A relief he couldn't explain worked its way through his body.

He strode into the living-room, giving the box as wide a berth as possible, aware of a childlike fear of the inanimate object.

'What time is it?' Kininsky asked irritably. He was seated in his chair by the window.

'It's three,' Hans said.

Kininsky opened his mouth to speak but a knock on the door cut him off.

'Open it,' he rasped to Joachim. 'Hans, get the box.'

The man who entered the room was very tall, perhaps six feet six. His hair was black and slicked back and his pallid, clean-shaven face was dominated by a large nose with deep

8

indentations in the flesh at either side. He was wearing a fawn trench coat and carrying an attaché case.

'Do you have it?' he said to Kininsky.

Kininsky nodded towards Hans as he entered the room carrying the box. A smile flicked across the Tall Man's face, a mixture of triumph and relief. He watched Hans place the box on a low table then turned back to Kininsky and raised the attaché case into the air.

'The money. Do you wish to count it?'

'Just leave it. I trust you,' Kininsky said, standing up.

He handed the Tall Man a key as Joachim took the attaché case. The man studied the key for a moment then turned towards the box.

'No.'

Kininsky almost shouted the word and the Tall Man spun back to face him.

'Don't open it here,' Kininsky added, more quietly now.

'Has something happened?' the Tall Man asked.

'Just take it and go.'

The Tall Man thought for a moment, then said, 'All right.'

'You are leaving West Berlin immediately?'

'Yes.'

Kininsky nodded slowly.

'Goodbye then.'

Carefully the Tall Man picked up the box. He left without saying another word.

'Pour me a drink,' Kininsky said and Hans went to the drinks cabinet.

Kininsky flopped into his chair, puffed out his cheeks and rested his head back. A lead weight lifted away from his shoulders. He sighed.

Hans gave him the whisky, two fingers neat, as he always had it, and he downed it in one swallow.

Joachim watched as the older man gently closed his eyes. A moment later he opened them again and the tension had gone from his face. A smile played briefly with the edges of his mouth.

'Do you need us any more?' Hans said.

Kininsky thought about that for a moment, then said, 'Stay

until tomorrow. By the way, there's a bonus in this for both of you.'

He hauled his tired body upright, picked up the attaché case and checked the contents with a glance. Then he drew aside the framed Van Gogh print on the wall to expose his safe. He fumbled with the mechanism, opened the door, pushed the case inside and closed it again.

'I'm going to sleep,' he said over his shoulder.

He entered the bedroom, closed the door then opened it again immediately.

'I'm leaving the door open,' he said, then added in a mumble, 'just in case.'

Joachim and Hans exchanged glances then Hans half smiled and said: 'Cards?' Joachim nodded and flopped onto the settee as Hans started towards the kitchen.

It was almost half an hour later that the door began to close. Very, very slowly.

The door was still three inches ajar when Joachim's head jerked up from a hand that consisted of an ace, two fives and two twos. It was the slightest, tiniest hinge-creak which had attracted his attention.

'Herr Kininsky?' he said.

The door slammed shut so violently that the door-jamb trembled and fragments of plaster fell from the wall and shattered into tiny white clouds on the floor.

Hans was at the door first, his chair clattering to the floor.

'Herr Kininsky, is something wrong?'

He hammered on the door with his fist then turned the handle and pushed. The door gave about an inch then stuck fast. It was not being held by a solid object, such as a wardrobe or cupboard. It was being held with a degree of elasticity, as if by a living creature which varied its holding pressure according to the force exerted from without.

Hans shouted again. 'Herr . . .'

Then the screams began. Terrible cries ripped through the apartment.

Hans threw his weight against the door and Joachim joined him but their combined thirty stones could not budge it. The screams continued, accompanied by a bumping sound as if the furniture in the room was being thrown about.

'It's no good,' Hans said, putting his hand on Joachim's

shoulder and pulling him back. He balled his hand into a fist and drove it into the right-hand panel of the door. The wood splintered and cracked and the second punch shattered a five-inch hole in the door.

Instantly an invisible force slammed into Hans's chest. It lifted his fifteen-stone frame clear of the floor and sent him flying back across the room. He thudded against the far wall, crashed to the floor, then rose to his knees, staring at Joachim, blood trickling from his nose.

'What . . .'

A scream, more high-pitched and terrible than ever, tore through the apartment.

Then silence.

The door shuddered open, very slowly.

Hans rose shakily to his feet and followed Joachim into the bedroom. It was as if a hurricane had passed through it. Every piece of furniture was broken, shattered. A section of plaster on the wall behind the bed had fallen to the floor, and the wall-paper was hanging in odd folds.

But it was Erwin Kininsky the men were staring at.

He lay spreadeagled in the centre of the floor, a gaping wound in the centre of his chest. Beside him his heart twitched, pumping blood onto the carpet.

PART ONE

The Coming

ONE

It was as Jon Hammond was hurrying along a chilly tunnel at the Leicester Square tube station that the tall, attractive black girl touched his arm and said: 'Excuse me. D'you have a light? I've left my lighter at home.'

He had left the Gare du Nord in Paris at two o'clock, crossed the Channel by hovercraft and travelled from Dover to Charing Cross by train. The tube journey from Charing Cross to King's Cross – from where he would get his train north – meant a change of trains at Leicester Square.

So there he was, looking down into the girl's deep brown eyes. They looked back boldly, too boldly, looking too deep.

'I'm sorry, I don't smoke,' he said.

'What do you like to do? Want to have some fun?'

He smiled. 'I'm always interested in fun but . . .' – he shook his head – 'I never pay.'

He turned away from her and strode on.

'It's your loss,' she shouted after him.

He grinned over his shoulder: 'I don't know about that. Women have been known to say they're never the same after I've had them.'

She pursed her lips and raised one finger in an obscene gesture.

He turned left and came out on the platform. The sign told him the train was four minutes away. He put his suitcase down and turned his coat collar up to keep the cold from his neck.

Paris. Memories of his week there came tumbling back now. The man feeding the pigeons in front of the Sacré Coeur; the Arc de Triomphe at night, lit up by great lamps; the mini-skirted, plunging-necklined prostitutes dotted along the Rue Pigalle; the Chinese restaurant near the Sorbonne where he'd had a three-course meal for twenty-five francs; the Eiffel Tower, which had disappointed him (just a pile of girders had been his first reaction when he saw it walking from the Bir Hakeim Metro); the Seine houseboats; the grimy saxophonist

15

who had nearly blasted his ears off with a rendition of 'Summertime' in a Metro compartment and then held his hand out for money; balmy nights in brasseries where they upped the charge for your drink drastically if you had it sitting down.

The train thundered up to the platform in a swish of wind just as he started to think about the grim-faced woman in the Gare de L'Est paper shop who had wanted to charge him the equivalent of seventy pence for a British newspaper. He had refused to pay and she had abused him. At least he had thought she was abusing him. His understanding of French consisted of half-forgotten grammar school phrases.

He swung his suitcase onto the train and settled his seventeen-stone bulk into the seat as the door clanked shut.

He was a massive-shouldered man, six-two in his bare feet, with the greenest of green eyes. His nose had been broken twice (once playing rugby at school and once playing centre half for a village football team) and its bumps and ridges conspired to give him the look of a bouncer in a better-class nightclub. He was in that mid-thirties, grey area of age, not young but not yet middle-aged. The first flecks of white laced his curly brown hair and thick moustache.

Paris. He started to recall his walk down the Quai des Orfevres where he had gone in memory of all the Maigret books he had read in his teens – then, suddenly, his thoughts took an abrupt turn. His eyes, wandering through the train, picked out a nurse, a dark coat dragged carelessly over her uniform, her eyes staring sightlessly out the window at the black tunnel beyond.

And, of course, the nurse made him think of Tanya.

He recalled the conversation in the White Lion a fortnight before.

'Great news,' he had said. 'Can you come to Paris next week?'

'Paris.' (She had spoken the word as if it was alien; as if she was saying 'Ulan Bator'.) 'Of course I can't go to Paris. I can't take holidays just like that.' She had snapped her fingers then.

'You could ask. A week in Paris, just you and me. It would be great.'

'But what . . .'

'You remember Harry Watt . . . you met him once when

he was up here covering that murder for the *Daily Mail* . . . well, he's got a friend who lives in Paris and is going on holidays next week. I can have his flat for the week for nothing. I could do another chapter for the book.'

(The book. It had been his pet project for a year. He intended to spend a week in various cities he had never visited before and write a chapter on each. He was going to call it *A Tale of Five Cities*. It would be a travel book with a personal angle. He would not just describe great statues, churches and museums but would write about the things that actually happened to him, the off-beat characters he saw, the silly, hilarious-in-retrospect things that happen on holidays, the places where tourists are mercilessly overcharged. So far he had done Stockholm and Madrid).

'It sounds too good an opportunity to miss,' she had admitted, but it was obvious the thought of him alone in Paris wasn't one she relished.

'Couldn't you just ask for a week off? At least try,' he had said.

'There's no chance. I'm not some newspaper editor who can take a week off whenever he likes and go gallivanting about the world.'

'Newspaper editor,' he had laughed, 'you have a way of making the *Batforth Courier* sound as if it's the *Daily Mirror*. I must be the only newspaper editor in the country with only one member of staff . . . and Ernie won't see seventy-five again.'

He was thinking of Ernie Spiers with his shuffling walk, his wandering right eye and his secret caches of dirty magazines when the train pulled into King's Cross and he stepped off and followed the signs up out of the tube station to the main railway station.

He put his case down in front of the destinations board, his eyes travelling down the lists of place-names printed in green letters. Batforth. There was a train in ten minutes. Platform 10. That was a stroke of luck, he thought as he grabbed his suitcase.

It was as he turned away from the board and started towards Platform 10 that he noticed the Tall Man. It was his height he noticed first but that would normally have solicited no more than a casual glance. What held his attention was the naked apprehension etched into the man's face, the intensity of anxiety in his eyes as they darted about the destinations on the board. Hammond studied the man as he drew nearer to him. He noted scuffed black shoes, a crumpled trench coat, lank black hair, a lock of which hung down over the man's pale, somehow unwholesome face. The man was hunched forward, almost on his toes, as if he desperately wanted to be somewhere else.

A package was tucked awkwardly under his left arm, a kind of box wrapped in a plastic bag. As Hammond drew level with him, the man took a quick step to one side and the package clanged, metal on metal. *A bomb*. That was the first thing that sprang into Hammond's mind. A terrorist with a bomb. But no, bombs didn't clang, not nowadays anyway and this man was no terrorist. Not this edgy, six-feet six-inch giant.

He reached the platform and strode along it, thinking about the Tall Man and his package. The image of the dread on the man's face clung to his mind like the aftertaste of an unpleasant drink.

He found an almost empty carriage, climbed aboard and hoisted his suitcase into the luggage rack. There were only six other people in the carriage – a woman with two little girls, about six and ten, two men in suits talking quietly over an open folder, and a young man listening to a radio through a set of earphones. He sat down, took out his notebook and flipped it open on the table in front of him.

Absently he flicked through the notes he had made in Paris as the carriage began to fill around him. He was half aware of the muffled thump of suitcases, the subdued hum of voices, the little girls in the seat nearby giggling excitedly at the prospect of the train trip.

He reached the section in his notebook on the Louvre and rested his head back, thinking about all he had seen there.

That was when he saw Mrs Lord taking a seat further along the carriage. Mrs Lord – that was how everyone knew her. There was no familiarity with Mrs Lord. Their eyes met and he smiled a polite greeting. She nodded curtly at him, an acknowledgement of his presence and no more. She owned the Riverside Tea Shop in Batforth and they had once locked horns over a plan for a block of flats near the river. She had opposed them, ('It would destroy the amenity of the area, wouldn't it Councillor Hardy?'). He had said in a *Courier* editorial that the flats should be built because people needed places to live and too many plans had been postponed or ruled unsuitable. The flats had gone ahead.

As she sat down and disappeared from his sight he glanced at his watch. One minute to departure time. He was pleasantly surprised to find the seats around him and across the aisle unoccupied. It meant he could have a pleasant, uninterrupted one and a half hour journey home, studying his notes or reading his book.

Then he glanced through the window and saw the Tall Man hurrying past, the lock of hair bobbing in front of his face. He was catching the same train. Perhaps going to Batforth?

Hammond's brow furrowed as he began thinking about the man again.

The Tall Man found a seat near the front of the train and sat down, holding the box in his lap. It was getting warm again and that alarmed him. He fidgeted unconsciously with the handle of the plastic bag which held it, then slipped his hand inside the bag and felt the box. It was more than warm, it was *hot*.

TWO

The face that suddenly appeared inches away from Hammond's, on the other side of the window, startled him.

At first it was just a primitive shape framed in the harsh glow of the platform lights, filled with shadows. Then he made out human features. Uncombed, dirty-looking hair, eyes close-set over a flattened nose, a dirty face half covered in a week's growth of beard. He realized the face was looking past him at the seats across the aisle an instant before it turned away and shouted: 'Hey, Eddie, there's f. . . . seats in here.'

A huge luggage trolley hove into view, covered in all manners of bags – sacks, suitcases, bulging cement bags and hold-alls. The man pushing the trolley – Eddie – was much smaller than the first man, no more than five-two or three. He had a small, oddly featureless face, and a bald head that shone. The lank hair he had at back and sides hung to his shoulders. He was wearing a filthy, torn rag of a blue pullover which had long ago said goodbye to its elbows and jeans which were through at the knees and matted in paint stains and years of accumulated grime.

'C'mon Lennie, let's get the f. . . . bags on the train,' Eddie said in a high-pitched whine.

As Lennie made for the trolley Hammond saw the taller man was dressed in a denim outfit which looked even more ragged, filthy and paint-spattered than his friend's clothes.

The two men loaded themselves up with bags, clambered aboard and stamped down the aisle, bringing a stale, unwashed stench into the carriage.

Halfway to their seats a hold-all slipped from under Lennie's arm. It hit Mrs Lord's leg on the way down.

'F. . . . it,' he yelled, angry beyond anything the event justified, and kicked it the rest of the way along the aisle.

He threw a suitcase onto the table in front of the empty seats and thumped a grimy hold-all onto Hammond's table. A half-full can of coke slipped out of the bag, clinked onto its side and spattered coke the length of the table. Some of it splashed onto Hammond's hands and over his notebook.

Hammond looked up, waiting for an apology. Nothing elaborate, just a mumbled 'sorry' or a gesture of regret would have done.

Instead the man snapped the coke upright and bawled, 'Shit.' Then he turned to his friend and said: 'I've spilt half our f. . . . coke. I hope you're right about the buffet car. I want coke with my vodka.'

Eddie unloaded his bags and turned back down the aisle. Lennie followed and they returned with their second load of bags, mainly sacks and cement bags this time and by the clanking sound coming from them it was obvious they were filled with bottles.

Hammond could feel his anger rising fast as he took out his handkerchief, wiped the coke from his hands and dabbed at the smeared writing in his notebook. The spilled coke dribbled across the table, leaving streaks of sticky residue, settled in the tiny, wooden gutters, then began to roll lazily towards him.

'I'll be glad when this f. . . . train gets going,' Eddie whined to Lennie as the men started distributing their bags about the floor, behind the seats and in the luggage racks.

'Stop f. . . . worrying,' Lennie said, snatching the hold-all from Hammond's table and throwing it into the luggage rack. 'We're all right now.'

He returned for his coke can then flopped into his seat.

It was as Hammond was wiping the coke from the table that he looked up and saw the woman with the two little girls. She was busy trying to occupy them with activity books. One girl was colouring in with a red pencil and the other was listening intently as her mother told her how to join up the dots in the book to make a pattern. The mother threw a glance in the direction of the two men and Hammond saw her face was fixed and tense.

Dammit, Hammond, she's scared. She's actually scared of these two foul-mouthed louts. And you're just sitting here doing nothing.

'Got a bottle of vodka there?' Lennie said to Eddie.

He had produced two paper cups and was pouring coke into them. Eddie bent under the table and began to flick open a series of cement bags.

'French wine. Spanish wine. Whisky.'

21

'F. . . . vodka,' Lennie said impatiently.

Hammond's gaze moved from the two children and came to rest on an old man in a check jacket. The man was leafing through a tabloid newspaper but not reading anything.

He's scared too, Hammond. Just like the woman.

The train gave a lurch, hesitated then moved forward again, gliding out of the station. The bottles clanged dully then settled down.

Hammond shifted his attention back to the two men.

'Got it,' Eddie announced and handed Lennie the bottle of Smirnoff.

Lennie unscrewed the top, gulped a mouthful from the bottle then filled the paper cups.

They're going to get drunk, Hammond. They'll be worse than ever.

Just then the door at the end of the carriage opened and a girl came in; about eighteen, fair hair hanging to her shoulders, duffel coat, jeans, a red bag hooked over her shoulder. She walked quickly down the aisle, looking for a seat, her head bent forward shyly, aware people were looking at her.

Lennie saw her, grinned and put his arm across the aisle, blocking her way.

'There's a seat here, darling.'

'Excuse me,' she said, blushing, trying to get past.

'Why, what have you done?' Lennie laughed. Eddie joined in.

'Please, let me get past.'

'Well, I might and I might not. What d'you think, Eddie?'

Hammond sighed.

'O.K., that's it, that's enough,' he said more loudly than he had intended.

Lennie looked at him as if seeing him for the first time, as if he hadn't realized there were any other human beings sharing the carriage with him.

Hammond reached over and shoved Lennie's hand aside. The girl hurried away.

'What the f. . . .' Lennie began.

Hammond had one elbow on his table now, his bulk turned towards Lennie.

'Now listen. You've both been Grade-A pains in the neck since you got onto this train. You splashed coke all over me and my table, coke that I had to clean up. You embarrassed that girl. You've done nothing but bawl and swear and be a bloody nuisance. There are kids in here. Their mother might not like them picking up the kind of language you've been using. Did you ever think of that?'

Lennie's eyes were wild, unreasoning.

'F. . . . off,' he yelled, leaning forward. 'And don't ever shove my f. . . hand like that again.'

Hammond started to speak again but swallowed the words when Lennie's hand moved towards the bottle. Lennie didn't reach for it as if he was going to pour another drink. He reached for it angrily, his fist inverted, as if he intended to use it as a weapon.

Eddie was amazed at how quickly Hammond got out of his seat. The big man was in the aisle in an instant, bent over the men's table, his hand folding over Lennie's, crushing it against the bottle.

'Now that was stupid,' Hammond said.

'He didn't mean anything,' Eddie whined. 'He wasn't going to do anything. You're not a cop are you?'

Lennie tried to pull his hand away but it was like a child's in Hammond's fist.

'He's got a bad temper,' Eddie said, 'but he wasn't going to hit you with the bottle.'

'Shut up,' Hammond growled into his face. Then he turned back to Lennie. 'O.K., you've got two options. You can go on the way you've been going in which case I'll get the guard to stop the train at the next station and get the transport police aboard. Would you like to answer questions about all this booze? I'd put twenty quid against a pound that you didn't come by it honestly.'

Eddie whined: 'We did. . . . we. . . .'

'Or. . . . you can let everybody enjoy their trip in peace. Do you understand?'

'Yeah. That's fair enough.' Eddie was nodding violently. Lennie was looking hard into Hammond's face.

Hammond peeled Lennie's fingers off the bottle, screwed the top back on and handed it to Eddie.

'Put that away before anybody gets hurt.'

Eddie was returning it to a bag under the table when Hammond sat down again.

The woman with the two children caught his eye. She smiled

at him and clapped her hands in silent applause. He returned the smile as he rested his head back and watched the black countryside rolling by.

Was it over with, he wondered. He had seen enough rotten, vicious types in his life to know one when he saw one and Lennie fitted the category perfectly. Would he let the matter drop or would he try something to get even? He was debating the pros and cons of that when he heard Lennie's voice again.

'Give me the vodka, Eddie.'

'No. . . . listen. . . .'

'Give me the f. . . . vodka.'

Hammond turned his head slowly.

Lennie jabbed a finger at him.

'And you can f. . . . off.'

Hammond shrugged, stood up and strode away down the aisle, preparing to search the train for the guard.

He had reached the area at the end of the carriage where the toilets were when he heard someone rushing up behind him. He spun and dropped into a crouch, his hands moving across his face and body in a karate motion.

'Take it easy, take it easy,' Eddie said. 'I don't want any trouble. You're not going to get the fuzz are you?'

Hammond dropped his hands to his sides. He nodded: 'Yes.'

'Look, the booze is not stolen. Honestly, I. . . .'

'I couldn't care less.'

'Lennie's had too much to drink. I'll keep him quiet. We're just going home after a month working in London. I don't want to spend the night in some police cell. I'll keep him quiet. Honestly.'

Hammond thought a moment then shrugged and said: 'O.K. but get the bottle away from him. He's had enough.'

'I will. I will.'

Eddie disappeared and Hammond went into a toilet. When he returned to his seat the two men were playing cards, loose change scattered about their table. Lennie didn't look up from his hand.

The temperature of the box in the Tall Man's lap had gone from hot to warm to normal to cool to very cold. Now a cold spot had started to form all around it. He had seen many things in his life but never anything like this.

A man seated across the aisle buttoned up his coat and turned up his collar.

He threw a glance at the Tall Man and said: 'They never seem to get the air-conditioning right on these trains, do they?'

THREE

Lennie threw down his cards, ran his fingers through his hair and started to pick up his winnings.

'I've had enough of cards,' he said to Eddie. 'I've got to stretch my legs. I think I'll go to the buffet car and get a beer. You coming, Eddie?'

Eddie nodded: 'Yeah O.K.'

They got out of their seats without looking at Hammond and disappeared up the aisle.

Hammond had been reading his book for half an hour without interruption. Lennie and Eddie had been so quiet he had almost forgotten they were occupying the seats across the aisle. Lennie had chuckled a couple of times when he won a comparatively large pot of money and made the odd comment about Eddie's poor qualities as a card player but that was all.

Hammond glanced at his watch. An hour and he'd be home. *Home*. He loved travel but going home was always one of the nicest parts. It was pleasant to be among familiar things again, in familiar places. Everything was the same, yet different. That was how he always felt and yet he could never really explain why. He supposed it was because being away changed his perception of the things around him.

Unrelated memories floated through his mind. Batforth High Street on a moonless winter's night, the rain drizzling down between the shops and houses, each individual drop sharply defined in the glow of the street lights. The barbecue the previous summer when Ernie Spiers had become so drunk he had fallen into the river and imagined he was drowning in two feet of water. His office with its old-newspaper smell, battered, scarred desk and the ancient Underwood typewriter he refused to give up.

He thought about Mary at the Blue Boar ('The best barmaid in the universe') and her plump hands pulling him a pint. And Councillor Ray Hardy who could deliver a Churchillian speech on the most trivial of subjects and usually did. And the tramp who had one leg shorter than the other, crippled Joe Minty, who was forever turning up at the *Courier* office with some dramatic but highly unlikely news story.

Then he thought of Tanya.

He looked out the window and saw they were passing through a town. Shielding the carriage-light from his eyes he pressed his face against the window. A complex pattern of lights stretched away to the north, south and east, tiny glowing dots against the pitch black of night. The buildings were just dim, featureless shapes, like a jumble of blocks gathered together in an abstract art form and glimpsed in a dark museum.

He was turning away from the window when the lights seemed to reach out for him and a prickly sensation crawled up his spine. He turned back and stared. Something inside him told him to rip his eyes from the scene and read his book or get some coffee or drink some of the duty-free wine in his suitcase – or do anything but watch what was unfolding beyond the train window. But he couldn't. He could just stare. He was a slave to the sight, his body numbed by it.

The lights were no longer glowing pinpoints; they were flickering like flames. And they were not static any more; they were moving across the blackness, gathering together, forming into a long straggling procession. The flames streaked the night as the wind whipped at them and glowing sparks spattered across the blackness like handfuls of diamonds.

Candles? No, not candles, Hammond. Don't be an idiot. They're too big for candles. Torches. That's what they are. It's a torchlight procession.

The torches stretched as far as the eye could see, a broad band across the blackness, a river of torches, a flood of torches. And they were moving steadily towards him now, swaying with the rhythm of the march.

He held his breath, straining to listen as the sound of singing moved into the outer reaches of his hearing. The sound faded in and out; men's voices raised high in a rousing marching song. He knew he had heard the song before but couldn't put a name to it. He strained to hear a word, a phrase that might strike a chord in his memory and bring the answer but he couldn't distinguish any individual words. The sound grew closer, louder, stirring and powerful, and he began to hum

27

along with it. He could make out the shapes of men now, their bare arms holding the torches aloft.

Then he blinked.

It was enough. It was as if some incredibly delicate soap bubble had popped. Instantly the sound disappeared, the torchlight procession was gone. Where it had been he saw once again the pattern of street lights, the smudges of light from curtained windows, the gleaming beams as cars moved through the night.

Lennie was still seething with anger as he strode through the train with Eddie in his wake. The anger was more intense than it had been when he had been arguing with Hammond but it was contained now. It worried away at itself deep down inside him, becoming more and more inflamed. He had always had a bad temper but four spells in Her Majesty's prisons had taught him how to keep it in check most of the time. Now he could put away his anger – like putting it in a bank, he always told himself – and save it for the right moment.

Eddie had been right, of course. They couldn't afford to have the transport police come aboard the train, not after what had happened the night before.

'Lager?'

He looked down into Eddie's face, realizing they had reached the buffet car.

'Yeah, O.K.'

They queued for their drinks then sat down at a table.

'You all right?' Eddie said, flicking the ring-pull off his can.

'What do you mean?'

'You've got that look.'

'What look?'

'You know. . . . like you want to break somebody's back.'

'I'm all right.'

'It's just that. . . . another couple of hours and we'll be home. We'll be in the clear. . . .'

'I said I'm all right.'

Lennie looked past Eddie, his eyes blank, thinking about Hammond. Big, smug, arrogant prick.

Lennie admitted that Hammond had annoyed him because he had told him what he could and couldn't do and because he threatened him with the police. What he didn't admit, and what was central to his anger, was that the man had been unbelievably strong, so powerful that he could probably have swatted Lennie like a fly. When his hand had closed over Lennie's after he had reached for the bottle it had made Lennie feel like a child and for an instant he had felt a deep intensity of fear. He had been *afraid*.

He drank his beer straight from the can in long gulps and finished it in a couple of minutes. He shook the can, rattling the dregs around.

'Hardly touched the sides,' he grinned. 'I must have been thirsty. Another one?'

'What are you brooding about?'

'Who's brooding?'

'You're not talking much.'

'Not compulsory is it. . . . talking?'

Eddie shrugged.

'Stop worrying. I'm not going to hit anyone. I've got more to lose than you have. You've never been sent down. Now, do you want another can?'

'O.K.'

He stood up, turned away from Eddie's worried face and strode to the counter.

They had gone to London a month before to work on a building site. The builder, whom Lennie had worked for before, had offered them the use of a caravan in a field adjacent to the site.

'You can have it for nothing so you'll have no accommodation expenses,' the builder had explained, making it sound like he was offering them a room at the Ritz.

They had still been reluctant to accept the jobs because the wages being offered were so low. But then the builder had added: 'You can still draw your social security. This will be on a strict cash-in-hand basis. I won't be telling the DHSS anything.'

That had made the proposition a lot more tempting but it was Lennie's plan which made it irresistible.

'What we'll do, see, is go down there, keep our heads down and work our backsides off,' Lennie had told Eddie. 'We'll stay out of trouble and take our cash. Everyone will think we're just a couple of honest lads from the north down to pick up a few quid. *But* all the time we're there we'll be casing a few places. On our last night we'll rent a van and knock all these places over. Simple. We'll spend the next day getting rid of the stuff. I've got a few pals down there, if you know what I mean, and they'll take the stuff off our hands in exchange for the readies. We might come out of it quite a few hundred quid ahead. By the time the fuzz start any real investigating we'll be hundreds of miles away.'

Eddie had found the work on the building site very hard and had quickly become fed up wandering the streets at night with Lennie searching for likely-looking shops and houses to be added to Lennie's 'shopping list' for the night of 'the operation'.

Privately he thought Lennie's code words were stupid. It also occurred to him that Lennie wasn't very good at what he was doing. For one thing if there was a sudden spate of burglaries in the area wasn't it possible the police might suspect two labourers who had been living in a caravan and had just moved on?

But he kept his thoughts to himself. He was no fool, he had seen Lennie lose his temper. With any luck they'd get away with it. If not, he'd do time. A man had to take risks in life.

Lennie never seemed to tire of adding houses and shops to his list and crossing others off, of making notes about methods of entry and revising again and again his estimates of how long it would take to get in and out.

By the end of the month his dog-eared notepad was filled with lists and notes and diagrams.

Then came the big night. Lennie had trimmed the list to three houses, two shops and a social club where the supply of liquor seemed to be protected by little more than a rickety door with hinges that could be removed in thirty seconds by any twelve-year-old with a screwdriver.

They did two of the houses first. The owners were away. ('It's the easiest thing in the world to find the houses where people are on holiday,' Lennie had told Eddie. 'First you check there are no lights on in the house for a few nights running. Then you can knock on the door and see if anyone's there. You can flip open the postbox and see if there's a pile of letters or see if milk's being delivered every morning. You can even ask a neighbour. If you say "Excuse me, do the Masons still live at Number Ten," chances are they'll say, "No, the Lincolns live there now but they're on holiday this week". Your average John Citizen is not very bright.')

The first two break-ins went smoothly enough. In each case Lennie managed to get inside without any trouble. Both times there was a lane beside the house and Eddie would park the van in the lane and wait beside the yawning van doors for Lennie to start passing things over the fence.

Half an hour after they had started there was a tidy haul in the van. TV sets, videos, transistor radios, two paintings and a table Lennie said was an antique.

There were minor hiccups at the shops. At the first one Lennie got stuck halfway through the narrow rear window and had to be helped by Eddie. At the second, Lennie knocked over some bottles and a dog started to bark in a house nearby. They stole only cigarettes from the shops because Lennie said they were 'dead easy to get rid of'.

The only problem at the social club was that there was more liquor than they had anticipated and it took a long time to load it into the van.

After that they drove to the last house on Lennie's list and that was where everything went terribly wrong.

Lennie had got into the house easily enough – one of the windows had been unlocked. He had brought out an old music centre, a television set, a painting and a handful of jewellery ('See those two rings there. . . . solid gold').

Then he had gone back inside to search a roll-top desk in the lounge. As he was trying to prise it open the light went on and he saw an old man standing in the lounge door in his pyjamas, his eyes fuzzy with sleep.

'What. . . .'

The old man had started to speak but in the same instant Lennie had hefted a chair, crashed it down on the man's head and started to run.

As they drove back to the caravan, Lennie became surly and began drinking vodka in long swallows.

Eddie had been in a panic. 'You didn't hurt him, Lennie, did you? I mean, you didn't really hurt him. He won't die or anything, will he?'

'How would I know? Now shut your mouth.'

'I mean, you know how these old buggers are. A little tap might kill one of them. How hard did you hit him. . . ?'

'*Shut up.*'

Lennie had continued to drink throughout the night and
into the next day as they drove around disposing of their haul.
By midday the surly mood had been replaced by a swaggering,
catch-me-if-you-can, nobody-touches-Lennie-Hughes kind of
mood.

They got rid of almost everything in the van but at prices
far below Lennie's estimates. By the end of the afternoon all
they had left were about forty bottles of assorted liquor and
three items from the last house – the music centre and the two
rings.

'I'm for ditching all of it,' Eddie said.

'We'll take it home.'

'We can't,' Eddie pleaded. 'If they catch us with the stuff
from the house where you hit the old bugger they'll know it
was us.'

'F. . . . 'em.'

'O.K., we'll keep the booze and get rid of the other stuff.'

'We'll keep it all.'

'We can't get rid of it up north. They'd trace it to us.'

'We're keeping it.'

So they'd packed what was left into hold-alls, cement bags
and sacks and headed for the station.

The Tall Man decided that if the cold spot got any worse he
would get off at the next stop, (Batforth, wasn't it?) and catch
a taxi the next 150 miles.

The man across the aisle shivered and said, 'I'd never have
believed a train could be as cold as this. There must be a door
open somewhere.'

And other people in the carriage were pulling on coats and
jackets and grumbling.

The Tall Man drew back the top of the plastic bag, studied
the box and thought about its long journey to his hands in
West Berlin. From Sombirsk to Moscow; from the Russian
capital to Brotz in Poland; from Brotz to Fiederfeld, East
Germany; and finally to the West.

That long journey had cost him a lot of money.

But it had been worth every penny.

FOUR

Tanya Bailey stepped out of her car when the drizzling rain stopped, turned up the collar of the red coat she wore over her nurse's uniform and strolled across Batforth Station's car park. She was a full-figured woman of medium height, with brown hair clipped short in a page-boy style and brown eyes set attractively but oddly very far apart. Her chin and nose were delicate and finely chiselled and seemed at odds with full lips many would have described as sensual ('Lusty Lips' was what Jon Hammond always called her when he was in a teasing mood).

She blinked as she walked into the harsh lights of the station's entrance hall and nodded to Charlie McMurty, the stationmaster, who was coming out of the ticket office.

'Hello, Tanya, what brings you down here?'

'Jon's coming in on the London train,' she told him. 'Is it on time?'

He glanced up at the clock on the wall.

'Should be. . . . maybe a couple of minutes late, no more. Where's he been?'

Charlie had never been one to mind his own business.

'Paris,' she heard herself answer.

'Paris, never been there. When are we going to be hearing wedding bells for you two?'

He had never been overloaded with tact either.

'I think that might be a little premature.'

'You've been seeing him for quite a while, haven't you?'

She pursed her lips, nodded without comment and strolled past him through the narrow door to the platform. Regular pools of light splashed holes in the black and grey-black shadows. There was no-one else about.

Marriage.

She thought about the word. She was twenty-six and had been close a couple of times. Once, when she'd been nineteen but twenty had come along and she'd grown out of Alex

33

Townson. She had come even closer with Richard at the age of twenty-three. They'd had an engagement party, the date had been set, but somehow it had never really felt quite right. She had been very fond of Richard. He was good-looking and fun to be with, intelligent and witty, but somehow he just wasn't *the one*.

She winced at the memory of the night she had told Richard it was all over. It hadn't been easy for her to explain why. She'd ended up by telling him she thought there should be something more than they had. She hadn't been sure then what that something else was. Some kind of magic, she'd thought, some kind of chemical reaction.

She had certainly found the magic with Jon Hammond. Too much magic. Sometimes it was as if he consumed her, as if she was in danger of becoming totally a part of his life with no separate identity of her own. He was so overpowering, both physically and mentally, and self-opinionated. . . .

She laughed to herself briefly in the darkness of the station. She could have gone on for an hour listing all his faults but it didn't make one jot of difference. For her, he had that certain something and no amount of analyzing seemed to produce an answer that even came close to putting a label on it.

He wasn't anything like anyone she'd ever met before. He was more self-sufficient somehow. He led a life along a course he chose, on his terms. Although he had few really close friends, he was popular around Batforth.

The men liked his dry humour, endless array of sporting stories, and ability to drink with the best of them.

Women liked him too, she thought, and a pang went through her thinking of him alone in Paris for a week.

What if he had met some London dolly-bird on holiday in Paris and looking for some fun, or a French widow with a lot more sophistication than a small-town nurse? She shrugged aside a tiny spasm of panic and started along the platform, the click of her heels echoing dully off the far wall.

It would be wonderful to have him back home again, she admitted, to hear his voice, his laughter. They'd probably eat at Bunty's Restaurant, have a bottle of the chablis that Jon liked, then go back to his flat and make love. She thought about the feel of his skin against hers, the smell of his hair, how it felt when he moved inside her.

She had never had an orgasm before she met Hammond. Before him, sex had been something she had never cared very much about. She could take it or leave it. She hadn't disliked it, it wasn't unpleasant but it hadn't been something that excited her very much.

And now?

She was thinking about that question when Charlie McMurty walked past her carrying a parcel. His arrival on the deserted platform startled her. When he glanced at her and their eyes met she had a sudden primitive feeling that he could read through her eyes what she was thinking and she felt a slight blush creeping across her face.

His size-twelve shoes clip-clopped along the platform and brought him to a halt outside a shed. He unlocked it and went inside. She strolled self-consciously past the open door and stopped at the end of the platform, peering into the gloom.

Then she saw the lights.

Lights?

She bent forward, narrowing her eyes. There were definitely lights there, a couple of hundred yards down the track. Two were stationary, two bobbing backwards and forwards.

A distant hammering sound hummed through the air as she turned and shouted to the stationmaster.

'Charlie.'

He came out of the shed and started to lock it.

'What is it?' he said.

'There's something out there, along the track.'

He looked past her and nodded.

'They're doing repair work on a whole section along there.'

'At night?'

'They don't work nine-to-five, you know. Anyway, it's the best time. Not so many trains. It's a go-slow area along here tonight, all the trains are just creeping through.'

She nodded her thanks as he turned away.

'The train should be in in ten minutes,' he said over his shoulder.

Tanya stood absently watching the lights for a long time before turning away and strolling back down the platform.

* * *

35

Lennie hooked his thumb twice over his shoulder indicating the toilets at the end of the buffet car and said: 'Back in a minute.'

Eddie grimaced as he watched Lennie lurch twice on his way up the aisle. Lennie had become quiet and surly again and Eddie feared trouble. What if Lennie did hit the big man who had threatened to get the police? What if the police got on board? What if they were arrested? How badly hurt was the old man Lennie had hit? Was he alive? His mind churned with questions.

The buffet car toilet was engaged and Lennie was forced to go to a carriage further down. He found a door with a 'vacant' sign and went in.

As he urinated he fantasized about what he would like to do to Hammond. He would take a note of which station the big man got off at, and one day he would come back and find him. He visualized a street at night, himself waiting behind a wooden fence, with a knife or an axe. . . . or better still, a gun. An automatic pistol. He would wait a long time and then he would see Hammond coming towards him, whistling, unaware of his fate. When Hammond drew level with him, Lennie would step out of the shadows and empty the gun into his chest.

He zipped up his jeans, imagining the look of horror on Hammond's face as the bullets punched into him, and turned to the sink. As he splashed water into his face he looked into the mirror.

The surface was not at all like a mirror, he noticed. It shimmered like water and his image was indistinct. He wiped at his eyes and looked again. There was a clear face-image in the quivering mirror surface now.

But it was not his own.

There was a stranger there. A gross, heavy man, in brown shirt and brown tie. The fat face was topped by an iron-grey crewcut and dominated by a pair of piercing blue eyes which stared at him with contempt.

Lennie froze, bent over the sink, water dripping from his face.

A chill ran up his back as if a strip of his flesh had just been exposed to a harsh snow-carrying wind.

He tried to speak but a half-dozen words tripped incoherently over one another. He swallowed and tried again.

That was when the mirror smashed and an immense fist shot forward out of it and seized his throat. His hands flailed, trying to knock the fist away but it was hopeless. He tried to scream but his larynx was smashed.

Remorselessly the fist closed tighter and tighter, crushing the life from him.

FIVE

It must have been my imagination. What else could it have been?

Hammond was staring at his book, which was open on the table in front of him, but he wasn't reading any of the words. Five times since he had seen the torchlight procession he had started to read the same paragraph. Five times it had been as if the words were jumbled and meaningless.

He couldn't rid himself of the strange fear he had felt as he had sat staring at the river of torches. It was something he had never felt before, a fear brought on by an experience he could not explain, something beyond the frontiers of his existence.

It had to be imagination. What else could it be? Mind-tricks. That was all it could be. Dreams could be so vivid, could seem so real. Couldn't daydreams be just as powerful? Yet it hadn't seemed like a dream at all. . . .

What are you trying to say, Hammond? That you had some kind of vision?

When people drank too much they saw things that weren't there. Their brains played tricks on them. Somehow his brain had obviously jumped a cog or two, suffered a momentary hiccup. Perhaps it was something he'd eaten or something he had had to drink. That last bottle of wine he'd had in Paris – the one he'd bought from a grocer's shop in a lane in the tenth *arrondisement* for eight francs – hadn't tasted quite right. It had been too strong, too acidy, and had lain uneasily in his stomach for a long time. Perhaps that was the problem?

He tried to recall everything he had seen from the train window but found that the memory was slipping away from him now, great chunks of it disappearing like sections of a crossword puzzle.

Just like my dreams.

When Hammond had particularly powerful dreams he would wake up and find the dreams there with him, clear and sharp. Then they would start to melt away, dripping rapidly back into his subconscious. Sometimes a few seconds after waking he could recall very little of a dream.

But I have to remember. He closed his eyes tightly. There were the bare arms holding the torches aloft, the flames flickering in the night, and the voices raised high, singing the marching song.

He opened his eyes and let his book snap shut. Impatiently he searched for a blank page in his notepad. When he found one he began to write down everything he could recall.

It was Eddie's voice that made him look up.

'Have you seen my pal?' he wanted to know. 'The man who got on the train with me,' he added as if there was a chance Hammond might have forgotten Lennie.

Hammond shook his head. 'Not since you both left together.'

Eddie shrugged: 'Can't find him anywhere.'

He turned away from Hammond and hurried back to the buffet car. There was still no sign of Lennie.

He went into the toilet at the end of the buffet car and looked behind the door as if there was an outside chance that perhaps Lennie was playing a trick on him.

He was beginning to panic. Where could Lennie be? Crazy thoughts surged through his head. What if Lennie had opened the wrong door and fallen off the train? Things like that did happen. Maybe he should get rid of the stolen property, just throw it out of a window? No, no, no, the bottles would smash and he'd be seen. Maybe he could just dump the music centre and the rings, the items which could tie him in with the assault on the old man?

Make sense, Eddie, a voice inside his head told him. *How can you throw a music centre off a train? Lennie will turn up. He has to be on the train somewhere.*

Mitch Sloane sat alone in the driver's compartment of the train as it gobbled up the endless miles of track which shone gold in the train's lights.

He had done this run a thousand times, alone in his dim capsule, javelining through the dark countryside. He liked being a train driver. He enjoyed that sense of being his own man, with no boss looking over his shoulder. It also satisfied a desire in him for movement, an urge to be going places or

39

coming back from them. He disliked being static for more than a few days and occasionally worried about what he would do about that feeling when he retired.

Sloane belonged to that rarest of groups – he was a contented man. Contented with his job, his marriage, his life. He and Effie had gone almost thirty years without so much as a minor hiccup in their marriage. They liked the same things – food, soap operas, the cinema, more food, football, Saturday nights at the pub.

The children were grown-up now and living their own lives and doing quite well, thank you. It was true that Frank was living in a squat but he wasn't the layabout some people said, and Mitch knew he would sort himself out one day. Bill was working on the North Sea rigs and living in Aberdeen. Doreen and Joan were both married and Joan was about to make him a grandad for the first time.

Nobody actively disliked him. He had a steady job, he was in the darts team and had a few trophies to show how good he was. All in all, life was quite pleasant. 'Can't complain,' was what he'd say when people inquired how he was – and he never did.

About an hour out of London he started to munch on the delicious ham and salad sandwiches Effie had made for him. He had just taken his third huge bite when he sensed there was someone beyond the door.

He half-turned, expecting Walter, the guard, to come in. But the door stayed firmly shut. He swallowed a half-chewed mouthful of ham, brown bread, lettuce, tomato and carrot and listened intently.

'Walter, you there?'

Had he heard something outside the door, some scuffling perhaps? Was that what had caught his attention? He racked his brain for the answer. If that had been what had happened he could have explained it away by saying that a gust of wind had knocked over a parcel in the guard's van. But he knew he hadn't actually heard anything.

He had just *felt* that someone was there, beyond the door. And he still felt it now.

Tiny alarm bells began to ring in distant corners of his brain, awakening an odd primitive fear he found annoying.

'Walter, are you out there? *Walter*.'

He coughed clear a tiny particle of bread that had caught in his throat and put down his sandwich.

'Walter, if this is some kind of joke, it's not funny.'

Walter would come through the door any second now, he told himself, and this tiny incident, this moment of inexplicable apprehension would disappear to be filed in his brain with all the other tiny inexplicable things that happen to human beings, sudden fears in familiar places that have no rational explanation, caused presumably by some maverick gremlin of a brain cell.

'Walter, if you're coming in, will you come in?'

The instant he issued the invitation the door lashed open with awesome violence and he saw the hunched figure of a woman standing there. Her head hung forward, her chin on her chest, so at first he could not see her face. What he saw was long, black hair in a style that had never been fashionable in his lifetime, an equally out-of-date navy blue suit which was covered in grime down one side, stockinged legs and mud-caked blue shoes.

'What are you doing along here?' he said.

There was no reply and he noticed with increasing irritation that the fear in his brain was growing, occupying new territory as each second passed.

'Passengers aren't allowed in this part of the train,' he told her. 'And. . . .'

He swallowed the rest of the sentence as her head began to rise, exposing her face to him. The features were what would usually have been considered pretty but her skin was so pale, the trenches under her eyes so deep and black, and her expression so indescribably tragic. The eyes watched him, somehow accusing him.

'What's wrong?' he said.

Her mouth opened slowly then worked soundlessly for a moment. It looked like she was in shock, Sloane thought. Maybe she'd been in some kind of accident.

'What's happened?' Sloane said. 'Has something ha. . . .'

She said a word then that he didn't understand. The sound was more like a croak.

'I'm sorry. . . . what?' he said.

She coughed, a soft invalid cough, and said the word again. '*Wasser*. . . .'

41

'What?'

'*Wasser. . . . bitte. . . .*'

'I'm sorry, I. . . .'

Suddenly her body seemed to rise from the ground and glide back from him, ascending at a forty-five degree angle. The door slammed shut.

'Hey!' he shouted, louder than he had intended.

Then he turned slowly in his seat and stared at the landscape, its smooth carpet of blackness smudged by farmhouse lights. A chilly sweat coated his body.

He was sure that at the instant the door closed the figure of the woman had reached the far wall and had begun to disappear into it. He shook his head as if to dislodge something unacceptable from his conscious mind.

She hadn't started to *disappear*. She hadn't *floated*. That was ridiculous. A swaying motion of the train had made him think that, had created the illusion that rather than stepping back from the door she was rising away from him.

Who shut the door then?

The question taunted him.

He reached for the sandwich, seeking comfort in it, as some men might in a cigarette or large whisky, and began to eat, chewing each mouthful vigorously.

That was when he heard the first scream, a terrible shriek of anguish.

He jumped and what was left of the sandwich slipped from his grasp. He snatched at it instinctively but it hit the back of his hand and disintegrated, the pieces scattering across the floor.

Then there was another scream and another and another until it was like listening to the sounds of a vast horde of men and women trapped in some living hell. He heard pounding too, and scratching, as if hands and fists were hammering and tearing at doors, desperately seeking escape from some terrible place.

The noises were coming from behind him, from the train. Something awful had happened. *A fire or. . . .*

He was about to apply the brakes when he saw it was dawn. The sun was rising above a distant horizon, reddening a bruised, mottled grey-blue sky, bringing warmth to a landscape strait-jacketed in snow. Gusts of wind pattered snow across the window in front of him and skirmished about a copse of stark, black, leafless trees away to his right, sending up tiny white puffs. The trees were the only features on the landscape. There was nothing else as far as the eye could see, just the blanket of snow.

Dawn. Snow. His mind panicked in a search for an instant answer. It couldn't be dawn. It couldn't be morning yet. And snow at this time of the year was out of the question.

The screams worsened, an endless cacophony of horror, like an outbreak of hysteria in a lunatic asylum for the incurably insane.

The brakes. He had to apply the brakes and stop the train.

As he made the motion to do so, he noticed the clothes he was wearing. Blue overalls, check shirt, a coarse blue jacket. And there was something on his head. He snatched at it. A blue cloth cap. These weren't his clothes.

Where was he? Who was he?

He jumped to his feet, turned towards the window, and froze. . . .

A grimy, oil-stained coat hung from a hook away to his left. There was a furnace there too. He could feel the heat of it through the blackened metal door. This wasn't even his train.

It was a steam train.

He was beyond panic now. Numb and trembling uncontrollably he stumbled to the window, snatched it open and looked back.

Windowless wooden carriages snaked back across the snow as far as he could see.

That was where the screams were coming from. There were people locked in.

He saw one carriage door tremble under the force of blows from within. Then he heard shouts, angry commands, threats, but couldn't see where they were coming from. . . .

Suddenly he was back in his seat. Had he really left it? He looked down at his clothes. They were his own.

This was his train, he realized, looking around him. But still the screams, the hammering and the pounding continued.

Outside, he could see the English countryside again, and the black of night.

He had to escape this nightmare. Somehow he had to get away. He accelerated, faster and faster, his mind a chaotic

43

mass of confused half-ideas related to the instinct for survival, the desperation to come out in one piece with his mind intact.

Then the dark countryside began to melt away again, fading to white. There was the sun again, peering over the far-away horizon, the blue overalls, the heat of the furnace.

'No. . . .'

He heard the sound before he realized it came from his own mouth, the essence of terror.

He could hear guttural voices behind him, shouting orders above the screaming and wailing and hammering, and realized he was yelling to drown out the sound. If only that sound would go away.

Darkness folded over him again. He was back in the English countryside. . . . but he could still feel the heat of the furnace and he was still wearing the blue overalls.

And the screaming went on.

Was he *there* or here? What kind of question was that? Where was *there*?

The furnace heat disappeared suddenly and he was wearing his own clothes but the countryside was beginning to whiten again and he could see the faint outline of the rising sun. He was going back yet again.

And the screaming went on.

The changes continued at random. The furnace heat, the sun, the white landscape, the black of the night, the clothes that were not his, everything changed rapidly.

The only constant thing was the screaming. That never stopped.

Suddenly the door was thrown open again and a woman stood there facing him. It was not the same woman as before. This was a much older woman, short and wearing peasant dress. Her hair was dishevelled, her eyes wild. She bared her teeth and her expression reminded him of a dog about to pounce on an unwelcome stranger.

She moved towards him quickly, too quickly.

Her mouth began to open wider and wider, distorting her face.

A shriek of unbelievable intensity peeled from the ever-widening mouth.

'Jeeeeeeeesus!' he yelled.

44

Fear stabbed a thousand needles into his skin, sparing no part of his body.

As she drew near, he threw a wild fist in her direction. She drew back, circled and came again, and again he threw a punch. This time she moved back against the wall, and raised her arms into the crucifix position, trembling violently.

Then she grew smaller, like a balloon with a tiny puncture. With a fluttering, whispering sound, she diminished to the size of a small girl, then a baby, and finally disappeared. He stared at the wide-open door. What would come through there next?

Batforth. He was getting near Batforth.

But the thought was distant, far-away, beyond the screaming and pounding that never stopped.

Batforth has a go-slow area. There are men working on the line.

But he wasn't in his own train, was he?

Then he saw the lights of the town up ahead, a rash of yellow dots against the darkness.

Batforth?

Was it Batforth or was it some fantasy place?

Then the black countryside began to lighten again.

SIX

The first time Hammond noticed anything unusual about the motion of the train was when his biro tumbled off his notepad and rolled away across the table. A couple of minutes later two empty cans of lemonade the little girls up the aisle had on their table clinked to the floor. The mother retrieved them.

These weren't very unusual occurrences in themselves. Hammond had seen similar things happen on trains before. On one particular occasion in Italy he had witnessed a man being thrown from his seat. But the London to Batforth journey was usually so sedate, so featureless.

The train swept swiftly around a bend, the speed and change of direction shifting even Hammond's bulk. His shoulder bumped against the wall.

A cement bag under Lennie and Eddie's table toppled over, spewing out bottles of vodka, wine and rum. Three wine bottles hit the floor together and smashed, spattering liquid and slivers of glass up the aisle and leaving an ugly pile of glass fragments. Behind him, Hammond heard other items falling to the floor and grumbling, irritated voices.

He looked through the window. The train was passing through a forest and it seemed to Hammond that the trees were going past very, very fast; too fast.

He glanced at the pile of glass fragments on the floor and decided they could be dangerous if just left there. As he stood up to move the glass to a safer place, he noticed the train had developed a severe swaying motion.

Surely it *was* going too fast.

He saw a figure approaching out of the corner of his eye and stepped back to let him pass.

When he saw it was the guard he said: 'Aren't we going a little too fast?' and gestured to the glass on the floor.

'Nothing to worry about,' the guard said. 'It's a fast part of the line.'

Then he was gone. Hammond stared at his retreating back.

46

Was he imagining things or had the guard looked worried, anxious?

He glanced out the window. The train was showing no sign of slowing down.

Then he saw the white buildings of Tawson's Farm. A minute or so and the train would pull into Batforth.

But there was a go-slow area this side of Batforth.

Men were working on the track. He had done a couple of paragraphs on that for the *Courier*. The train should have slowed to a snail's pace by now.

He turned and started after the guard. Through the glass panel of the carriage door up ahead he could see the guard was two carriages down now.

And he was running.

The guard, Walter Darrow, was puffing when he reached the driver's compartment. He snatched open the door, stepped inside and gasped:

'Mitch. What the hell are you doing? We're nearly into Batforth. Slow down.'

Mitch Sloane didn't seem to hear him. He sat as stiffly as a man turned to stone, staring out the window in front of him.

'Mitch. . . .'

Darrow touched the driver's shoulder. Sloane turned as quick as a snake, and in the instant before his punch hit Darrow on the chin, the guard saw a wild face, a quivering mouth and two staring, terrified eyes.

The force of the punch sent him back through the door and he crumpled to the floor, stunned.

The train can't be more than a minute or two now, Tanya Bailey thought, glancing at her watch then looking up the line. She tapped her foot impatiently.

Admit it, my dear, you've missed him like hell, and you can't wait to see him again.

She grinned wryly. It was true. But he was such an odd character, so different from all the other men she had known. For one thing, she had never seen herself falling for a fitness freak. She thought about his massive shoulders, huge biceps and the heavy corded muscles of his chest and stomach. He ran at least two miles every day and five on a Saturday, and it seemed like he was always working out with weights. She had asked why, of course. It all seemed a little pointless to her. 'Because it makes me feel good,' he'd told her at first. But later, when they'd got to know each other better, he'd said. 'The truth is, when I was about fifteen I was already over six feet tall and I was the skinniest, scrawniest fifteen-year-old you ever saw in your life. A puff of wind would have blown me over. I loved sports. I wanted to play rugby but I was too light. I wanted to play football but I didn't have the strength in my legs. So I decided to do something about it. After I got started on body building and physical fitness it became a habit.'

She had started to walk down the platform again when she heard the rumble of the train. A moment later it swung around the shoulder of Moulson's Hill and hurtled towards her, its huge light making her blink.

Her brow furrowed. Hadn't Charlie McMurty said this was a go-slow area? This train seemed to be going very fast, as if the driver had no intention of stopping at Batforth.

She stared at the huge light, which swayed violently from side to side, and waited for the first sign of the brakes being applied.

It never came.

Instead the light jumped into the air once, twice, three times, then shot sideways. The train smashed through the white fence above Moulson's Pond and slewed down the embankment. The lights at the carriage windows and the human figures beyond were a blur as they swept down after the train.

Hammond had reached the guard's van when the locomotive jumped the tracks. He was thrown forward against a wall as the train suddenly decelerated, its right-hand wheels gouging a trench along the top of the embankment, its left-hand wheels churning through a score of sleepers.

A voice in his head began to yell hoarsely. *We're off the tracks, we're running off the tracks, Hammond. We'll never stop. We'll hit the station. Tanya. . . .*

His eyes stared wildly out the window. He saw Moulson's Pond, a black smooth mass, scarred across the centre by uneven ridges of moonlight. It danced violently before his eyes like a flickering television-set image with the horizontal hold malfunctioning.

Suddenly the train jerked sharply to the right and he was knocked off balance.

We're going over the edge, down the embankment.

His fingers scrambled up the wall, desperately searching for a handhold.

Then the floor was whipped away from his feet as the train plummeted downwards. He was thrown sideways. Instinctively he covered his head and turned up his shoulder for protection.

He crashed through a pile of boxes that did nothing to slow him down and felt his right foot scuff the floor briefly. Then he seemed to spin in mid-air. He saw the heap of mail sacks an instant before he thudded into them.

The impact drove all the wind from his body. A searing pain bit into his shoulder and lanced across his chest. He tried to push himself into a sitting position as the floor danced crazily beneath him but his left arm was numb and weak and he flopped back onto his stomach.

An instant later there was a terrific *crack* and he found himself skidding across the floor in a jumble of mailbags, paper bundles and broken boxes.

He didn't see the low shelf until it was too late. It struck him just above the temple, snapping his head around.

The Tall Man was standing by a door at the end of his carriage when the train crashed.

He had decided ten minutes before that his best course of action would be to get off the train at Batforth and complete his journey by taxi. The cold spot had become too alarming for him to stay on the train, and he had become worried that someone might call the guard and the guard might suspect the cold had something to do with the box and want to see what was inside it.

Of course, the cabbie would notice the intense cold too but he had decided to say he was a scientist or a doctor taking a frozen specimen to a laboratory. He would promise the cabbie a tip big enough to eliminate his curiosity and stop him asking any questions.

In the moments before the crash he had trouble keeping his

feet because of the swaying motion of the train and managed to steady himself only by propping his shoulders into one corner.

When the guard had rushed past him less than a minute before, he had said: 'How long to Batforth?'

'We're there,' the guard had shouted over his shoulder.

The Tall Man had pulled down the window on the door, ready to reach outside and unlock it as soon as the train drew alongside the platform. The wind had whipped at his lank, black hair as he peered out the window, his eyes picking out the lights of the town.

That was when the train jumped the lines.

He was tossed around like dice in a cup, flung against the far wall, then onto his knees. Another jerk knocked him onto his back. He scrambled to his feet, desperately holding onto the box. Then the train plunged over the embankment and he was thrown against the door, bent double. His legs, hips and stomach hit metal but the top part of his body jack-knifed through the open window.

He felt the box slipping through the fingers of his left hand and grabbed at it, snatching it towards him. It hit his chest and bounced free. He juggled it between his hands for a moment and then it was gone.

SEVEN

The box hit a bush, crashed down through its weaker, less mature top branches, then rebounded and shot away at a right angle to the train. It tumbled and bounced down the steep embankment and travelled about a hundred feet through the tussocky grass of a field. Its inertia spent, it trembled for a moment on the bank of Moulson's Pond before slipping over the edge and sinking slowly into two feet of water.

At first Tanya heard no sounds at all, but later she decided this must have been an illusion.

As the train jumped the rails and ploughed down the embankment, her entire world was filled with silence, a hollow, vacuum of a silence.

Then a wall of sound hit her.

A huge oak tree exploded as the train shouldered it aside, smashing it into a thousand pieces. The train toppled onto its side with an ugly thud and continued its journey down the slope and into the field, shuddering like a dying thing. Metal shrieked as the third carriage broke in two and the fourth began to climb over it. The sound of smashing glass ripped through the night.

Jon. Jon. Jon.

The noises ceased and for an instant there was silence again. Tanya stood frozen for a moment, then blinked as if hoping none of it had really happened.

Then the cries for help and the screaming started.

You're a nurse. For God's sake MOVE! Don't stand around like the vicar's daughter on her first date.

As she started to run down the platform she heard the stationmaster behind her.

'Call the hospital, Charlie. Hurry up!' she shouted, looking back at him.

A moment later she had jumped into the darkness at the end of the platform and started across the field.

A woman came towards her, hurrying away from the train, her dress ripped open at the front, blood on her face. Tanya grabbed at her.

'What happened,' the woman babbled. 'What happened. . . .'

Tanya checked the head wound. It was just a graze.

'You'll be all right,' she told the woman. 'Stay here. Help will come soon.'

Then she ran on, half of her desperately wanting to see Jon, wanting to know he was alive, the other half knowing it was her duty to find the most badly hurt and tend to them.

She almost collided with a woman carrying a little girl.

'I'm a nurse, where's she hurt?'

'It's her leg.'

'Put her down.'

Tanya studied the deep gash which pumped blood, then whipped off her belt and used it as a tourniquet.

All around her was bedlam.

Eddie regained consciousness, tried to stand up and fell back into a seated position. He saw a door opposite him but slightly *above* him. Then he realized the floor was at a thirty-degree angle.

He couldn't remember much about the crash, just being thrown forward and tumbling over and over.

He scrambled up the floor, forced the door open and jumped out.

'Lennie,' he said in a whisper, then looked around him and shouted his friend's name again. 'Lennie.'

To hell with Lennie, he thought suddenly. Lennie was probably away by now. Safe. Eventually someone would be sorting out the baggage, what belonged to who. They'd want to know who owned the music centre and all that booze. He shook his head. Hanging around was not the thing to do, he decided. There was nothing in his own bags of any real value and his profits from his stay in London were in the wallet in his hip pocket.

He turned and started to run towards the lights of the town.

The Tall Man was also unhurt after the crash.

He moved backwards and forwards along the train, through

the crowds of injured and confused people, searching for the box.

The search became easier when police and ambulances arrived at the scene and shone their lights along the train. But still he could not find the box.

He began to search further out into the field, but again, met with no success.

Perhaps the box had been smashed, ripped to pieces on impact. Perhaps there was nothing left of it. Perhaps it had been crushed under a carriage.

He found himself searching an area he had searched three times before. It was useless, he decided. He would have to come back in the morning, in the daylight.

He climbed up the embankment, walked along the tracks to the station, and went through a door that brought him out into the main street. Ten minutes later he had checked into the Batforth Hotel.

Hammond rolled out of the open door in the guard's van and dropped onto his feet. He winced as he touched the egg-shaped lump above his temple. He began to shuffle forward, moving instinctively away from the crash. Then he saw Mrs Lord. She was dead, lying flat on her back, but she didn't seem to have a mark on her. Her eyes stared sightlessly up at the stars. A man draped a coat over her, tucking the edges in under her body as if in an effort to give her some dignity in death.

As he raised his eyes from the corpse he saw Tanya. He stood with his hands on his hips, watching her soothing a woman, carrying a little boy to an ambulance, then coming back in his direction.

She was no more than ten feet from him, hurrying through the crowd, when she turned her head and saw him. She covered her mouth with both hands in an instinctive gesture, stared at him for a moment, then ran over and leapt into his arms.

'Are you all right?' she said, standing back and looking at him.

'I'm fine,' he said. 'Just a little bump on the head.'

A man shouted, away to her left. She glanced in his direction, then looked back at Hammond.

'I've got to go.'

He nodded as they touched hands for an instant before she

rushed away. Hammond closed his eyes, rubbed his temples with the palms of both hands, braced his shoulders and started walking, heading for the station. He had trouble climbing onto the platform. His limbs felt rubbery and weak. He found the phone box and called Ernie Spiers.

The phone rang for a long time before his one and only reporter answered.

'Yeah.'

'Ernie. It's Jon. There's been a train crash.'

'Where?'

'Here. Batforth, by the station. I was on the train. Get a photographer, will you? Henry or Bill. I don't care which. Tell him we'll buy all the pictures, that's the deal. Standard rate plus any we sell to the nationals we'll split fifty-fifty. As soon as you've done that, get down to the hospital and get what you can. I'll be here for a while. I'll ring all the people we're stringers for with some kind of holding story. Got all that?'

'Yeah,' Spiers said, then added, 'You O.K?'

'I'm not quite sure at the moment,' Hammond said.

'Your voice sounds funny, a bit slurred.'

'I'll be all right. Got to go now. Bye.'

He scribbled the basic facts of his story on the back of the phone book then rang all the nationals, provincials and wire services that he worked for as a stringer and gave them a story. One definitely dead, probably more, he told them. Many injured. He'd get back to them within an hour with more information.

When he had completed his last call he went back the way he had come.

Beside the train he found Sergeant William Joss talking to two other policemen he had never seen before. He supposed they had been brought over from Ruttlake.

'Hello, William.'

'Jon, what's happened to you?'

Hammond touched the lump on his head and found it had grown bigger, more tender.

'I was in the crash.'

'That's a heck of a bump. Maybe a doctor should see that.'

'It's just a lump. I'm not concussed, I know the symptoms. Besides I've got work to do. How many dead, William?'

'Two for sure.'

'I knew about Mrs Lord, but who else?'

'We found a man in a toilet carriage that broke in two.'

'Was he a local?'

'He was a bit of a mess but I'm sure I'd never seen him before.'

'Any idea how many went to hospital?'

'I'd say about fifty, maybe more.'

'Thanks, William.'

He rubbed his chin thoughtfully, then added, 'By the way, there's something I should tell you.'

'What's that?'

'I think the train was going too fast as it came into Batforth. It really was going very, very fast. The guard realized it too, I think. He was running up towards the driver's compartment when I last saw him.'

Joss nodded slowly. 'I'll look into that, Jon. You might have to make a statement. I'll get back to you.'

'Any time.'

As he turned away, the sergeant took his arm: 'Seriously Jon, a knock on the head like that, you should get someone to look at it.'

'Yeah, I will, definitely.'

He went back to the station and through it to a pub on the main street. He drank a large whisky and repeated the calls he had made earlier, updating the information in the stories. When he finished, he realized he felt worse than before, dizzy and rubber-limbed. Maybe the sergeant had been right. He called a cab, and when it came he climbed in and said: 'Batforth Hospital.' Halfway there he changed his mind. He was sure there was nothing seriously wrong with him. He wasn't concussed. There were no bones broken. The hospital had far more serious cases to deal with tonight. He was just shaken up, that's all.

'Forget the hospital,' he told the driver and gave him the address of his flat.

When they arrived, he paid off the cabbie, went inside and flopped into his large easy chair with a loud sigh. He called Batforth Hospital and asked for Ernie Spiers.

'You're in charge now, Ernie,' he told him. 'The latest story I've filed is, two dead, more than fifty in hospital. Stay at the hospital for a couple of hours. If the numbers change, ring around and update the stories. Get the pictures as soon as you can and find out who wants to buy.'

'Where will you be?'

'I'll be in bed, Ernie. I'm feeling pretty rotten. I think it must be some kind of shock after the accident.'

'O.K. I'll take care of things.'

'Goodnight, Ernie.'

'G'night.'

He undressed, drank a large whisky and went to bed. He was asleep a few seconds after his head hit the pillow.

And that was when he had the dream for the first time. The dream that had no pictures.

PART TWO

The Town

EIGHT

The alarm on the Tall Man's watch woke him at six o'clock. He dressed, paid his hotel bill and returned to the crash scene.

Two cranes had been manoeuvred into position beside the carriage which had broken in two and a lorry was parked alongside. A gang of men was working on the train and he could see the sparks of the welding torches. He searched all around the train and as far as the bank of Moulson's Pond, then retraced his steps, checking the ground again.

'Lost something?' one of the workmen shouted from the top of the train.

'Yes, I was on the train last night when it crashed. I was looking for something I had with me.'

'A lot of cases have been taken up there,' the man told him, jerking a thumb towards the station.

The Tall Man thanked him, hurried to the station and found the left-luggage office. A boy of about eighteen, with ugly acne and greasy hair, confirmed that he was in charge of the cases collected from the crash scene.

The Tall Man told him about the box.

'About that size,' he said, measuring the box with his hands. 'It was made of metal with a padlock. It was in a plastic bag.'

The boy shook his head. 'Definitely nothing like that, just suitcases mostly, two handbags, cardboard boxes and mailbags from the guard's van. That's all.'

The Tall Man sighed. 'It must be somewhere.'

'What was in it?'

'Just some personal things,' the Tall Man said evenly.

'Some kids were chased away from the train last night, late on. The police think they might have pinched some things.'

'Could I look at the luggage that has been collected?'

'Well. . . .'

The Tall Man took out his wallet and put five pounds on the counter.

'I just want to look.'

The youth shrugged, pocketed the five pounds and showed the Tall Man where the luggage was being stored.

A thorough search of the racks was unsuccessful. He thanked the youth and returned to the crash scene. He reconnoitred the area again but gave up after twenty minutes.

It was gone. Irretrievably gone. Stolen by boys or smashed, or. . . . whatever. But gone.

The thought brought a sudden bleak feeling of emptiness and defeat. He turned his collar up against the breeze and trudged back to the road.

Martin Silver, Batforth Tractors chief security man, was in a foul mood when he arrived for work and he knew the reason why. It was the date – September 14. Exactly one year since Wendy had left him after twenty-five years of marriage.

He had tried to put all that behind him but without much success. He could still remember the moment he walked into the house and saw the small white envelope on the kitchen table, held down by his favourite coffee mug. He could recall the letter word for word and the sense of betrayal he had felt. He had been furious, of course. What kind of woman was she, to run away with an insurance salesman after all he had done for her?

It was his married daughter who had helped to put things in perspective. Elizabeth had never been one to mince words.

'You're a bully, Dad, and the person you bullied most was mum. You treated her more like a servant than a wife. You never gave her a chance. Why she put up with you for so long is beyond me. You were bad enough in your days as a policeman but when you took on your security job you became like some kind of Batforth Mussolini. You never had a kind word for anyone, especially for mum. You always had a jaundiced view of the world, you saw everyone as being some kind of cheat or liar or thief. . . . but you never took a good, long look at yourself and you never realized what a gem mum really was. The truth is, she was always far too good for you, too kind, too considerate; she saw good in you that never existed. Well, she's gone now and I hope she finds some kind of happiness that she could never have had with you.'

Silver had been unable to believe what he was hearing. *No one* had ever spoken to him like that. *No one.*

For once he had actually been stuck for words. He hadn't bellowed or banged his fist on the table. He had just stood open-mouthed as Elizabeth put on her coat, took her handbag and left without a backward glance. He hadn't seen her since that day.

His job was all that he had had left and in the past year he had tackled that with a new vigour. It was his boast that no one could steal even a screw or a cardboard box from Batforth Tractors and avoid prosecution. He had become such a bully with the security men that they dubbed him 'the Reichsführer'.

He drove through the front gate at Batforth Tractors shortly after six a.m. ignoring the brief wave of recognition from the guard in the gatehouse, parked his car and headed for his office.

He told himself he had come in three hours early because he had some paperwork to catch up on but really it was because he couldn't stand to be alone in the house, alone with his memories and the nagging thought that maybe Elizabeth had been right.

It was as he passed the stores building that he heard the dull, metallic *clang*.

He stopped and listened. No one was supposed to be in that building at this time of day. The storemen didn't come on until nine.

The sound came again. *Clang*.

There was somebody in the building. No doubt about it now. Probably one of the night shift men pilfering, he thought. Well, he was in for a big surprise. A venomous thrill ran through him as he tiptoed towards the door.

Clang. The sound came again. Like a heavy metal object bumping against the wall or the floor.

He reached the door and found the padlock in place. He ran his fingers over it gently, then tugged at it to make sure the lock was holding. It was.

Had they used a window? Or managed to open the huge doors to the delivery bay?

He thought about shouting but decided it would be better to catch whoever it was red-handed.

He hurried around the building, walking on the lawn now to avoid making any noise. He checked two windows and found them closed.

Clang.

The sound was still coming from the front of the building, near the padlocked door. It occurred to him that it sounded like the tolling of a church bell.

He reached the back of the building and jerked at the roll-up delivery bay doors. They were locked securely.

He jogged back the way he had come and stopped at the second window. Cupping his hands around his eyes to block out the morning light, he peered into the building. He saw orderly rows of boxes, the counter, a desk, a lorry parked silently at the delivery bay shelf. Nothing more. Nothing out of the ordinary.

Clang.

The noise startled him this time and a tiny uneasy lump began to form in his stomach.

'Who's there?' he shouted, surprised at the high-pitched tone of his own voice.

There was no answer, only the morning silence.

'Who's there? It's Martin Silver here. I. . . .'

Clang.

He jumped, and for the first time, realized he was actually afraid. But why? What was there to be afraid of? If anyone was in there he could soon overpower them using the neck-lock he was so proud of. Unless they were professional boxers or wrestlers they wouldn't stand much of a chance. And there were other possible explanations for the sound, weren't there? So why the fear?

He considered going to the gatehouse for help or running to his office to call the police but rejected these thoughts immediately. He was the head of security. It was his job to sort out trouble, not run away from it.

A vicious anger began to pump through him as he turned from the window and strode back to the front door, snatching his keys from his pocket.

He snapped off the padlock and stepped into the dark interior.

'All right, I'm not playing games. Who's in there?'

There was a strange clamminess about the place, a dankness that was normally associated with castle dungeons or the basements of disused stone buildings, not modern structures like this one. Silver shivered despite himself.

The room was illuminated only by two great funnels of light which came in through the uncovered windows. His eyes searched the shadowy lanes between the rows of boxes.

It was as he turned and swatted his hand down across the row of switches that the sound came again.

Clang.

It was much louder now of course.

He swung around, burying his fear in a wave of anger.

'Hey.'

The sound had come from the area of the third or fourth row of boxes, he guessed; probably between the fourth row and the wall that cut the interior of the building in two.

He marched forward as the fluorescent tubes above him sprang into life, splashing an ocean of sharp, eye-pinching light through the building.

The first two lanes were empty. He paused before the third, dropped into a fighting crouch, then shuffled quickly forward. There was nothing there. The third lane was as bare as the first two.

On the balls of his feet, he took half a dozen quick steps to the corner of the fourth lane, hesitated, then jumped forward.

At first he thought that lane was empty too, but as he started to turn away he saw the black shape of a crowbar, about forty feet from where he stood, near the base of the wall. He paused in a half-turned position and stared at it. If that had been banged against the wall it could have made the sound he had heard. But who had done the banging?

He turned back and started towards the crowbar. He had gone about ten feet when the fluorescent lights high above him began to dim as if their power was being slowly diminished. The lane grew darker and darker and he stopped and looked up at the lights. The tubes were dull and grey now, giving out hardly any light at all. He heard a brief rasping sound up ahead of him and in that instant the lights returned to full power. His eyes dropped back to the crowbar.

It had moved. It was at least four feet from where it had been before. That was what the rasping noise had been.

Goose bumps formed on the back of his neck as he started forward again. How could it have moved? It couldn't possibly have shifted. It had to be his imagination.

He covered another ten feet in an even, measured tread.

Then twenty. It had been a trick of the light. The crowbar hadn't moved at all. It. . . .

Suddenly the fluorescent lights died and he was surrounded by blackness.

Clangngng.

The sound was deafening. Right beside him, head-high. He wanted to run but instead he crouched down and covered his head like a frightened child aware of a thudding in his chest, a bad taste in his mouth.

The lights returned as the last reverberations of sound ceased. Silver fell forward onto all fours and stared at the crowbar like a mouse at a snake. It had moved again, at least three feet. It was nearer the row of boxes than the wall now.

It had made the noise. It had been banged against the wall.

He started to back away from it, still on all fours. Five feet, ten feet, fifteen.

Then it moved. In two quick motions it rasped across the floor and covered half the distance between them.

'Stop. Stop it,' he said, as if trying to calm an angry guard dog.

When it moved again – only an inch or so this time – he sprang to his feet and started to run.

He had taken four paces when he heard the angry, rasping sound again. Then something hit him on the side of the head and as he fell, he saw it spin away. His shoulder hit the concrete floor but instantly he was on his knees, using a pile of boxes to drag himself upright. Blood was running into his left eye and he tried to blink it away as he staggered forward.

The crowbar. It had been the crowbar.

Where was it now?

What. . . .

As he reached the end of the row of boxes and swung towards the door, he saw it flailing through the air at him again, and threw up an arm to protect his head. The crowbar crunched into his forearm, snapping the bone.

It had been on top of the boxes. Waiting for him.

He tried to galvanize his rubbery legs into a run but could only manage a shuffling, stumbling motion as the crowbar thudded into his back and legs and arms.

As he reached the door it seemed to attack more vigorously,

thudding and stabbing into him as if wielded by a powerful, invisible hand.

Don't fall. Don't go down.

He snatched at the handle, dragged the door open and fell outside. The sudden silence of the morning was overwhelming.

It hadn't followed him.

He rolled onto his back, groaning in agony, and looked up at the sky.

He was alive. Thank God. He was alive.

Then he heard the sound again.

Clang.

It was ringing in his ears as he lost consciousness.

NINE

The box lay exactly where it had landed during the train crash.
It was propped up by debris which littered the bottom of the
pond; a rusted metal bar, a broken brick, a tin can. The wind
whipped at the water above it, creating white-shouldered
ripples on the grey surface. But the box did not move. A fish
nosed up to it, searching for morsels of food but found none.
With a flick of its tail it spurted away, searching for warmer
water.

There were two dominating aspects of the dream that was to
become a part of Jon Hammond's life.

The first was sound. The dream always began with the
distant, rhythmic *rrup-rrup-rrup* of marching feet. This grew
louder and louder as if a great host of men was moving
remorselessly towards him. Then it would be joined by the
sound of men singing, and the song was the same marching
song he had heard on the train when his mind had conjured
up the torchlight procession. The second dominating aspect
of the dream was the fact that there were no images, no
pictures, no shapes. He saw nothing at all. It was as if he was
suspended in a black void.

The emotion of the dream began with a mild irritation at
not being able to see anything (dreams always had images,
didn't they?) but this was rapidly replaced by an inexplicable
terror as the marching feet drew closer and closer and the
singing louder and louder. He couldn't explain why he felt
such an intensity of fear but it increased in direct relationship
to the marching noise and reached a peak when the sounds
became a roar in his ears.

And that was always when he woke.

The first time Hammond had the dream was the night of the
train crash. He awoke as he always would, the fear slicing
through him as the sounds reached a great, twisted crescendo

as if being spat at him through a malfunctioning loudspeaker. He sat bolt upright, staring around him and trembling violently. For a moment, a haze of sleep hung before his eyes, then the familiar items of his bedroom began to take shape. The wardrobe, his watch, his wallet, the transistor radio on the dressing-table, his keys. After the blackness and terror of his dreams they seemed to take on an almost magical beauty, the keys so intricately formed, the yellow colour of the transistor radio so sharp.

He sat there as the memory of the dream slipped away, leaving only a residue of fear and a drumming headache that seemed synchronized to the sound of marching feet. His body was bathed in sweat. He could feel it running down his back and seeping out of his hairline and dribbling across his face.

He climbed wearily out of bed and took two tablets for his headache, crunching them between his teeth. He felt as if he had been dreaming all night, as if he had had no proper sleep, no real rest. He shaved then studied the bump on his head in the bathroom mirror. It was just a discoloured swelling now but painful to touch. He showered and called his office.

Jemma, the office girl, answered.

'Morning, Jemma, is Ernie there?'

'No, he hasn't come in yet. He left a note for you on your typewriter.'

'Read it to me, will you, Jemma?'

He heard the clunk of the phone being put down and the click-clack of her walking feet, then she spoke again.

'It says: "Jon, number of dead is now three. The guard died at four o'clock this morning. I've updated all the stories you filed and written my piece for this week's *Courier*. The only local person killed was Mrs Lord. The guard's name has been released but the police are still trying to get a positive identification of the other dead man. Apparently he came from Newcastle. Leonard Hughes was the name in his wallet. It is now six a.m. and I'm going home. I'll see you when I get up, probably mid-afternoon. I've had a couple of nibbles for the pictures and Jemma will be sending them in the morning." It's signed, Ernie.'

'O.K. thanks Jemma. I'll be there in about an hour. Bye.'

'Bye.'

He hung up and glanced across the room at the clock on

the dressing-table. It was almost eleven a.m. He dressed and headed for his car, which was parked at the rear of the block of flats, his keys jangling in his hand.

As he started the engine, he thought about the dream again. It was the blackness he remembered, the lack of any shape or form. . . .

We have temporary loss of vision, he thought as if hearing a television announcer's voice. He laughed briefly as he set the car in motion.

Ten minutes later, he parked the car in the gravel driveway in front of Tanya's small stone cottage, a hundred yards beyond the last line of houses at the edge of Batforth. There was no answer when he knocked.

He waited and knocked again, then used his own key.

He found her in the bedroom, a sleepy face peering at him over the edge of a quilt.

'I'm sorry, did I wake you?' he said.

She nodded: 'Uh-huh. I didn't get away from the hospital until six o'clock this morning.' She rolled over and turned her face into the pillow. 'Don't look at me. I must look terrible.'

He crossed the room, sat on the bed and kissed her neck.

'You look just fine to me.'

'Men are such liars,' she mumbled into the pillow.

'You just get back to sleep,' he said.

She sighed and whispered some response that he didn't hear.

'Just sleep,' he said.

He drew the quilt back, slipped the nightgown straps off her shoulders and tugged the blue material down to her waist. He began to massage the muscles between her shoulderblades. She sighed again and wriggled deeper into the bed.

'Go to sleep,' he said softly.

A few minutes later, her breathing became rhythmic. He paused before pulling the quilt back, studying the shape of her neck, her arms, her tapering back, the swell of her small muscles under the woman-flesh. *Vive le differance*, he thought with a smile, covering her up again.

He drove back across Batforth and was behind his type-writer writing a colour piece on the accident for the next edition of the *Batforth Courier* when the town hall clock chimed noon.

When he had finished he yawned, stretched and called the police station.

'Sergeant Joss, please,' he said and a moment later a voice said: 'Joss here.'

'It's Jon,' Hammond told him. 'I wondered if you'd had a chance to follow up on what I told you last night, about the speed the train was going.'

'I've spoken to a few people about it and put in a report,' Joss said. 'Several people from the train said they agreed it seemed to be going too fast. But the guard is dead and the driver's in a coma. Until the driver comes round we can only guess at what happened.'

'I didn't know about the driver,' Hammond said.

'The doctors are optimistic but they can't say when he's likely to come round. . . . a day or a week.'

'O.K. thanks, William. Nothing else happening?'

'Not much.'

'See you.'

He hung up and realized the headache he had had since waking was getting worse.

That night Hammond told Tanya about the torchlight procession he had seen from the train and about his dream while she cooked his favourite meal of steak, fried potatoes and eggs.

'They seem to be related. . . . you see that, don't you?' he said when he had finished. 'Marching men. . . . and the same song.'

'You've had a knock on the head, Jon. You've still got the headache to prove it. I'm sure that's all there is to it.'

The steak hissed and spat as she prodded at it with a fork.

'But I hadn't had a knock on the head when I saw the torches from the train.'

'You've been away for a week. You're probably overtired, that's all. I doubt very much if you actually saw a torchlight procession.'

'I'm not suggesting it was really there,' he said.

'Well, what are you suggesting?'

He shrugged: 'I don't know.'

She began to serve the meal, ferrying plates and glasses from her tiny kitchen to the table in the lounge. He shifted from the settee to the table and began to uncork the red wine.

'Did you get your luggage back?' she said, sitting down.

'Yeah, I picked it up from the station today. Lost my notebook though. I'll have to reproduce those notes from memory before I forget everything.'

They talked small talk during the early part of the meal but inevitably the conversation turned to Paris, the train trip and the accident.

'By the way,' Hammond said, 'the third dead person. . . . was there a confirmation of identity when you were at the hospital today?'

'Yes there was, late this afternoon. The police brought a man down from Newcastle.'

'It *was* the man from Newcastle then?'

'Yes.'

'Leonard Hughes?'

'Yes.'

'You know the men I told you about, on the train, the ones with the bottles. One of them was called Lennie.'

'Which one?'

'The one who wanted to start trouble. I just wondered if it was the same man. You didn't see the body?'

'No, I didn't. But there were probably half a dozen Leonards on the train.'

He shrugged: 'Probably.'

'How was the steak?' she said as he wolfed down the last mouthful, placed his knife and fork on the plate and sighed with satisfaction.

'Sheer perfection. I think I can say with all due modesty that I've trained you well. Gone are the days when you used to place burnt offerings before me.' He shook his head as if in sad reflection. 'Now, you've got it just right.'

She pursed her lips as if in mock anger and cocked her head to one side: 'And it's all down to the fact that you taught me how it's done?'

He looked at her innocently and said: 'I thought we were talking about cooking.'

'One-track mind,' she said, standing up and taking the plates into the kitchen.

He took the wine bottle and a glass and returned to the settee as she cleared the table.

'How's Martin Silver?' he said, sipping at his wine.

'Not very well. Nothing too serious though. . . . a broken arm and lots of cuts and bruises.'

'Yes, I got a call from a contact at Batforth Tractors late this afternoon. He said there had been some kind of break-in and Martin had been hurt. I rang the police but Joss seemed reluctant to tell me anything. He wouldn't even confirm that there had been a break-in. He became very formal and started using terms like "police investigations are continuing". All I've been able to find out is that for one reason or another Martin was beaten up.'

'Pretty savagely beaten up,' Tanya said. 'The nurses who were on this morning were saying he was quite a mess when he was brought in. Apparently he said a crowbar was used on him.'

'If it was a break-in, it's an odd time for one to take place, at six in the morning. And they've got two security guards on all night. It doesn't make much sense to me.'

The table cleared, she came back into the lounge and stood watching him.

'More wine?' he said.

She shook her head slowly: 'One glass is my limit. After that I get sleepy, you know that.'

'Come here,' he said, putting his drink down on an occasional table.

She walked across the room and stood in front of him.

'I missed you,' he said, looking up at her.

'I missed you too.'

He leaned forward and ran his hands across the backs of her knees then up under her skirt.

'Why, Mr Hammond, is this in the nature of a medical examination,' she said.

'No, it's more in the nature of a sexual advance.'

'I admire your frankness, Mr Hammond. What did you have in mind?'

He grinned up at her. 'I thought we might have a game of naughty night nurses,' he said and started to laugh.

'You quiet ones are always the worst, Mr Hammond.'

He stood up then, towering over her.

'Enough jokes,' he said, kissing her, his powerful hands pulling her body against his.

*   *   *

71

The last thing Hammond remembered before he fell asleep was the softness of Tanya's breasts travelling briefly across his chest as she shifted in her sleep. It was as if he was being lowered into a valley of warm feathers, all the everyday tensions eliminated.

Then oblivion.

How long his peaceful sleep lasted he could not recollect when he woke, but at the end of this indeterminate period, which could have been a minute or several hours, the dream began.

Far, far away, he heard the sound of marching feet, the rhythmic *rrup-rrup-rrup*.

He tried to turn away from it, to close his ears to the sound, but it was as if he was bound securely in some dark capsule, unable to escape. And the noise grew louder and louder.

Half a mile away, in the last terraced house at the edge of Batforth, Miss Agnes Davenport glanced out of her window at the dark fields which swept away towards Ruttlake, then tugged her curtains closed and got into bed. She sipped her cocoa and took up the romantic novel which would sweep her away from the life of a drab fifty-year-old spinster into the world of tall, handsome strangers, South Sea islands, true love and happy endings.

She had not even finished the first paragraph when she heard the first scream.

She raised her head from the book and listened. It had come across the fields, from somewhere near the picnic area by the river. Probably youngsters, teenagers capering about, she thought.

Then she heard the second scream, a shriek of naked terror.

TEN

'Alex, is that you? Can we talk?'

'Who is this? Who's calling?'

'It's me, Janet. Just say if Margaret's there and I'll hang up.'

'She's just gone next door for a coffee. Why are you calling me here? I've told you never to call me at home.'

'I've got to see you. I must.'

'When?'

'Tonight.'

'Don't be silly. I can't tonight. I didn't know John was away.'

'He's not. I've just got to see you.'

'Has something happened?'

'Yes. . . . no. . . . I'll explain tonight.'

'I've told you. I can't come tonight.'

'You *must*. Say you're going for a pint. I've got to see you even if it's only for an hour.'

'You know Margaret's been ill. . . . I. . . .'

'*Please.*'

'All right, but only for an hour.'

'Pick me up at the phone box on Wellington Street at eight.'

Alex Wright thought he did a good job of fooling his wife an hour after Janet called.

'Any beer in the house?' he said casually as they watched a quiz programme on television.

'No, I don't think so,' she said, still trying to think of the capital of Yugoslavia.

'I really do feel like a beer.'

'Belgrade,' the grinning quiz-show host said from the television set.

'Belgrade,' Margaret exploded, annoyed that she hadn't thought of it.

'Now this is a very, very important question,' the host in the loud check-jacket told an already nervous woman from

73

Yorkshire. Then he paused, making it even tougher on the woman.

Margaret leaned forward.

'Who was the first. . . . man. . . . to. . . . run. . . .'

'I think I'll go to the Blue Boar and have a pint,' Alex interrupted.

'*Alex*. . . . you made me miss the question.'

'Sorry, I was just saying. . . . I'm going to nip out for a pint. Want to come?'

'You know I watch this programme every week. You go if you want to.'

'All right.'

The host yelled the answer to the question but Margaret didn't catch it.

'What was that? Did you hear what he said, Alex?'

'No, I didn't. Sorry. See you in about an hour, darling.'

She raised her cheek for a tiny peck of a kiss then he was gone. She knew the next answer. She yelled 'The Battle of Bosworth' as her husband's car reversed down the gravel driveway.

He picked up Janet McLure at the phone box ten minutes later.

'Where to?' he said as she got in.

'Anywhere. Just drive.'

'What is it? What's wrong? Is something wrong?'

'Everything's wrong.'

She was in her melodramatic mood. He had seen her like that before.

'I can't stay with John much longer.'

He drove out of the village and along the road towards Ruttlake.

'What's happened this time?'

She sighed, halfway to a sob.

'You know, we. . . . John and I. . . . haven't. . . . made love. . . . for more than a year. Well, last night, he wanted to. It was horrible.'

'I thought for a minute maybe he'd found out about us. Or he'd beaten you up or something.'

There was something about his tone that surprised her and she said: 'Don't be so callous. Think about how I feel.'

He swung off the Ruttlake road about a quarter of a mile

74

from Batforth and parked by the wooden table in the picnic area beside the river.

'I'm not being callous,' he said.

She folded into his arms and held him tightly.

Their relationship had started after an adult education art class six months before. They met once or twice a fortnight at Janet's house, whenever John McLure's work as a representative for a car firm kept him away from home. The problem was that, emotionally, it had grown more and more powerful for Janet but had become shallow and boring for Alex.

For the last month he had been regretting all the promises he had made early in their relationship.

There's no fool like a forty-six-year-old fool who finds himself with a willing twenty-five-year-old girl, he thought suddenly, as he ran his fingers through her hair.

'We've got to do something,' Janet whispered.

'What. . . .'

'About the future. We have decisions to make.'

'Yes, I suppose we do,' he said vaguely.

That was when he heard the scraping sound on the car roof.

'What was that?' he said.

'What?'

'That noise.'

She listened but heard nothing. 'A twig on the roof probably,' she said.

'It didn't sound like a twig.'

It had sounded like an animal's movement, yet too light for an animal. A bird?

He glanced to his right, at a clump of bushes that ran along one side of the picnic area all the way to the river. A shape moved quickly across his field of vision, between him and the bushes.

'What's that?' he said, pointing towards the bushes.

'What?'

'There.'

His finger moved towards the front of the car. The shape had moved between them and the large wooden picnic table and had stopped in front of a tree. It was without substance, shimmering like clear water.

'It looks like a patch of mist.'

'It's not mist. It moved.'

'You're scaring me,' Janet said, looking at him.

'Let's go somewhere else,' he said and snapped the keys into the 'on' position. The engine whined and died.

'Shit.'

He tried again. This time it gave a triple whine, spluttered, then was silent again.

'It can't be the battery. I've just put in a new one.'

'Alex, *look*.'

The fear in her voice made the back of his neck prickle.

'What?' he said, almost shouting.

'There.'

It was her turn to point and he looked towards the tree again. The shimmering shape remained but there was something else there now. It was darker and looked like the outline of a thick-set, shortish man.

'What is it, for Christ sake?'

'Alex, I'm scared.'

'*You're* scared.'

He fumbled to find the keys again and when his fingers missed them in the dark, he panicked and snatched at the dashboard, accidentally turning on the light switch. The headlamps punched two funnels of light into the darkness.

For an instant they both saw the figure of a man, hunched, mis-shapen, his face heavy and very pale, his eyes wide, watching them. The figure began to waver, quivering like an image on a malfunctioning television set. Then it faded and disappeared.

'Did you see that?' Janet shouted.

'I saw it. I saw it.'

His fingers had found the keys again and jerked them round. The engine whined and coughed, then convulsed once and fell silent.

'It's not going to start.'

'Let's just leave it.'

'I think we should stay in the car. I don't. . . .'

He stopped dead and swallowed. The car had started to fill with a horrible smell. It was as if they had entered a shed where a cat had died and lain unburied for months.

Janet retched. 'What is that, Alex? Oh God, what's happening?'

He snatched at the keys again. A whine and a rumble, nothing more. He forced the key back again with such venom that the thin metal almost snapped. A whine, a double-cough, then silence.

'Oh God,' she said and put her hands on his shoulder, seeking human contact. He could feel them there, trembling like two frightened birds.

His eyes followed her gaze, looking away to their left. Half a dozen shapes moved about the clearing now. Some were just shadows, but others had the vague form of men, translucent shapes, their substance strengthening and weakening like sputtering radio signals sent from far away.

In the split second that Alex tensed his wrist to flick the ignition key again, he heard the click of his door handle.

Someone was trying to get in.

He jumped around, falling back against Janet.

Three faces looked through the window. They were pale and haggard with dark trenches under their dull and lifeless eyes. Two looked like old men, their hair matted and filthy, but the third was a young girl, about twenty, and her tongue jutted obscenely from her mouth.

As the door swung open, Alex scrambled across Janet, jerked at her door and pushed her out. As he tried to follow her, he felt chilly fingers scrape down his neck and a hand grasp the collar of his jacket. He shrugged his shoulders out of it and flopped onto the grass beside Janet. He was on his feet in an instant, dragging her up by the arm.

'Run, Janet. For God's sake, run.'

She felt as if an electric charge had passed through her legs. She sprang to her feet and ran as she had never run before, gripping the hand Alex held out for her. A face loomed up in front of her, black hair, sharp nose, a grinning mouth of badly-decayed teeth. She screamed when she saw the eye sockets were empty. A hand plucked at her dress and she slapped it away, hearing the dress rip, feeling cold air wash over her back.

Another face loomed up at her now and she closed her eyes, shutting out the sight, running blind. Something cold and chilly that felt like thawing meat brushed her leg and she screamed again.

She felt Alex's hand jerk as he stumbled and then her arm

77

being pulled almost from its socket as he fell, dragging her down with him.

She opened her eyes and clawed herself upright along his back, then held his arm as they began to run again.

There were people all around them now, reaching for them, touching them. Ugly, mis-shapen people who carried a stench of death with them; ragged, hunched people with putrid sores on their faces who shuffled and hobbled about. Some were clear and tangible but many were still wavering shapes, half images without substance.

Something soft and yielding touched her face and as she knocked it away she realized she was no longer holding Alex's arm.

He was gone.

She ran on, dodging between the figures, flailing her fists about, grunting with repulsion at what they touched.

Suddenly she found she was alone, running into the blackness. There were no faces any more, no shapes, no hands that touched her. Just the dark night, the bushes and the trees. Relief rushed through her.

I'm free. I've managed to get away from them. Just a nightmare. Some kind of nightmare. That's all it was.

Then the terrible yell turned her spine to ice.

'*Janeeeeeet.*'

She faltered and stopped.

'*Janeeeeeet.*'

She spun around and looked back towards the picnic site.

At first it appeared that Alex was suspended in mid-air, about seven feet from the ground. Then she saw the quivering, trembling, amorphous mass beneath him and hands extended from it, holding him aloft. As she watched, the mass divided and separated and became a crowd of people then merged again into a single, quivering entity.

She wanted to go back to help him, to save him but found herself turning away, running again, into the blackness.

ELEVEN

Tanya awoke with a start, pushed her face away from the pillow and stared at Hammond. In his sleep he had thrown all the blankets back from his body and she could see he was trembling violently from head to foot, almost convulsing. Each muscle of his body was tense and rigid, bulging against his flesh. His eyes were closed tight (as if the eyelids had been clamped into place, she thought) and his mouth was pulled back in a grimace of sheer terror.

'Jon,' she said, then louder, 'Jon!'

She leaned over and touched his face. As if in response he sat upright, throwing her backwards, and held his hands out in front of him as if to fend off some invisible attacker.

He began to gasp, to moan and the sight started a chilly sensation running up Tanya's spine.

'Jon!' she shouted, 'Jon!'

She tried to shake him but he was too big so she slapped his face firmly.

'Jon.'

He opened his eyes abruptly, staring wildly around him and his hands fell to his sides.

She held him tightly.

'It's all right, Jon, it was a dream. You were having a dream.'

'A dream. . . .'

'Yes, a dream, it's all right now.'

Gradually the wildness left his eyes and his breathing became more even.

'Not just a dream,' he said.

'What do you mean?'

'It was the same dream I had yesterday. Exactly the same.'

'The sound of marching men. . . .'

'Yes.' He cut her off then sat deep in thought for a moment. 'I have to find out the name of that song they were singing. I've heard the song before but I just can't remember. . . .'

'Lie down, Jon, try to get back to sleep.'

He sighed, blinked sleep from his eyes and glanced at his watch.

'I can't,' he said.

'Why? What time is it?' she said.

'Seven-fifteen.'

'You don't have to. . . .'

'It's publication day tomorrow, remember?' he said sweeping back the blankets. 'I've still got a couple of pages to lay out, headlines to write, stories to edit, printers to watch over and a couple of stories to chase up.' On his way to the bathroom he added: 'What time do you start?'

'One o'clock,' she said.

'We'll have lunch at Bunty's then. Shall we say midday?'

'O.K.,' she said through a yawn. 'Do you want some breakfast?'

'No, you get some more sleep. I'll get something at the office.'

He shaved, then stepped into a steaming hot shower and let it wash away the memory of the dream.

He returned to the bedroom after towelling himself dry and found Tanya sound asleep. He dressed, tiptoed out of the house and drove through Batforth to his office.

Jemma had an advertising file open on her desk and as he walked in the front door she said: 'That used car firm haven't paid up for two months.'

'Send them a reminder,' he said without stopping.

Ernie Spiers was battering at an old typewriter, a biro stuck behind his ear, his eyes narrowed against smoke that dribbled from a cigarette in his mouth. The last lock of hair (which was six inches long) in his otherwise bald head hung down over one side of his face.

'Anything happening?' Hammond said, flopping into his chair.

Spiers tossed his head, flicking the lock of hair back into place and took the cigarette out of his mouth.

'Might be,' he said.

'What does that mean?'

'There was some kind of incident at the picnic area by the river last night. Haven't been able to get much on it. There was a police car out there and people reported hearing screams.'

'Screams.' Hammond nodded thoughtfully. 'That sounds promising. Have you called the police?'

'They wouldn't say anything.'

'Was Joss there?'

'No, he wasn't.'

'I'll give him a call later.'

He took off his jacket, rolled up his shirt sleeves, loosened his tie and designed the *Courier*'s front page. The entire page was given over to the accident and was dominated by an excellent picture of the wreckage of the train with people being loaded into an ambulance in the foreground. After that he designed an inside page which consisted entirely of other pictures of the crashed train.

When he had finished the second page, he told Jemma to make some coffee and called the police station.

'What happened out at the riverside picnic area?' he asked Sergeant Joss.

'There isn't much I can tell you, Jon,' Joss told him. Hammond thought he sounded tired.

'I. . . .'

'I don't want to stir up a hornet's nest, Jon.'

'What does that mean?'

'I'll give you a statement that you can use in tomorrow's paper and that's all.'

Hammond flicked open his notepad and took up a pencil.

'You can say. . . . Batforth police are anxious to trace the whereabouts of Mr Alexander Wright, aged 46, salesman, 43 Andover Street, Batforth, who left his house at 8 p.m. on the evening of September the 14th and was last seen near the riverside picnic area on the Ruttlake road.'

There was a pause then Hammond said: 'That's it?'

'Uh-huh.'

'Off the record, William, can you tell me what's going on?'

'I wish I knew,' Joss said.

'That sounds mysterious.'

'Sorry, Jon, there's no more I can tell you at the moment.'

'O.K., thanks William. Bye.'

He was typing up the statement, thinking about all that it didn't say, when the telephone rang.

Jemma answered it.

'It's for you, Ernie,' she said and transferred it to Spiers's extension.

Hammond heard Spiers say: 'Yes. Uh-huh. An accident. Where? O.K. . . . yeah, thanks Tom.'

As Spiers hung up, Hammond looked at him with raised eyebrows.

'Accident on the Ruttlake road,' Spiers said. 'Car spun off and hit a tree.'

'Anyone hurt?'

'Apparently a man's still trapped in the car. Want me to go and have a look? I could get a photographer if it looks particularly horrific.'

'No, it's O.K., I think I'll go.' Hammond stood up, shrugging his shoulders into his jacket. 'I was thinking about doing a road safety feature next week anyway. There have been far too many accidents around here recently.'

On his way to the crash scene he passed Emmerson's record shop and it occurred to him that Jack Emmerson would be just the man to try to put a name to the marching song that plagued his sleep. Hadn't Emmerson once said to him: 'I can name any tune; any tune in the world no matter how obscure. Just hum me a few bars?' And it was no idle boast. He had seen Emmerson display his memory for music at a couple of parties and no matter how hard people tried they hadn't been able to trip him up. A few seconds of thought and he had come up with the answer every time.

Hammond started to hum the tune to himself but found he was humming another tune altogether. He tried again and again he got it wrong. It was ridiculous. How could he forget the tune that had burst into his life on the train and ravaged his sleep ever since?

Relax, Hammond, he told himself. *Don't rush it. It'll come to you. That particular gremlin hasn't gone out of your life yet.*

He turned left along the Ruttlake road and two minutes later arrived at the accident scene. The rear of the crashed car was intact apart from the smashed window still half-filled with shattered glass, but the front which was wrapped around a tree was a tangle of twisted, ripped metal. There was no one inside the car.

A police car was parked on the grassy shoulder of the road

and a constable inside was talking on the police radio. Another policeman stood behind the crashed car, making notes.

Hammond drew up on the other side of the road and got out.

'Morning,' he said, flipping open his wallet to expose his Press card.

The policeman looked up from his notebook and nodded.

'Jon Hammond, *Batforth Courier*,' Hammond told him.

'I know who you are,' the policeman said.

'They got the man out O.K?'

'Yeah, he's on his way to hospital now.'

'Badly hurt?'

'He'll live but his leg doesn't look too good.'

'A local?'

'No, he was a tourist.'

'Foreign?'

'No, just up from Devon, heading north.'

'Odd place for an accident to happen,' Hammond said. 'You couldn't find a much straighter road than this.'

The policeman half smiled, mirthlessly: 'You could build the perfect road and people would still have accidents.' Then he shrugged and added: 'But you do have a point. No skid marks either. It's as if he just jumped from the road straight into the tree.'

'Mind if I look at the car?'

'No.'

Hammond strode through the long grass to the car and looked inside. The entire front of the car had been pushed back a couple of feet and the twisted remains of the dashboard dangled only inches above the front seat. Chunks of shattered glass were scattered about like confetti and there was blood on the driver's seat and the floor. Hammond felt his stomach churning (the way it always did when he saw the remains of smashed cars) and turned away.

'Where have they taken him, Batforth or Ruttlake?'

'Batforth Hospital.'

'O.K., thanks for your help.'

He climbed into his car and headed back towards Batforth. A quarter of a mile along the road, he slowed and dropped the car down a gear when he saw three policemen in the middle of a field away to his left, walking slowly along the riverbank.

They're not out for a Sunday stroll, Hammond.

He drew the car to a halt and studied them for a moment. They were hunched forward, their eyes on the ground. . . .

Searching for something.

He set the car in motion again and swung along the track towards the riverside picnic area.

That was when he remembered Alexander Wright, the missing salesman, and the statement he had received from Sergeant Joss, the statement that had been most notable for what it hadn't said. 'Last seen near the riverside picnic area'. Wasn't that what Joss had told him?

He found three police cars in a neat row, facing a red Citroën Visa and parked behind them.

Something's up, Hammond. Something is definitely up.

He opened his car door to get out and saw a police constable hurrying towards him. He recognized the man – one of Batforth's younger bobbies.

'Hello, what's. . . .'

'I'm sorry, you can't stay here, Mr Hammond.'

'What's going on?'

'You'll have to ask a senior officer. Call the police station.'

'Is it about the missing man?'

'I'm sorry, Mr Hammond, I'm going to have to ask you to leave.'

'What are you searching for?'

'Mr Hammond. . . .'

'All right, all right, I'm going. . . .'

He drove back into Batforth and was only two streets away from his office when he remembered his lunch date with Tanya. He glanced at his watch. It was eleven-fifty. He had said he would meet her at twelve. He turned the car around, drove along the High Street to Bunty's Restaurant and left the car in the parking area at the rear.

Tanya was waiting for him, sitting at the bar, sipping a glass of Perrier water.

'Hi,' he said, giving her a kiss on the cheek. 'Order me the fish,' he said, 'I've got an important phone call to make.'

'Rush, rush, rush,' said Bunty Robinson, coming out of the door behind the bar and wagging a finger at him. 'Relax. Tension is bad for your digestion.'

'Hi, Bunty,' he said over his shoulder, going through a glass door into a narrow hall that led to the toilets.

He snatched up the pay phone in the hall and called the office.

'Give me Ernie, Jemma,' he said and waited. A moment later Ernie Spiers came on.

'Now listen, Ernie, something's happening out at the picnic area. I think it's something to do with a missing man called Alexander Wright. The place is crawling with cops. If a big story is breaking in Batforth I don't want to read about it in the nationals. You know that old cop. . . . the one you always call your best contact on the force. . . . give him a ring and see if you can find out anything. Joss wouldn't tell me a thing this morning.'

'All right, I'll do that. By the way, Joss called while you were out. He said could you be at the police station at one o'clock. He said to tell you it was very urgent.'

'Did he say what it was about?'

'No, he wouldn't say. He just said to stress that it was very urgent.'

'O.K. I'll be there. Thanks Ernie. Bye.'

He hung the phone up slowly then turned and went back into the restaurant.

'A Perrier water for you too, darling?' Bunty said from behind the bar, smiling her teasing smile at him and drawing a pint of lager.

He returned her smile and said: 'No, Bunty, I think I'll continue my gradual descent into alcoholism.'

He and Bunty had been the closest of friends for almost six years, ever since their affair ('our mad fling' Bunty called it) had petered out. Bunty was pushing fifty now – fourteen years older than Hammond – but worked very hard on her appearance and could have easily passed for a woman in her late thirties. She was an attractive, laughing woman with blue eyes, auburn hair and a figure and a way of moving that still drew men's eyes. She also had the attribute Hammond always found very attractive in women – the ability to laugh at herself.

'You're the only ex-lover I've ever become close friends with,' she often told him when Tanya wasn't around. Tanya didn't know about Hammond and Bunty. 'Tell her if you like,' Bunty had said, then added: 'But be warned. She might not

85

like us being friends after that. I know what women are like, darling. Jealousy is never far away, particularly where a hunk like you is the body in question.'

Bunty was an ex-actress and dancer who had seen the inside of most of the dressing-rooms in the theatres and clubs of Britain during twenty-five years in show business. 'I was never a show stopper,' she always said, 'but, by God, I was a tryer, and I was in love with the business. Then age caught up with me and all I had left was my dream of opening a restaurant, my own place, and my fatal flaw.' What Bunty always referred to as her 'fatal flaw' was her desire for younger men, the younger the better. 'I just can't help myself,' she'd told Hammond, with a smile. 'When I was nineteen, my men had to be in their forties or older. Now, anything past thirty is a has-been. There's perversity for you.'

She handed Hammond his lager, winked at Tanya then rested her elbows on the bar and looked up into Hammond's eyes with a sigh and the look of a love-sick teenager.

'If only I was ten years younger,' she said.

Tanya laughed but Hammond gave Bunty a brief, disapproving glance.

TWELVE

After lunch Hammond dropped Tanya at the hospital and drove to the police station. He found Joss in the outer office, talking to a constable.

'Hello, William. You wanted to see me?'

Joss turned and Hammond saw there was a grim, worried expression on his face.

'Yes, Jon, I did. I'd like you to step into my office. There's someone I'd like you to talk to.'

'What's up, William?'

Joss ignored the question, crossed the room and knocked on the door of his office. The gesture struck Hammond as very odd. Why would Joss be knocking on the door of his own office?

Joss pushed the door open and Hammond caught a glimpse of an erect, dark-suited figure behind the desk.

'Inspector Jensen, Mr Hammond is here,' he heard Joss say.

Then the sergeant waved him into the room and as he entered the man behind the desk stood up and smiled a stiff, official smile. He was about fifty, Hammond guessed, with short, iron-grey hair and a clipped moustache.

The man stretched out a hand. 'My name is Jensen, Inspector John Jensen,' he said as Joss closed the door, leaving them alone.

Hammond shook hands with him briefly then the inspector said: 'Please, be seated. I'll try not to keep you too long.'

As Hammond lowered himself into the chair he thought the inspector's words sounded too much like a dentist saying: 'I'll try not to make it too painful.'

'What's this about?' he said.

The inspector leaned back in his chair, pursed his lips and made a steeple with his fingers. He had an aura of arrogance that Hammond disliked immediately.

'Mr Hammond, you are in a position to help us a great deal.

What I'd like you to do for me is to tell me the story of your train journey from London, leaving nothing out. Tell me about all the people you saw, everything that happened, no matter how insignificant it appeared at the time. Would you do that?'

'What for? Why?'

'Because it might help us with a problem we're trying to solve. I'm sorry to be vague but you would be helping me a great deal if you would do that.'

'What's this to do with? The crash?'

'Just tell me everything that happened on the train trip. Everything.'

Hammond thought a moment, his brow furrowed, then shrugged and said: 'All right. I got on the train about ten minutes before it was due to leave. I. . . .'

Ten minutes later he had finished. He had outlined all that had happened on the journey, consciously leaving out only one thing: the torchlight procession.

'Now will you tell me what this is all about?'

The inspector nodded, thinking.

'This. . . . how shall we describe it. . . . difference of opinion you had with this man Lennie. Were any blows exchanged?'

Hammond stared silently at the policeman for a moment then said testily: 'I've told you exactly what happened. No blows were exchanged. Now what is this all about?'

Jensen ignored his question. 'And when the two men left to go to the buffet car, you never saw this man Lennie again, although you did see his friend?'

Hammond shook his head slowly. 'Look, I'm not answering any more questions in the dark. I've done what you asked. I've told you exactly what happened. Unless you tell me what's going on, I'm leaving.'

The inspector stood up, strolled to the window and glanced out. When he turned his head in Hammond's direction again he said: 'What if I was to tell you, Mr Hammond, that a post-mortem examination has just been held into the death of Leonard Hughes and the findings are that he did not die in the crash but was murdered some time previously?'

'Murdered,' Hammond breathed. Then he was silent for a long time, letting the word sink in. When he spoke again, he said: 'Until this moment, I didn't know that the Lennie that I argued with and the Leonard Hughes who died on the train were one and the same man. I wondered about it but I didn't know for sure.'

'Murdered,' the inspector said evenly, 'and whoever did it must have been very strong.'

Hammond grinned humourlessly: 'And you're trying to say that I might fit the bill.'

'You're certainly strong.'

Hammond studied Jensen for a moment then he spoke again, his voice hard and angry.

'If I'm a suspect you should have warned me of my rights at the beginning of this conversation. You know that.'

'I didn't say you were a suspect.'

'Don't play games with me. You should have told me at the beginning what this was all about.'

The inspector sighed: 'Mr Hammond, I've spent the last two hours being told by Sergeant Joss that it's incomprehensible that you could be the killer. My purpose in inviting you here today was to try to eliminate you from our inquiries and to find out if you knew anything that might be of help to us. As it happens I'm satisfied with your story. You told me about your argument with Lennie. If you were the killer I don't think you'd have done that. There's no way you could have known that I already knew about your argument with Lennie.'

'How?'

'I've been speaking to a rather poor specimen called Eddie. We traced him in Newcastle and brought him down to identify Lennie's body. He confessed to being involved in a series of London break-ins with Lennie a couple of days ago. . . . but he's not our killer either. Eddie is not physically strong enough to do what was done to Lennie.'

'What *was* done to Lennie?'

'He was attacked with such ferocity that his neck was broken, his head almost torn off, a leg and both arms were broken, his ribs were crushed. I've never seen anything like it in my life. Whoever attacked him must have gone berserk. Anyway, I needn't detain you any longer, Mr Hammond. Just one last question. Could you tell me your whereabouts last night. . . . shall we say between the hours of seven and nine-thirty.'

'Last night?'

'Yes.'

'Why?'

'Please, Mr Hammond, it would be a help.'

'I was with my girlfriend.'

'Her name?'

'Tanya Bailey.'

Jensen wrote that down on his pad.

'Where can I get in touch with her?'

'She works at Batforth Hospital.'

'All right, Mr Hammond. Thank you for all your help and I apologize for the inconvenience.'

Hammond left the room and Joss met him in the outer office.

'I'm sorry about all this, Jon.'

Hammond shrugged then said: 'Why did he want to know where I was last night?'

'I can't comment on that, Jon, I'm sorry.'

'Stop apologizing, William, for God's sake. What about what happened at the picnic area, can you tell me anything about that yet?'

'No, I'm afraid not.'

Hammond sighed – a professional exaggeration of a sigh – and said: 'When are the Press going to get an official statement on this murder on the train? Can you tell me that much?'

'I believe Inspector Jensen plans to release a statement at about three o'clock.'

'Thanks.'

Hammond strolled to the door, pulled it open, then hesitated.

'By the way, William, I believe you put in a good word for me, with the inspector, before I arrived.'

Joss looked puzzled. 'I told him you couldn't possibly be the killer if that's what you mean.'

Hammond nodded and smiled: 'Thanks, William. It's nice for a man to be reminded who his friends are once in a while.'

Joss returned his smile as he went out the door.

'Well?' Hammond said to Ernie Spiers as he entered his office fifteen minutes later. 'What did your contact on the police force have to say?'

Spiers stubbed out a cigarette and flipped open his notepad.

'Facts,' he said. 'A man was driving along the Ruttlake road last night and came upon a woman, a Mrs Janet McLure. She was hysterical and he drove her to Batforth Hospital where she's been under sedation ever since. It seems she was with a man at the picnic area, a Mr Alexander Wright. Mr Wright is missing and the police have found blood on some bushes near his car. Secondly, my contact says there is to be a statement from the police this afternoon. . . . one of the men who died on the train didn't die in the crash, he was murdered. He. . . .'

'I know all about that. Get back to the picnic area incident.'

'You've heard all the facts I've got. The rest is speculation. My contact says the man in charge of the case – an Inspector Jensen – believes the murder on the train was committed by some kind of psycho and he's afraid that this Alexander Wright is dead and may have been killed by the same man.'

Hammond nodded, pieces of a jigsaw falling into place in his mind. So that was why Jensen had wanted to know where he was the night before? It was just as well he had a watertight alibi. Surely now he'd be crossed off the list of suspects for good.

He went to his desk and flopped into his chair.

'Ernie, get onto the printer and tell him to hold the front page until we get a story on this train murder.'

It happened when Tanya was in the drugs cupboard and was over in an instant. Later, she would remember every detail.

She was standing facing an array of bottles and boxes lined up like parade-ground soldiers on the shelves. In her hand she had a tray carrying four bottles of tablets. Her eyes were searching for a box containing hydrocortisone cream.

Suddenly, something hot and sticky (like a fat man's hand covered in oil, she thought later) touched the back of her knee. As she recoiled from the touch, the *thing* thrust its way up her leg and touched her obscenely.

She dropped the tray, staggered back, snatched open the door and stumbled into the corridor.

Nurse Moira O'Malley was passing. She hurried over to Tanya, her face concerned and puzzled, and put one hand on each of Tanya's shoulders.

'What is it, Tanya?' she said, her voice filled with alarm. 'What's wrong?'

Tanya felt foolish. What could she say? What was there to say?

'Just a dizzy spell,' she muttered, then repeated it, insistently: 'A dizzy spell. . . . that's all. I haven't been sleeping well lately. I'll be all right in a minute.'

Then she forced a brief smile for Moira's benefit and went back into the cupboard to tidy up the mess and replace the tablets she had dropped.

What could it have been? What could have caused that particular sensation of being touched? A muscle spasm? What?

All the time she remained in the cupboard she felt as if eyes were watching her, as if some unspeakably vile Peeping Tom was standing in the corner, leering at her. Invisible.

THIRTEEN

The tin can which supported one corner of the box settled deeper into the sand at the bottom of the pond. The box shifted a couple of inches and several air bubbles escaped, plopped to the surface of the water and sent tiny clouds of steam up into the air.

The box was hot again.

It was five o'clock and Hammond had just finished redesigning his front page with the Lennie Hughes murder story as the lead when the phone rang.

'It's for you,' Jemma said and transferred the call to his extension.

'Hammond speaking,' he said.

'Jon, it's William Joss here. There's something I'd like to talk to you about, something personal. I can't talk about it on the telephone but it's very important.'

'Yes, all right. We can have lunch tomorrow if you like. A pint and a pie in the Blue Boar.'

'No, it has to be tonight.'

'That's a bit difficult, William. Tonight's the night we print the *Courier*. I've got to be at the printers. Is it. . . .'

'It's very important, Jon.'

'Care to give me a hint at what it's about?'

'I can't explain it over the telephone.'

Hammond looked at his watch.

'Pubs are open. . . . let's have a pint at the Blue Boar.'

'No. Somewhere private.'

'You're sounding very mysterious, William,' Hammond said with a sigh, then added: 'All right, I need something to eat anyway. I'll grab a hamburger and meet you at my flat.'

'That would be fine.'

'Shall we say half an hour?'

'I'll see you then, Jon.'

'Bye.'

Hammond hung up slowly and raised his eyebrows at Jemma.

'Problems?' she asked.

He shrugged: 'I don't know.'

Hammond bought a hamburger and chips at the fish and chip shop opposite his office and drove to his flat. He had finished his meal, washing it down with two cans of lager, by the time Joss arrived.

'Come in, William,' he shouted in answer to the rapping on the door and added, 'Sit down,' as Joss strolled into the lounge. As the policeman took off his coat and hat and dropped into an easy chair, Hammond went into the kitchen to fetch himself another can of beer.

'Want a beer, William?'

'No thanks. . . . oh yeah, O.K., I will.'

Hammond thought his voice sounded thick, worried.

He handed a can to Joss, snapped the ring pull off his own can and sat down opposite the policeman.

'O.K., William, what's the big mystery?'

When Joss hesitated he said quickly: 'Any broad hints about what's going on at the picnic area? Off the record if you like.'

'Off the record the official situation is that a woman was picked up by a motorist on the Ruttlake road last night in a hysterical condition. She was taken to hospital, babbling something about this man friend of hers who'd been attacked. A couple of constables went out to the area and found the man's car and a lot of blood on some bushes. There is a possibility. . . . at least Inspector Jensen thinks there is a possibility. . . . that the same man who killed Lennie Hughes killed this man. We can't find a body and the woman in the hospital is still under sedation. We haven't even been able to question her yet. But all that is definitely off the record.'

'Have I ever let you down before?'

Joss shook his head.

'Now, what was this personal matter you wanted to see me about?'

The police sergeant shifted uneasily.

'It's not a personal matter exactly. What I meant when I said that was it's not a police matter. I can't discuss what I've got on my mind with Mary. She wouldn't understand. And apart from you my only friends are policemen and I can't discuss this with another policeman.'

'You're beating around the bush, William, get to the point.'

'I'm sorry, it's just that it's not easy to say. The problem is that what I've got on my mind doesn't really make any sense to me. I thought if I put it to somebody else they might make sense of it.'

'What?' Hammond said, an edge of impatience in his voice.

Joss gulped a mouthful of beer, put his can down on an occasional table and leaned forward.

'Jon, this has always been a peaceful town,' he said earnestly. 'It's always been a quiet little place. I spend all my time dealing with vandals, Saturday night drunks and a very rare break-in. Nothing. . . . really unusual ever happens around here. But in the last couple of days, since the train crash. . . .'

'What?'

'Let's start with Martin Silver. The official story is that he was attacked by person or persons unknown and beaten up with a crowbar. Do you know what Martin told me privately?'

Hammond shrugged.

'He told me there was no one in the warehouse. The crowbar flew through the air at him. He said it was like. . . . like whoever did it was invisible.'

Jon grinned: 'Sounds like Martin's been smoking some of those funny cigarettes.'

'Laugh if you want to,' Joss said. 'But that's not all. The way Lennie Hughes was murdered. . . . it was hideous, unbelievable violence. And this woman at the picnic site. The nurses said when she was brought in that she kept telling them about people who appeared and disappeared. And then there's the car crash.'

'Which car crash?'

'The one on the Ruttlake road today.'

'Oh yeah, I was out there looking it over.'

'I talked to the driver this afternoon. He swears he was doing forty miles an hour, no more. He says something pulled the steering-wheel out of his hands. He said he tried to wrestle against it but he couldn't.'

'A steering fault?'

'Maybe, but it was a brand new car.' He snatched up the beer can and took two quick gulps. Wiping his mouth with the back of his hand he said slowly: 'Ever since the train crash, haven't you noticed a kind of heaviness, a kind of ugliness in the air, a sort of darkness about Batforth?'

Hammond shrugged and studied Joss, puzzled. The words were so unlikely coming from down-to-earth, both-feet-firmly-on-the-ground police sergeant William Joss.

'I don't know,' Hammond said. 'I can't say that I have. I've been too wrapped up in my own life. I haven't been sleeping well since the accident. Bad dreams.'

'It's there, believe me.'

'What point are you trying to make, telling me all this?'

'I don't know.'

'What are you suggesting?' Hammond waved his hand about as if trying to pluck an answer from the air. 'Are you suggesting. . . . some kind of mass hysteria as a result of the accident? Irrational behaviour? What?'

Joss drained his can of beer. 'I don't know. But there is one thing I haven't told you yet.'

'What's that?'

'I was driving home last night after work. A couple of streets from my house, I suddenly saw a group of children run onto the road, right in front of my car. I braked hard but there was no way I could miss them. I threw the car into a four-wheel drift and tried to swing towards the pavement at the far side of the road. But it was no good. I ploughed into them, Jon. I saw my bonnet smashing into one of them. I felt the bump as the car ran over several others. I came to a halt and got out. . . .' He hesitated, shivered briefly. 'There was nothing there, Jon. No kids. Nothing. The street was empty.'

Hammond studied the sergeant's puzzled face for several minutes without speaking then he said: 'I don't know if I can give you any answers, William. But there's something else that happened. Something you don't know about. It happened to me on the train.'

Then he told the policeman about the host of marching men, their arms held high bearing torches, and the song they sang.

That night at the printers as Hammond struggled to put his newspaper to bed, all the things Joss had said worried away at the back of his mind like a pair of terrier pups with an old blanket. They gnawed, chewed and tugged at him. There were facts, there were questions, but there were no answers. A couple of blows on the head could have twisted Martin Silver's memory of what happened to him. The motorist's car could have had faulty steering. Joss could have been overtired when he thought he saw the children. But why were all these things happening at once? Had the train crash and the deaths caused some kind of shock to the collective consciousness of Batforth, creating some kind of hysteria? Was that what a lecturer in psychology would say? People were just imagining these things.

But nobody was imagining Lennie's murder or the blood out at the picnic area or the train crash. And what had happened to cause the train crash? The driver *had been* going too fast? *Why?*

And what about the torchlight procession? He had seen that himself. Whether or not it had come from his own mind, *it had been there*, and that was before the train crash.

By eight-forty-five the presses were humming and Hammond had the first half-dozen copies of the *Courier* tucked under his arm. He thought they looked pretty good and knew that the local angle stories he had on the train crash and the Lennie Hughes murder would ensure a boost for sales. He rang Tanya from the printers.

'I'm finished up here,' he said, 'I can pick you up at nine o'clock if you like.'

'All right,' she said.

'We can drop in at Bunty's if you feel like a drink.'

'No, I don't think so. I've got a bit of a headache.'

'O.K. I'll drive you home. Have an early night if you want to. See you in. . . .' He glanced at his watch. '. . . .about ten minutes.'

'Bye,' she said.

'Bye.'

Questions came in a fresh wave as he drove to the hospital. He was looking forward to discussing his thoughts with Tanya but as soon as he saw her, standing alone at the front of the hospital, he knew something was wrong.

'What's up?' he asked, putting his arm over her shoulders as they walked to the car.

'Nothing, just a bit of a headache.'

'What's up?' he said insistently, ignoring her answer.

97

'I'll tell you in the car,' she said as he held the door open for her.

He slammed it shut and slid into the driver's seat.

'O.K. what is it?'

'Drive, Jon, I want to get away from the hospital.'

He stared at her then turned away, started the car and set it in motion.

'Now, tell me what's the mystery?'

She outlined the incident in the drugs cupboard and added: 'I know it sounds silly. I wouldn't tell anyone but you, but ever since then I've had this feeling that somebody's watching me. It's really uncanny. I can't remember the last time I felt as scared as this. I don't want to be alone tonight, Jon. I'm actually scared to be alone.'

Bunty Robinson was thinking about Tom Wyler as she flicked off the lights in her restaurant, locked up and headed for her detached bungalow in North Batforth. Wyler was more than twenty years younger than Bunty and the latest in a long line of what she called 'my young men'. In the two months she had known him she had become very fond of Wyler despite the fact that he was very limited in the brains department and his conversation was almost non-existent. (Who needs conversation? she had once asked herself with a half-grin as they lay in a tangle of limbs on her huge bed after making love). At least he made a change from Arthur Manners, the jobless would-be poet with the body of a boy, who had preceded Wyler in Bunty's affections. Arthur had actually tried to get Bunty to read Kant.

Wyler was a man of medium height with skin which was oddly dark for an Englishman and the hard, whipcord muscles of a man who had taken karate very seriously for fifteen years. But it was his hair which Bunty had noticed first. It was thick and brown and hung almost to his shoulders in a great tangle.

A smile played on her lips as she pictured Wyler waiting for her, lying on the settee, wearing nothing but the quilted maroon dressing-gown she had bought for him, sipping a whisky and watching the video. He was the most relaxed man she had ever met. There was something totally calm about him, an aura that suggested he never thought about yesterday or tomorrow or worried about anything. She adored that because it contrasted with her own bustling nature.

It had been a week since she had seen Wyler and in her eagerness to feel his lean, hard arms wrapped around her she drove a little too fast across Batforth. She glanced at her watch as she parked the car in her driveway (hoping that she hadn't kept Wyler waiting too long) and saw that it was one a.m.

It was as she crossed the lawn in front of her house that she heard the brief rustling away to her left in the tangle of trees and shrubs that separated her garden from Nelson Street. Her stride faltered as she peered into the gloom, holding her bunch of keys tightly to stop them jangling.

A cat? she thought.

'Puss, puss,' she said. 'Puss, puss.'

The sound had ceased now and it occurred to her that there was a strange stillness about the entire garden. *Nothing* moved. There was a total, unreal silence. Not a rustle, not a whisper, not the distant sound of a car on Nelson Street or a dog barking. Nothing.

That wasn't unusual in North Batforth at this time of night, she told herself. It was one o'clock in the morning after all. Most civilized people were in bed asleep. Why should there be noise? And there was no wind. That was why everything was still. What was odd about that?

Yet, no matter how rational she tried to be about it, it *was* too still, too quiet.

Suddenly it occurred to her that the flowers and shrubs and trees were like a crowd of tense, silent, intimidated witnesses who knew something she didn't.

Witnesses.

What had made her think of that word? Witnesses to what? Why was she thinking such crazy things?

She was hurrying now and she almost fell as she stepped up onto the porch. Her fingers fumbled for the front door key, found it and thrust it into the lock. It was as she snapped it round and pushed the door open that she looked back and caught a glimpse of what looked like the dark shape of a man beside the tall oak at the bottom of the garden. Her eyes darted across it then returned an instant later. But it was gone the second time she looked.

99

'Tom,' she rasped into the dark garden. 'Are you playing tricks on me, Tom?'

There was no answer from the stillness and a cold shiver ran up her spine.

Had there been a. . . . shape? A man?

She spun around and looked into the house. The hall was in darkness. At the far end a weak shaft of light shone from the slightly ajar lounge door.

'Tom,' she called, 'are you there?'

She flicked on the hall light, finding a degree of satisfaction at eliminating the interior darkness. Then she stepped inside and shut the door quietly behind her.

Why had she done it so quietly, she wondered. Why was she afraid to make a noise? Why was she acting like a burglar in her own home?

'Tom!' she shouted. 'Tom.'

She started down the hall on her tiptoes then forced herself to walk normally.

What *was* wrong with her? If Tom wasn't answering it was probably because he had fallen asleep. Or maybe he had gone for a walk. So there *was* a shape in the garden she had mistaken for the outline of a man. . . . so what? In the morning she'd be able to pick out which shrub it was. Wouldn't she?

She reached the lounge door and pushed it open with her fingernails.

'Tom,' she said. 'Are you there, darling?'

The room seemed normal; warm and inviting. A log glowed in the fire. The clock on the mantelpiece tick-tocked. It was when she took three quick steps forward, passing the Japanese room divider, that she saw the occasional table in front of the fire had been knocked over and the pool of blood drying into the carpet.

An instant later her eyes sprang to the settee and she saw Tom's naked body, bloody and battered. He had been beaten until he no longer resembled a human being, smashed like a doll might be smashed by an enraged child. He lay on his side, one leg twisted halfway up his back, his head dangling at an unnatural angle over the edge of the settee.

She stared at him, shock rendering her incapable of making sense of it all, incapable of comprehending what had happened.

Then, as she became aware that she was sobbing loudly, she heard something move behind her.

She spun around with such force that she stumbled sideways and had to grab the back of the settee to stay on her feet. When she righted herself, she stood staring at the man who had come into the room, her blood chilled.

FOURTEEN

The man who faced Bunty Robinson watched her through two dull, uncomprehending eyes. He was about her own height with massive shoulders encased in a ragged flannel shirt. Strands of filthy reddish hair hung down over a grimy, unshaven face dominated by a mis-shapen blob of a nose.

She was frozen with fear but her mind remained strangely calm. It was as if she had been plunged so far into terror that she had reached the eye of the terror, the centre, a place of insane, dangerous tranquillity with horror on every side.

She thought: That face. It's not. . . . it's not. . . .

Real.

The word came to her like the sharp pain of cold air washing over the exposed nerve of a tooth.

That was the word she had been reaching for. *Real.* The face wasn't real. It was like a mask, a parody of a face.

'What do you want?' she heard herself say and was surprised that her voice was calm, even.

He shifted his weight from one foot to the other but didn't answer. The movement exposed the right side of his face and neck and she saw a discoloured lump on his jaw and fresh blood pumping out of a neck wound and running down into his shirt.

Tom did that, she thought. Tom inflicted those injuries with karate blows before he was killed. Her eyes flicked over his body searching for other wounds and settled on his forearm. The arm was twisted at the elbow and a shaft of jagged bone protruded from the flesh three inches above the wrist.

Yet the man showed no sign of pain. . . .

'What do you want?' she repeated but again he made no reply.

Suddenly a voice in her brain shrieked: 'What are you doing? Why are you talking to this man? Why are you studying him like he's a museum exhibit? *Tom is DEAD and this is the man who killed him.*'

She took a single, hesitant, awkward step backwards. She had to run, she had to get away. But where, how? Her eyes flicked around, searching desperately for an answer. The windows were locked of course and the man was between her and the door.

Then the man made a sound. It wasn't a word, more a rasping clearing of the throat. Like a growl, she thought. Her eyes darted back to his face and she saw that he was grinning at her now. The dullness had gone from his eyes and he seemed to be seeing her for the first time, staring at her with a burning intensity.

Suddenly he raised his one good hand and lunged at her. She side-stepped the outstretched arm and spun away from him, a tiny scream escaping from her lips. *Scream*. That was her chance. If she screamed someone was sure to hear her. There were houses all around. She was in the middle of a town. She screamed again as she leapt the fallen occasional table but it wasn't much of a scream, hardly more audible than a sob; the panic and physical exertion had taken her breath away. A hand grabbed at her shoulder but she shrugged it aside.

As she darted past the settee something brushed her leg and a clear, sharp voice in her brain dug at her like an ice-pick saying: *That was Tom's head.*

Instinct made her snatch down the clock on the mantelpiece, spin around as she reached the dining-table and fling it into his face. There was a dull *slap* as it struck him, smashing his right cheekbone, but he came on as if nothing had happened. She threw a chair down in his path and jumped around the table, stopping at the far side to watch him, her heart thumping against her ribcage like a trapped animal.

The grin was still fixed on his face, lop-sided and more terrible now because of the broken cheekbone, and the eyes still burned with an intensity that plunged her even deeper into terror.

He took three quick paces to his right, circling the table and she moved quickly to her right, keeping the same distance between them. His grin broadened. He took a short step to his left and she did the same.

Then, as if tiring of the game, he looped his one good arm

under the huge oak table and flung it effortlessly against the wall.

She was cornered now. There was no way past him. She jumped back and half turned away, her eyes searching wildly for some way of escaping or a weapon to defend herself. Anything that would give her a chance.

Her shoulder bumped into something. *The drinks cabinet.* If she could just get the door open and get her hands on a heavy bottle, a half filled whisky bottle. . . .

It was as she reached for the cabinet that his massive body crashed into her, thudding her to the ground.

She struggled desperately but her arms were clamped tightly to her sides.

What now? the voice in her head wanted to know. Rape? Was that what the man wanted? Would he rape her then kill her like he killed Tom?

She thrashed with her legs, trying to shift her body sideways, but he was too heavy, too strong. Then she felt something forcing her mouth open, wider and wider. Terrible pain stabbed from the edge of her jaws up to her temples. She tried to see what he was doing but the top half of her face was pushed so far back that her eyes were half shut.

Something was forced into her mouth, something living. . . . yet not living. Like a powerful jet of air, she thought. It was as if she had opened her mouth in the face of a hurricane. Then it was through her mouth, diving down her throat. Dispersing into her.

Suddenly her jaws relaxed. The man was gone. The room was silent.

She lay still for several minutes then climbed unsteadily to her feet and began to shuffle towards the door.

Rrup-rrup-rrup, rrup-rrup-rrup, rrup-rrup-rrup.

In his dream, Hammond jerked and twisted his head wildly as the sound of marching men drew closer and closer. It was as if he was paralyzed from the neck down and suspended, weightless, in a black capsule, the sides of which he could not see. The desperate motions of his head rolled his body over and over in slow, uneven loops but there was no escape from the synchronized thud of heavy boots on an invisible road.

Then came the singing, a roar of voices joining the slow-motion wave of sound which threatened to engulf him. Panting with a fear he could not explain, he listened intently and managed to pick out a couple of words, or pieces of words, but they made no sense.

Not in English anyway. Words from another language, Hammond. Words from another language.

The noise was contorted now, like the shriek of a hi-fi if an accidental slip pushed the volume control all the way up.

In a frenzy, he thrashed about, but there was no way out. No escape from the din and the fear and the darkness.

Hammond woke with a start and sat upright but this time he knew immediately where he was and what had happened. He climbed out of bed with a sigh, shaved, showered and dressed, then kissed the still sleeping Tanya on the cheek and headed for his car.

He took out his pocket diary and flicked it open. There were two scribbled entries. One said: Funeral, Mrs Lord one p.m. The other said: Check condition of train driver and woman in picnic site incident.

He climbed into his car and sat at the wheel looking out across the fields.

After Tanya had fallen asleep the night before, he had lain awake for hours, going over and over everything in his mind and he was certain now that everything that was happening in Batforth was connected. What he didn't know was how or why or what it all meant. It was like a vast jigsaw puzzle of which he had only a few of the pieces. But where could he start to get the rest? Perhaps the marching song was a clue, he thought. Perhaps that had some significance he had missed.

He started the car and drove to Jack Emmerson's record shop just off Batforth High Street. On his way there his jaws began to ache and he realized his teeth were clenched. What was happening to him? What was happening to all of them?

As he got out of his car, he realized with a deep sense of frustration that once again he couldn't remember the tune. He tried to dredge it up from his subconscious but failed miserably.

The grinning red face of Jack Emmerson greeted him from the back of the store: 'Hello, big Jon. How are you?'

'I've got a slight problem, Jack. . . . with a tune. You know how a tune buzzes around in your head? Well, I've got this tune buzzing around in mine.'

'And you want me to name it.'

'The problem is it's slipped out of my head for the moment.'

'What kind of tune is it? Pop? Classical?'

'No, it's a marching song.'

'Military music is over this way,' said Emmerson, leading Hammond towards the back of the shop. 'Take a few records, play them in a booth, see if it jogs your memory.'

'I suppose I could try that. It's a foreign marching tune I think.'

'French? German?'

'I don't know.'

A customer entered the shop and Emmerson said, 'I'll leave you to it,' and went to attend to the customer.

Hammond had selected five LPs and was heading for a booth when the bell above the door rang as the customer left. Suddenly the tune was there, in his head again.

He hurried over to Emmerson.

'This is it, Jack, this is the tune,' he almost yelled.

Slowly and carefully, he started to hum it to Emmerson. The shopkeeper gave a disparaging half-laugh and cut him off.

'That's too easy, Jon.'

'Easy?'

'That's the Horst Wessel song, the Nazi marching song. Where did you hear that?'

'I don't know.'

'Must have been some documentary on TV. It's not the sort of thing you hear on Radio One.'

'TV. Yes, it must have been on TV,' Hammond said, deep in thought. 'Anyway, thanks Jack, you've been a big help.'

He left Emmerson's and drove to his office.

A Nazi marching song. Why? What did it mean?

'Morning, Jemma. Morning, Ernie,' he said as he strode to his desk.

Jemma returned his greeting. Ernie grunted.

'What's happening?'

Ernie looked up from the crossword he was doing and said: 'I had a call from one of the nationals, trying to find out if we know how the murder hunt's going and asking if there's any truth in the rumour that they've heard that the murderer might have struck again. I gave them a story. Couldn't say anything about the missing man though, linking it with the Hughes murder, because officially the police haven't linked the two yet. But I said I'd let them know if anything happened.'

Hammond nodded slowly.

'O.K. Good. I'm going to call the hospital. I want to get a condition check on the train driver and the woman who was at the picnic spot.'

'I've already done that,' Ernie said. 'Train driver's still in a coma. The woman's still under sedation. One of the sisters there is an old friend of mine. She says the woman's lost her marbles.'

'What do you mean, lost her marbles?'

'Well, I think her exact words were, "Every time she wakes up she's incoherent, babbling". She keeps trying to tell the nurses about strange things she saw out at the picnic site. Apparently they've called in a psychiatrist.'

Maybe the woman did need a psychiatrist, Hammond thought. Maybe she had lost her marbles, as Ernie put it. Or maybe she was just in the same boat as a lot of other people in Batforth. Maybe if she needed a psychiatrist so did Sergeant William Joss and Nurse Tanya Bailey and Martin Silver and a certain motorist who lost control of his car and didn't know why. . . . and newspaperman Jon Hammond.

And God knows who else.

FIFTEEN

Shortly after the shower of rain began, raising a white rash on the back of Moulson's Pond, the box began to tremble violently, tap-tapping against the metal bar, brick and tin can which supported it.

A moment later, it toppled onto its side, shouldering its way into the soft sand.

Hammond arrived at St Giles Church for Mrs Lord's funeral at ten to one. As he was about to enter the church, a police car drew up and he turned and strolled towards it when he saw William Joss getting out. The sergeant's face was grim and tired-looking. He took Hammond by the arm and led him away to one side.

As they walked among the gravestones, Joss said: 'The man missing from the picnic area, Alex Wright, the salesman, the one who. . . .'

'Yes, I know who you mean,' Hammond interrupted.

'We found his body this morning. In some reeds about a mile downriver from the picnic site.'

Hammond spun around and faced the sergeant.

'And?'

'Killed the same way as Lennie Hughes. Savagely battered and beaten beyond belief. One of his legs was almost ripped off. It was almost as if he'd fallen into some kind of machine. Jensen thinks we have some kind of karate freak on our hands. . . . a psycho who killed Lennie Hughes and Alex Wright and may still be in the Batforth area. He may even be a resident, Jensen thinks.'

They started walking again, back towards the church.

'And what do you think?'

'I don't know what to think, Jon. I was confused when I spoke to you last night and I'm even more confused now.'

Hammond rubbed his forehead vigorously with the tips of

his fingers as if it might relieve the headache which had begun to pound at his temples.

'A couple of other things have happened, William.'

Hammond told him about Tanya and his visit to Jack Emmerson's shop.

'The Horst Wessel song,' Joss said.

'That's right.'

'Why *that* song?'

Hammond shrugged.

'I don't know. Why did you run down children that weren't there?'

When they reached the church, Hammond said: 'You go on in, William. I've got a phone call to make.' He hurried down the gravel path, crossed the road and called Ernie Spiers from the phone booth on the corner.

'Ernie, this picnic site incident is definitely a murder. They've found the body. The police are linking this with the Hughes murder. I want you to get on to Inspector Jensen at the police station, get everything you can and file stories with all the newspapers we deal with as soon as you can. Got that?'

'Yeah, O.K.'

'And put away that crossword puzzle.'

There was a short silence then Ernie Spiers said: 'How did you know I was still doing the crossword?'

Hammond was going to say: 'Because you were doing it first thing this morning and they usually take you all day.' But instead he found himself saying jokingly: 'Let's just say I'm psychic.'

As soon as he said the word psychic, he froze, staring at the blank wall of the phone booth. *Psychic.* That was what they needed. He'd been dodging around the issue, trying to make the irrational rational. This was the paranormal (whatever that was), wasn't it? They needed a psychic or a spiritualist or a professor of parapsychology or a priestly exorcist because whatever was happening to Batforth, it didn't fall into the realms of what you could call normal.

'Roy Stevenson,' he said aloud.

'What?' said Spiers. 'What did you say?'

'Oh, nothing, Ernie. I had better get to the funeral now. I'll see you later.'

'O.K.'

Yes, Roy Stevenson. He's your man, Hammond. Why didn't you think of him before?

The funeral service had already begun when Hammond tip-toed into the church and took a seat on a pew at the back. The church was packed with relatives and friends and people Hammond imagined were just there to show sympathy for a fellow Batforthian who had died in a particularly nasty way. Tragedy had a way of bringing people together, he thought; tragedy and Christmas, you could always bank on those two.

He watched the minister as he spoke, not really listening to the words. He wondered idly about his earlier thoughts about the paranormal and about the need to find somebody to attempt to explain what was going on in Batforth. The minister? He rejected the Reverend Kent as the man for the job instantly. Kent was a feeble, easy-going, grey-haired old man, who was pleasant to old parishioners at tea parties and kind to children. No, Roy Stevenson was his best bet.

The congregation had begun to sing. Hammond joined in only one of the hymns, 'Abide with Me', because it was the only one he knew.

Then Mrs Lord's two sons and four of her nephews carried the coffin to the grave. Hammond scanned the crowd as the final formalities of death were completed, nodding to many familiar faces. He heard a woman sobbing at the front of the crowd and felt the sudden shaft of sadness and grief he always felt at funerals – even of people he knew hardly at all or not at all.

Never send to know for whom the bell tolls, Hammond. It tolls for thee.

He craned his neck to see over the crowd and saw that it was Mrs Lord's sister who was crying. A man he didn't know was trying to comfort her.

He shifted his attention back to the burial. The coffin was suspended on cords over the mouth of the grave now, being gently lowered by the young men.

Suddenly the coffin seemed to quiver. Hammond blinked, thinking it had been a trick of his eyes then realized a hush had fallen over the crowd. The six men holding the cords were leaning back now, straining as if the coffin had become heavier.

'Be careful,' the minister shouted, unable to understand what was happening.

The casket began to rock violently from side to side, bumping against the earth walls of the grave.

'Hold on,' the minister shouted as one of Mrs Lord's sons dropped his cord then snatched it up again.

A woman's scream broke the hush and seemed also to snap the crowd out of a spell which had kept them transfixed like an engrossed audience watching a fascinating play. Several men ran forward to help and Hammond began to push his way through the crowd. He couldn't see what was happening now but he could still hear the irregular wet-earth thumps as the coffin bumped about. He had reached the small knot of men at the graveside when he heard somebody shout: 'God, no. . . .' This was followed almost immediately by the sound of smashing wood and another voice shouting: 'They've dropped it, they've dropped the coffin.'

Hammond shouldered past the last line of men and looked down into the grave. The coffin lay on the bottom, broken-backed. The lid had shifted with the impact and an arm hung out.

And the arm was moving, thrashing violently about.

'She's alive,' the man next to Hammond shouted. Then he looked back over his shoulder and called: 'Doctor Harrison, come down here quickly, she's alive.'

'And what happened then?' Jemma said, her face filled with horror and disbelief, as he told her the story in the office later.

'I lowered Doctor Harrison into the grave and he searched for signs of life. . . .'

'And?'

'She was dead. Beyond a shadow of a doubt. Well and truly dead.'

'But. . . . how did he explain the moving arm?'

'He said the fall must have left the arm in an awkward position and it jerked forward. . . . in the same way that if you leave a pencil balanced on the edge of a table it might fall off.'

'And she's buried now?'

'Yes.'

'Do you think. . . . Are *you* sure she was dead?'

'Oh, she was dead all right.'

Yeah, she was dead all right, Hammond. But something made that coffin thrash about. And Harrison's explanation of what happened to the arm wasn't very convincing really. If Roy Stevenson can't come up with the answers, you'll have to find someone who can.

He returned to the story in the typewriter, reading over what he had written.

'Are you going to write all about that?' Jemma asked. 'The coffin jumping about and the quivering arm?'

He sighed: 'I went there to do a colour piece, a kind of "Batforth Says Farewell to Prominent Resident" kind of thing, but I'll have to mention the. . . . accident. I won't sensationalize it. That would upset too many people.'

The door burst open and Ernie Spiers took three steps into the room.

'Have you heard?' he said.

'Heard what?'

'About Bunty Robinson and Tom Wyler.'

'What about Bunty and who the hell is Tom Wyler?'

'Wyler was Bunty's latest. . . . boyfriend. He worked at Batforth Tractors. He's dead, killed like the others. They've just found his body. And Bunty's missing.'

'Missing?'

'Yes, missing. But the strangest thing of all is that police inquiries have turned up a man who says he saw someone answering Bunty's description walking out of Batforth along the Ruttlake road in the early hours of this morning. He hadn't been able to sleep. He got up to make himself a cup of tea and looked out the window. . . . and there she was, walking out of town, heading towards the picnic area.'

SIXTEEN

'Oh, *that* Tom Wyler,' Hammond said to William Joss.

He had been prevented from entering Bunty's house by a very tall, very thin police constable who had agreed after some argument to fetch the sergeant from the house.

'Yes, that Tom Wyler,' Joss said.

Hammond nodded: 'I remember him now. We used to call him the karate kid . . . it was a bit of a joke at the Blue Boar. I believe he really was very good at karate, a black belt, God knows which dan. . . .'

He paused and studied Joss's face then added: 'It must be one helluva powerful killer you're trying to get your hands on . . . if he was capable of killing Tom Wyler like that.'

Joss shifted his weight uneasily from one foot to the other.

'I take it Jensen is still pursuing his psycho-on-the-loose theory?' Hammond asked.

'Of course,' Joss said, studying Hammond's face. Then he took the journalist's arm and guided him down the gravel driveway. Out of the constable's hearing, he said: 'O.K. Odd things are happening in Batforth. But do you really think they could be related to the murders?'

Hammond shrugged: 'I don't know what to think. Have you told Jensen all the things you told me?'

'No, of course not.'

'Why not?'

'Because it wouldn't do any good. He'd just think I had a screw loose if I said I'd seen children who weren't there. . . .'

'But you did.'

'There are a lot of explanations.'

'Name one.'

Joss shrugged.

'You saw what happened to Mrs Lord.'

Joss sighed: 'Yes, I saw that. But what can we do about it?'

'I think I know someone who might be able to help,' Hammond said. 'I'll give him a call tonight. In the meantime

113

I'm going down to the river to help in the search for Bunty.'

'Good, we need all the help we can get. We found a second man who said he saw her. Positive identification.'

'Why would she go down there?'

'Shock,' Joss offered.

Hammond raised his eyebrows: 'You don't believe that any more than I do. See you, William.'

He gave the sergeant a brief wave over his shoulder as he headed for his car.

Then he drove to the Ruttlake road picnic area, found the man co-ordinating the search for Bunty – a thick-set police sergeant from Ruttlake with a clipped ex-sergeant-major's way of speaking – and asked how he could help. The policeman sent him to join a team searching along the riverbank.

Hundreds of people came out of Batforth to help in the search for Bunty, many of them still wearing the Sunday clothes they'd had on for Mrs Lord's funeral. Hammond was in a team of fifteen strung out in an uneven line on the north bank of the river.

He and Councillor Ray Hardy shared the worst position in the line, nearest the river, where the mud was deepest and the soaking grass and the reeds grew highest.

'What do you make of all this, Ray?' Hammond said.

'Jesus, I don't know, Jon. But why Batforth, that's what I'd like to know.'

They trudged on for a minute, their eyes scanning the ground, then Hardy added: 'I've heard they're bringing up some experts from Scotland Yard. Maybe they'll be able to find our killer. All I can say is they'd better catch him soon.'

They searched all the way from the picnic area to the point where the river swung east along the shoulder of Moulson's Hill but found nothing.

The search was called off when darkness fell. Some people stood around for a long while, talking in groups, apparently reluctant to leave, but most joined the steady procession of cars headed for Batforth, their collective exhaust fumes wafting off the road into the dark fields like a thick mist.

Hammond drove back to his flat, his shoes and socks and the lower half of his trousers soaked and smeared in mud. At the flat he threw off his clothes and stepped into a hot shower. Afterwards he pulled on a dressing-gown, consulted an address book then sat down at his desk and dialled Roy Stevenson's number.

'Hello,' a voice said on the other end of the line and he recognized it at once.

'Hello, Roy. It's Jon Hammond here. How are you?'

'*Jon*,' Stevenson almost yelled. 'It's good to hear from you.'

The delight in Stevenson's voice was so obviously genuine that Hammond felt his spirits lift. They had been good friends for a long time until Stevenson had sold his home in Ruttlake and moved to Devon and Stevenson's voice seemed to carry the essence of many memories. Hammond felt a twinge of regret at not having kept in touch.

'How have you been keeping?' Stevenson said.

'I'm fine, just fine. How's life in Devon?'

'Great.'

'And the job?'

'Quiet.'

'It must be two years since you left Ruttlake. Or is it more?'

'Four. Are you still with the *Courier*?'

'Yeah. I'm starting to think I'll be in that place until they carry me out in a pine box.'

'At least you are your own boss there, Jon. You know how you are with authority figures. You never did like taking orders.'

'That's true.'

'So what brings you on the line now? If it's about my four-year-old invitation to come and spend a week in Devon, the offer is still open.'

'No, it's not that, Roy. We have a problem here in Batforth.'

'You mean the murders? I heard about them on the lunch-time news. Two dead, isn't it?'

'It's three now . . . and there might be more to it than just simple straightforward murder.'

'Like what?'

Hammond hesitated: 'There's something not right in Batforth at the moment. There's something happening that I think is . . . abnormal. The paranormal if you like. The murders might be linked to them and I thought you might be able to help, using all those gifts that the university discovered you had.'

There was a long pause and when Stevenson spoke again his voice was quiet and even: 'They didn't discover anything at that university I didn't know already, Jon. I've had those gifts, as you called them, all my life and believe me, they're gifts I'd rather not have. It's more of a curse than a blessing. I always hated it. Cast your mind back . . . How many times did we discuss my psychic powers when we were friends way back when?'

'Not often.'

'True. Do you know why?'

'Nope.'

'Because I always felt a bit like a freak. And because some of the things that happened to me scared me a lot, particularly when they were doing the tests and making me stretch my powers. I try to forget all about it nowadays. Coloured TVs are magic enough for me. I don't dabble in anything I don't understand. Of course sometimes. . .'

His voice trailed away and he left the sentence unfinished. After a pause, he said: 'Most people down here don't even know that I am psychic and that's the way I like it. They don't know anything and I don't want them to. What was it you wanted me to do in Batforth? Find some missing body? I'm sorry, Jon. I can't help you. I had a very bad experience just before I left Ruttlake. I'll tell you about it one day. I decided then I'd never tamper with psychic phenomena again.'

'It's not about finding a body, Roy. It's far more serious than that. Just let me tell you what's happening, then you can make up your own mind.'

For the next fifteen minutes Hammond outlined everything that had happened in Batforth from the train crash to the incident at the funeral, leaving nothing out.

'If this is the paranormal,' he said when he had finished, 'then somebody has to identify it and tackle it before more people get hurt. I'm very concerned about my girlfriend. She's as level-headed as they come and the state she was in last night was unbelievable.'

'What do you want me to do, Jon?'

'I've got to know one way or the other whether something like psychic phenomena is occurring here or whether it's just a case of Jon Hammond suffering from post-train-crash depression or something like that.'

'I don't know, Jon. As I said, I try to stay away from things like this nowadays.'

'So you think it is the . . . paranormal?'

'It sounds possible . . . but I'd have to be there to be sure.'

'Will you come to Batforth? I can put you up. In fact, you can have my flat while you're here. I'm staying at my girlfriend's house until all this is over.'

'Jon, I. . .'

'If it wasn't for Tanya, I wouldn't ask this of you, Roy.'

Stevenson sighed audibly then said: 'All right, I'll come.'

'Tomorrow?'

'Yes, I'll catch the first train. That should get me there about noon.'

'I'll be waiting . . . and thanks, Roy.'

'Just one thing, Jon.'

'What's that?'

'No newspaper stories about this. I like my privacy.'

'No problem there.'

'See you, Jon.'

'Bye.'

The instant he hung up, the phone rang, startling him.

'Hello,' he said, snatching up the receiver.

'Jon, it's Ernie here. I thought you might like to know the train driver is out of his coma and being interviewed by the police right now.'

'Thanks, Ernie. Oh by the way. I want you to take charge of the murder story. I'll be tied up on something else for a couple of days.'

'Yeah, O.K.'

'Bye, Ernie.'

'Bye.'

He hung up and rang the hospital.

'Tanya Bailey, please.'

'Is that you, Jon?'

'Yes, Diane.'

'She's gone home. Got off early because she wasn't feeling well.'

'Thanks . . . tell me, is Doctor Farmer still there?'

'Yes.'

'Can you put me through to him?'

'Certainly.'

There was a click then Dr Farmer's voice said, 'Yes.'

'Jon Hammond here. I was wondering if it might be possible for me to see the train driver? It's nothing to do with the newspaper. I'm not looking for a story. I was in the crash and there's something I want to talk to him about.'

'When? Tomorrow?'

'Yes.'

'I think it'll be all right, provided he wants to see you of course.'

'Can I call you in the morning to find out?'

'Do that.'

He hung up, threw off his robe and began to dress, preparing to go to Tanya's cottage. He wasn't surprised that Tanya had decided to work only half a shift. She had slept very little the night before and the few hours she had managed had been interrupted by bad dreams. She had probably called the office looking for him, he supposed, and Jemma had told her that he was out helping in the search for Bunty.

He was thinking of the train driver as he headed for his car. Would the driver have a vital piece of the jigsaw or would he just confuse things even more? So far, Hammond thought, all I've got is a confusing mass of information that adds up to a big fat zero.

An irritating headache had started by the time he got behind the wheel of his car. Roy Stevenson would make sense of it, he told himself. Roy would come up with some answers.

Tanya awoke, propped herself up on one elbow and studied the face of her watch on the bedside table. Seven o'clock. But was it morning or evening? She blinked sleep from her eyes and glanced outside through the narrow slit where the curtains on her bedroom window failed to meet. It was evening. She had been asleep for two hours. She recalled coming home from the hospital and flopping into bed at five o'clock with a cup of hot chocolate. The drink lay untouched on the bedside table.

She rested her head back on the pillow and stared at the ceiling. Her sleep had been blissfully dreamless. Not at all like the night before. She had spent the evening and early hours of the morning describing her experience at the hospital to

Hammond over and over again, at each telling adding some minute detail she had left out earlier. At first she thought she saw a kind of horror etched in the lines around his eyes and in the set of his mouth and she had had the strangest sensation that he knew something that she didn't. Later, his face had relaxed. He had poured her a large brandy and that had made her feel slightly better.

At three o'clock, with the blankets tucked in around her, and her arms gripping Hammond as if she never intended to let go, she had dozed off. Into a sleep crowded by terrible dreams. Horrible faces leered at her; men in uniform laughed but there was no mirth in their laughter, it was cruel, ugly laughter; she saw firing squads and bombs hitting villages and had a terrible falling sensation.

She had woken once and found Hammond still awake, staring into mid-air, deep in thought. She had started to speak, but he had covered her mouth with his hand and said, 'No, just sleep. Don't worry about anything' and she had drifted off again, returning to the domain of those terrible dreams.

She stretched, then swept back the blankets and stepped out of bed. Her nurse's uniform lay crumpled on a chair, where she had thrown it as she got into bed. She tut-tutted at her untidiness, picked up the uniform and hung it in the wardrobe. Then she padded barefoot into the kitchen, took a cardboard container of apple juice from the refrigerator and began to pour it into a glass.

As she turned to put the container back into the refrigerator, she saw the man standing outside the kitchen window, watching her. The verandah light was on and she could see him as clearly as if it was daylight.

SEVENTEEN

Tanya froze, staring at the man at the kitchen window. He was about six feet tall and was wearing some kind of black uniform with flashes on his hat, shoulders and collar. Tanya guessed he was about thirty-five. The features of his face were neat and regular as if organized with military precision.

But it was his eyes which seized and held her attention. They were pale blue and burned in the rigid, emotionless face, glaring at her with a hideous malevolence that chilled the marrow in her bones.

For what seemed like a long time but was probably no more than three or four seconds it seemed as if there was nothing in the world except those eyes. It was as if she was trapped by them, rendered powerless. She stared back wide-eyed, like a rabbit at a cobra, her mind a chaos of primitive impulses, word fragments and half thoughts which scurried about trying to sort out her predicament and coming up with no answers at all.

Suddenly she found she was moving, walking stiff-legged out of the kitchen, away from the man. Something told her not to run, not to show any sign of panic, just to leave calmly and quickly. In the hall she discovered she was still carrying her apple juice. She put it down on a small table then walked quickly to the front door and checked that it was locked.

The back door. Check the back door, a voice in her brain said. *Hurry up.*

She tried to recall if she had locked it when she came in but couldn't remember. The numbness that she had felt in the kitchen in the presence of those eyes was thawing out now and she felt a kind of hysteria beginning to work its way through her.

She took three steady paces towards the back door then broke into a run. As she reached it, she saw the handle start to turn.

He's trying to get in.

Her eyes fell to the key. *It's not locked. Idiot. You didn't lock it when you came in.*

Instinctively she threw her shoulder against the door and flicked the key round, snapping the ancient lock into place.

The door handle turned again, quickly this time, and the door was banged violently backwards and forwards.

She stared at it helplessly, her back pressed against the wall, hysteria engulfing her now.

Surely the old lock would break any second or the groaning hinges would lift out of their sockets.

'Go away,' she heard herself shout. 'Go away. What do you want?'

What could he want, she thought, this black-uniformed man with piercing blue eyes. What could he want with her? What was he doing in Batforth? Who was he?

She began to move away from the door, sliding along the wall as if contact with it gave her a degree of security.

What should she do?

Try to get out of the house and run for it? Get her hands on some kind of weapon (a knife from the kitchen, perhaps) and try to fight him off?

Or hide?

As she drew level with the half-open lounge-room door her eyes fell on the telephone. She hit her forehead with the heel of her hand. How stupid. The telephone. Why hadn't she thought of it before? That was the first thing anyone thought of in a situation like this. Yet it had never occurred to her.

She rushed into the lounge and snatched up the receiver.

Jon's number. What was Jon's number?

A jumble of numbers sprang into her mind and she repeated several combinations out loud but none of them was right.

It was stupid - *crazy, crazy, crazy* - but the number wouldn't come.

The police station. What was the number of the police station? Or the hospital. Any number. And where was the address book she always kept on the telephone table? When had she moved it?

A number. Think of a number, a voice in her head shrieked.

Instantly she thought of nine-nine-nine.

She dropped a trembling hand onto the telephone and stabbed a finger at the nine. She caught the seven by accident then banged at the telephone until the dial tone returned.

Then she dialled a nine . . . and a second nine.

Suddenly the banging at the back door ceased and the shock of the silence which filled the house made her drop the receiver.

She listened intently and picked up the sounds of his footsteps going around the house, back towards the kitchen window.

Finish your call, the voice in her head urged.

She was reaching for the receiver again when she heard a sliding, scraping sound coming from the kitchen. For an instant she couldn't work out what it was. Then she knew.

He was opening the window. It was the one she couldn't bolt because the frame was warped.

She ran back into the hall and glanced into the kitchen. The window was wide open now and his knee, arm and shoulder were already visible as he climbed into the room.

She stumbled sideways, terrified that he would turn his head and she would find herself looking into those horrible blue eyes again. She bumped into the hall table and her glass of apple juice tumbled to the floor, the liquid spattering along the carpet. She splashed through it, fumbled to open a door and found herself back in her bedroom.

She knew she should have gone back to the telephone and finished her call but it was too late now.

She closed the door carefully behind her and considered hiding under the bed. *Under the bed*. A hysterical giggle was stillborn in her throat. Nobody actually hid under beds, she told herself. That was the first place anyone looked.

She flicked off the light, hurried to the wardrobe, unlocked the door and stepped inside, pulling the door closed behind her.

There was no way she could lock the wardrobe door from the inside, she realized. She dragged a coat off a hanger and crouched down and covered herself with it. At least now if he did search the wardrobe there was a chance he would mistake her for a pile of clothes, particularly if he didn't turn the light on. But she didn't rate her chances very highly.

Squelch.

The muffled sound chilled a thousand nerve ends in her body and made her shiver violently.

Squelch.

122

It came again. He was in the hall, moving slowly along, stepping in the apple juice, probably listening just like she was.

She heard the squeak of the lounge-room door then a moment later the telephone being hung up.

Then silence. Several minutes later, she heard the distant sound of another door opening and closing.

Was it the front door? Had he gone? Was she safe? Had all this really happened?

She restrained a powerful urge to step out of the wardrobe. She would wait. She had to wait. She would give him fifteen minutes. If there was no sound for fifteen minutes, she would begin a search of the house, as quietly as possible.

How could she count fifteen minutes? She did a quick sum in her head. Fifteen minutes was nine hundred seconds. If she counted very slowly to a thousand that would be about fifteen minutes.

She had counted to seven-hundred-and-forty-six when she heard the bedroom door being thrown open.

EIGHTEEN

Seven-hundred-and-forty-six.

The number stuck in her mind, repeated over and over again.

Seven-hundred-and-forty-six.

Footsteps moved from the door to the bed, a measured tread. She heard a creak as something brushed the edge of the bed.

Seven-hundred-and-forty-six. The number in her head was like the tolling of a bell. She tried to stop it but couldn't.

She held her breath, her mind paralyzed, a nervous tic twitching in her right eyelid.

There was a dull clunk. Something had been moved on the dressing-table. A bottle of perfume . . . or her jewellery box?

Seven-hundred-and-forty-six.

He was heading for the wardrobe now, walking straight towards her. Each footstep bit into her like the lash of a whip on her back. She was trembling so violently that she realized if he opened the wardrobe door she would have no chance of remaining undetected.

Seven-hundred-and-forty-six.

A hand bumped the wardrobe door then pulled on the handle. The hinges squeaked as the door swung open.

A silent shriek filled her brain and hot pokers of fear seared up from her groin to her chest as she felt a hand close over the coat and begin to pull it aside.

She closed her eyes tightly and lashed out with her feet then she drew them under her and sprang forwards and upwards with a scream, scratching and clawing. Her nails found flesh and she dug into it.

Two powerful hands grabbed her arms and clamped them to her sides and a voice said: 'Tanya, Tanya for God's sake, what is wrong? What's wrong?'

She opened her eyes as soon as she heard Hammond's voice and looked up into his face, sobbing hysterically. He folded his arms around her.

'Tanya, what happened? It's all right now. What happened?'

'There was a man. I saw him at the kitchen window.'

'When?'

'About ten minutes ago. He tried to get in the back door but I managed to lock it. Then he climbed through the kitchen window.'

'What did he look like?'

'He was wearing a kind of black uniform. He was tallish, fair-haired and he had. . . .'

She hesitated, shivering at the memory of the hate-filled eyes.

'He had piercing blue eyes . . . I came into the kitchen to get a drink and he was standing at the kitchen window.'

Hammond led her to the bed and made her sit down.

'I'll have a look around,' he said.

'Be careful, Jon,' she said as he left the room.

He went into the lounge, took a poker from the fireplace and searched every room in the house. The kitchen window was unbolted but firmly shut. He went outside and carried out a thorough search of the garden. Then he went back to Tanya's bedroom.

'There's nobody here now,' he said.

'I saw him coming in the kitchen window,' she murmured distantly.

'The window's closed now. You said when you first saw him, he was standing outside the kitchen window?'

She nodded.

'Among the rose bushes?'

'Yes, he would have been standing among the roses. Why?'

'I just searched there. The earth is soft. I left footprints but there were no footprints when I arrived there.'

'Are you saying I'm imagining things?' she said in a high-pitched voice.

'No, just calm down, Tanya. How far back was he standing from the window?'

'No more than a foot.'

'You'd have seen him clearly in the verandah light.'

'Yes.'

'And you actually saw him climbing in the window?'

'Yes.'

He nodded slowly then got her dressing-gown, slipped it around her shoulders and led her into the lounge.

He poured her a large brandy and handed it to her. She was trembling so violently she spilled some of the brandy and it ran across her chin. She didn't bother to wipe it away. She sat staring at the pile of fresh logs in the fireplace for a long time.

'Why were there no footprints?' she said suddenly, without looking up. 'Jon, what's happening to me?'

'It's not what's happening to you, that's not the question. It's what's happening to Batforth.'

'What do you mean?'

He studied her quizzical expression for a long time then said: 'You're a grown woman. I've got no right to keep things from me. I'm going to tell you everything.' He sighed and then said: 'O.K., here goes. . . .'

She was wearing a confused, disbelieving expression when he stopped talking.

'So that's it,' he said. 'I just hope Roy Stevenson can come up with answers. In the meantime, I don't want you to be out here at the cottage alone.'

'Jon, you're making me more frightened than ever.'

'It's your day off tomorrow, isn't it?'

'Yes.'

'Go shopping, stay with the crowds . . . or better still, is there someone you can visit?'

'I could drop in and see Mary Joss. But. . . .'

'I know all this sounds crazy and maybe I'm being overcautious but I'd rather have it that way until I can speak to Roy. I've asked Ernie to take over the murder case. He can file all the stories to our people and keep up with Inspector Jensen's theories . . . That will leave me clear to try to get to the bottom of this.'

He took her glass away then knelt down in front of her. He kissed her softly but she returned the kiss with passion, urgency, as if seeking escape in lovemaking. It was as if she wanted to push away her ugly thoughts and kick a door shut on them, to be alone in a world with only him.

Hammond understood and he covered her face, neck and shoulders with kisses, his hands moving across her body.

A few minutes later, he lifted her as if she were no heavier than a doll and carried her into the bedroom.

They didn't talk very much that night. After they made love they went into the kitchen and Tanya cooked a meal while Hammond sat with his feet up on a wooden stool, sipping a glass of beer. After they had eaten they watched the news on television and a documentary about Chile then went to bed. She huddled against him, her face buried in his chest.

'Try to sleep,' he said.

'Sleep,' she murmured. 'I don't want to sleep. I'm afraid to sleep because I might dream about . . . that man . . . those eyes. I might even dream your dreams. Who knows? I don't know anything anymore.'

He stroked her hair. 'Just relax,' he told her. 'Try to relax. Roy Stevenson might come up with some answers. . . .'

Roy Stevenson *has* to come up with the answers, he thought, staring up at the ceiling.

NINETEEN

Neither of them had a good night's sleep. Both were disturbed by dreams.

First thing in the morning Hammond phoned the hospital and asked for Dr Farmer. The doctor hadn't arrived for the day and he spoke instead to Meg Richards, the duty sister.

'Is it about the train driver, Jon?'

'Yes, it is.'

'Doctor Farmer left a message that it's all right for you to see Mr Sloane. The man's quite happy to meet you. He knows you were on the train when it crashed.'

'Could I see him at about eleven o'clock?' Hammond asked.

'Yes, I'm sure that would be all right.'

'O.K. I'll be in at eleven then, Meg. Thank you. Oh, and by the way . . . could you tell me the condition of Mrs McLure, the woman who was with Alex Wright the night he was killed?'

'Mrs McLure is no longer in the hospital. She's been transferred to another hospital. She's in need of a long rest.'

'What other hospital? What for?'

'Officially, you'll have to ask Doctor Farmer. Unofficially, I can tell you she's had a complete nervous breakdown.'

'Thanks, Meg,' he said slowly. 'Goodbye.'

He hung up and joined Tanya for breakfast.

'I must look awful,' she said, running her fingers through her hair.

'No, you don't look awful,' he said.

She buried her face in her hands and sighed: 'I wish I could believe you. God, I wish this nightmare was over.'

He felt a wave of helplessness at not being able to set things right immediately. But what could he do that he wasn't already doing?

He dropped her off at Mary Joss's house on his way to the hospital.

'I'll come back here for you in the middle of the afternoon, all right?' he said, kissing her lightly on the cheek.

She nodded and gave him a brave smile and a half-wave as he drove away.

He arrived early at the hospital and sauntered uneasily up and down the corridor outside the waiting-room for fifteen minutes. He had hated hospitals since he had spent a month cooped up in one at the age of seven with glandular fever. There were similarities about all hospitals which triggered bad memories for him. Echoing corridors, the whisper of nurses' uniforms as they passed, that strange antiseptic smell, empty wheelchairs, trays of pills, unused crutches propped in cupboards. These things brought with them the memory of his feeling of loneliness and isolation. Oh, the nurses had been kind enough and his mother had managed to get a bus the fifty miles to see him three times a week from the small village where his father had been a miner until the accident which had cost him his leg. But however comfortable it was, it wasn't home. What he had needed was his own bed, the sound of his mother's voice in the morning, his father telling him wildly unlikely stories about life with the Eighth Army in North Africa during the war, and his brother, Malcolm, to play with. Even now, he thought, the memories still bit deep, still brought a wave of strange insecurity.

At eleven o'clock Meg Richards showed him into Mitch Sloane's room with a warning. 'Remember, he's still a sick man, Jon. Don't be too long. Shall we say fifteen minutes?'

'Fine.'

The train driver was helpful, eager to tell his story, full of apologies for what happened.

'The crash was my fault,' Sloane told Hammond. 'There's no other way to put it. I don't know what happened to me. I can't explain it. I've told the police everything.'

Then he told Hammond the full story and said: 'That's it. You explain it. I've got to live with this accident for the rest of my life, live with the fact people are dead because I started seeing things. I hadn't been drinking. I've never taken drugs. Yet there it is; I was hallucinating.'

'I can't explain it now, but there may be another explanation. You may not have been hallucinating,' Hammond told him.

He had intended the statement to be helpful but all it did was puzzle Sloane and when Hammond left the train driver was propped up in bed watching him with a quizzical expression. As he walked down the corridor, Hammond felt a twinge of guilt at not telling him more.

What could you tell him, Hammond? You don't know anything yourself.

He's just given you one more piece of a giant jigsaw. Be thankful for that.

He drove up the High Street and parked outside his office. He was surprised how weary his legs were as he climbed the stairs. The knock on his head in the crash, a few nights of bad sleep and a pile of worry had all taken their toll of his fitness, he realized.

Jemma was bent over a low drawer in her filing cabinet when he entered the office, her jeans stretched taut over her thighs, like a second skin. Ernie Spiers was watching her candidly over his newspaper. He glanced at Hammond as he entered and said, 'Finest bum in Batforth,' then turned his attention back to Jemma.

'Dirty old man,' Jemma said, still searching the drawer.

Spiers was about to answer but Hammond cut him off.

'Any news on Bunty?'

'No, the search has started again. Are you going down there?'

'No, I can't today. I have to meet somebody off the midday train.'

'What are you working on?' Spiers said.

'I can't explain it at the moment, Ernie.'

'Must be important if you want me to take over the murder story.'

'It's important all right.'

'This is a big story for me to be handling at my age,' Spiers said as Hammond headed for the door again.

'You'll manage.'

As the door swung shut behind Hammond, he heard Spiers shout: 'Don't you realize I'm decrepit?'

He parked at the station and met Charlie McMurty, the stationmaster, outside the ticket office.

'London train on time, Charlie?'

'About ten minutes late.'

'Thanks.'

He went into the café, bought coffee and sat at a table where he could see the platforms. He had just finished his second cup when the train pulled in, a full twenty minutes late.

He strode to platform one and stood with his hands in his pockets, watching the windows gliding past, his eyes searching the carriages for Roy Stevenson.

Then the train jerked to a halt, doors banged open and people began to climb off. He searched the faces away to his right and was turning to his left when he heard a voice shout: 'Hi, big fella.'

He grinned as his eyes picked out the short, fair-haired figure of Stevenson getting out of a door a few feet away, his thin frame leaning to one side to counterbalance the weight of a medium-sized suitcase.

'It's good to see you, Jon,' Stevenson said as they shook hands.

'You haven't changed a bit,' Hammond told him, then added: 'Here, let me take that suitcase before you do yourself an injury.'

'O.K. Mr Universe.'

'The car's this way,' Hammond said and they walked off together.

Hammond grinned down at him: 'It's about time you built up some of your muscles.'

'I suppose I should have eaten my crusts as a boy,' Stevenson said, 'but what the hell, I could still thrash you at squash any time.'

Hammond pointed to the suitcase. 'I suppose this means you'll be able to stay a few days.'

Stevenson nodded and his grin faded. 'If I have to,' he said, 'but frankly, I didn't like the sound of what you told me one bit.'

'We'll have a beer and I'll explain everything,' Hammond said as they entered the car park.

As he reached the car Hammond realized that Stevenson had fallen behind. He looked back over his shoulder and saw that Stevenson had stopped in the centre of the car park and was standing unsteadily, loosening his tie. His face had turned pale and his mouth was turned down at the edges, like a man about to be sick. Hammond put down the suitcase and hurried back.

'What is it, Roy? What's wrong? Are you ill?'

'Can't you feel it?' Stevenson said, looking up at him.

'Feel what?'

'This place . . . this town. There's something here.'

'Tell me.'

Stevenson shook his head slowly: 'I don't know. It just hit me like . . . like the stench of a dozen dead cats might hit you.'

News of the third murder brought the media pouring into Batforth – newspapermen, a tall brunette from a wire service Ernie Spiers had never heard of, camera crews and a sprinkling of household names from the world of television.

The *Courier*'s telephone never stopped ringing and it was Ernie Spiers who had to take all the calls.

No, he didn't know anything they didn't. No, he had no new angle he was working on. No, he hadn't known any of the three victims very well. Yes, he knew the missing woman. Yes, she was the same Bunty Robinson who had once appeared in a television play called 'Hotspur' about the colour problem.

At three o'clock Spiers said to Jemma: 'I'm going out. I'm out all day. Even when I come back into the office, I'm still out.'

At five o'clock, the task force which had been sent from Scotland Yard called a Press conference and Spiers went along just in case there was an important announcement. 'You never know, the flatfoots might have actually caught someone,' he told Mary, the Blue Boar barmaid.

But they hadn't. An inspector read a prepared statement which said the team were in Batforth in an advisory capacity only and Inspector Jensen remained the man in charge. They had nothing to say on specific theories but did not rule out the possibility that the killer might strike again (*Clever, clever*, Ernie thought) and warned everybody to make sure they locked all their doors and secured their windows.

Spiers yawned and muttered to the journalist beside him: 'It doesn't matter how you wrap up nothing, it's still nothing. Right? And that's just what they've got . . . nothing.'

It was George Murdoch who first spotted the box lying at the bottom of the pond but Henry Low disputed that fact.

They were a pair of middle-aged Batforth no-hopers, variously known as the Deadly Duo, Bill and Ben, and Back and Shoulder. The latter nickname came from the fact that whenever the Job Centre offered George a job he would suddenly develop a sore back and if one was offered to Henry he would speedily point out the trouble he had with his right shoulder. Both of them had skilfully managed not to do a day's work for more than a decade. Henry lived in a boarding-house on the High Street and had a weakness for sherry. George had his own cottage on the outskirts of Batforth where he lived with three goats, a budgie and a mean, scrawny dog. Not much was known about Henry's private life before he had arrived at the boarding-house, but George, who had lived all his life in Batforth, had once had a family. His wife had walked out fifteen years before, taking the three children.

George had been the one who had suggested going fishing at Moulson's Pond. The idea had come to him that morning when he had been exploring a shed in his garden which he hadn't opened for years and found two fishing rods.

They were walking around the edge of the pond when George hesitated, stopped, and said, 'What's that?'

Henry bent forward, rested his hands on his knees and peered into the water.

'It's a box,' he said. 'Some kind of box with a lock on it . . . and I saw it first.'

'You did not see it first.'

'I did. I saw it from back there,' he said, gesturing over his shoulder.

'No, you didn't.'

George put down his fishing rod, took off his coat and rolled up his right shirt sleeve.

'I think I can just reach it,' he said, kneeling down.

He plunged his arm into the water until it almost reached his shoulder then ran his fingers along the top of the box, searching for something to grip.

'That's funny,' he said.

'What?' said Henry.

'It's warm . . . the box is warm.'

Then he grunted and his face was a mask of concentration. Finally he said, 'Got it' and lifted the box gently out of the water and set it down on the bank.

'It is warm,' said Henry, touching it.

George tugged at the padlock but it held firm.

'If it's locked, there must be something valuable in it,' said Henry.

'That's nothing to do with you,' said George. 'It's mine.'

'I saw it first,' Henry protested. 'At least we could go fifty-fifty.'

'Fifty-fifty,' said George, spitting out the words. 'Why should you get half just for being here?'

'We're friends, aren't we?'

'I'll tell you what I'll do. If it's valuable, I'll give you a share. But not half.'

Henry seemed satisfied with that.

'It might be something that's stolen,' Henry said. 'Maybe we shouldn't be seen with it.'

'That's a good point,' George agreed. 'You carry the rods.'

He wrapped his coat around the box then tucked it under his arm.

'I've got some pliers at my house. We'll get the padlock off in no time,' he told Henry.

They hurried around the pond and started up Moulson's Lane towards the High Street, their heads together, discussing what the box might contain.

TWENTY

Hammond and Stevenson had a busy afternoon. After Hammond went through everything that had happened over lunch at the Blue Boar, going into more detail than he had been able to on the telephone, he called Martin Silver and the Batforth Tractors chief of security agreed to talk to Stevenson 'provided nothing goes in the papers'. They met twenty minutes later at Silver's office and the grim-faced ex-policeman gave them a detailed description of what had happened to him.

'I don't really like talking about it,' Silver said. 'First of all, it sounds so loony . . . and secondly, it scared me. Even thinking about it scares me.'

After leaving Silver's office, Hammond called William Joss and told him about Stevenson.

'I'll talk to him,' Joss said, 'but you can't bring him to the police station. I'll be at your flat in half an hour.'

Hammond drove Stevenson to his flat and they sat sipping coffee as they waited for Joss. Stevenson's natural personality was that of a jovial extrovert, the typical chirpy little man, just like he had been when Hammond had met him at the station. But since the incident in the car park he had been quiet, thoughtful and edgy. *Brooding* was the word that sprang to Hammond's mind. He had tried to talk to Stevenson about it but the little man had made it obvious it wasn't something he wanted to discuss.

'Let's just get all the facts first,' Stevenson had insisted, 'then we'll have a long talk.'

It seemed to Hammond that Stevenson was trying to be business-like, matter-of-fact (trying to cling to the side of him that made a living as an accountant, Hammond thought) but underneath he was a man in turmoil.

When Joss arrived, Hammond introduced them then left them alone while he made some more coffee. When he came back, Joss was talking animatedly about the incident when he had ploughed into a crowd of children who weren't there.

Stevenson listened to everything Joss had to say, his face impassive, but his left hand which constantly fidgeted with his jacket pocket and the endless drumming of his right foot told another story.

When Joss was finished, Hammond said, 'I hope you can help us get to the bottom of this, Roy. After what's happened, I'm prepared to believe almost anything.'

Hammond saw Joss to the door then turned to Stevenson and raised his eyebrows questioningly.

'Not yet,' Stevenson said. 'I'd like to talk to your girlfriend.'

Hammond nodded. 'O.K. I'll go and pick her up. You must be tired after your journey. Why don't you put your feet up and have a rest? Help yourself to a beer from the fridge. I'll be back in fifteen minutes.'

That was when Stevenson said something that brought a sudden chill to the back of Hammond's neck and made the hair there bristle.

'No, Jon,' he said. 'I'll come with you. I don't want to be left alone.'

Stevenson didn't speak at all on the journey to Mary Joss's house. It had started to rain, a fine drizzle from a sky filled with low, dark clouds and it seemed to Hammond that the only sound in the world was the rhythmic flick-flack of the windscreen wipers.

Stevenson gazed down empty streets and into parks and studied the schoolyard, turning his head to look back, his eyes narrowing. Once he sighed like a man with a huge burden of worry and as they turned into Mary Joss's street he jumped as if startled, then composed himself.

Hammond went inside and fetched Tanya and they drove back to the flat.

After Tanya had told her story, Stevenson said: 'The only witness we have to murder is this Janet McLure. If there's no way I can talk to her, is there any way I could get one of the nurses who was on duty on the night she was admitted to tell me some of the things she was saying?'

Tanya looked at Hammond. 'Meg Richards was on that night,' she said. 'She saw Mrs McLure.'

'Could you get her to talk to Roy?'

'I could try.'

Tanya rang the hospital and spoke to Meg Richards. The

sister lectured her on nursing ethics and pointed out that not even the police had been allowed to talk to Janet McLure. After five minutes of argument Hammond shouted at Tanya, 'Tell her everything, for God's sake try to make her understand' —and Tanya did.

When she had finished, there was a long silence, then Tanya handed Stevenson the receiver and said, 'She'll speak to you.'

Stevenson talked to the sister for ten minutes then hung up, strode to the window and stared out into the street.

'For Christ sake, Roy,' Hammond exploded, 'this has gone on long enough. Tell us something. At least tell us what you think is going on.'

Stevenson turned slowly and studied Hammond's face for a moment. Then he said: 'All right. I'll tell you.'

The pair of pliers George Murdoch had used to try to open the box lay on the floor of his shed now, twisted beyond use.

George and Henry were kneeling in one corner of the shed, their heads buried in a large, rusted chest which was filled with tools, car spare parts, gardening implements and bits of an old television set.

'Have you noticed how cold it's getting in here?' Henry said.

'Never mind the cold. Keep looking,' George said irritated. 'I know there's a bigger pair of pliers here somewhere. The really big kind. I can't even remember what I used them for but I've seen them in here.'

His fingers swept aside a cobwebbed trowel and a bundle of screwdrivers held together by an elastic band.

Henry shivered. 'It's just that . . . it wasn't this cold when we came in here.'

'You don't have to stay,' George said. 'You can get out whenever you like.'

'I'm staying,' Henry said. 'I'm not going to be cheated out of my share . . . I've been thinking . . . I think this box might have fallen off the train during the crash.'

George nodded slowly then said: 'That's the most intelligent thing you've said in years.'

Henry shifted a filthy oil-filter box and saw a crowbar.

'This'll open it,' he shouted, snatching up the crowbar and turning back to the box.

'It's worth a try,' George conceded.

Henry thrust the crowbar eagerly into the padlock's ring and jerked it up and down violently, using the edge of the box for leverage. Still the padlock held firm.

'I've got an idea,' George said.

He slid half the length of the crowbar through the padlock, rested it on the edge of the box and jumped on the end of it with both feet.

The padlock snapped open.

'That's it, that's it,' Henry yelled.

He withdrew the crowbar, took off the padlock and threw both into one corner. Then he placed both hands on the box's lid and lifted it carefully.

'Jesus,' said George, stepping back quickly.

Henry looked up at him, speechless, an instant before the door slammed open with such violence that the entire shed shook.

TWENTY-ONE

'You were right, Jon,' Stevenson said, lighting a cigarette and drawing the smoke deep into his lungs.

The rain hammered against the window behind him which was misted with condensation. Night was falling and silhouetted against the black rectangle of the window his fair hair gave him a boyish, choirboy look.

'You mean there is some kind of psychic phenomena here?' Hammond asked.

'Yes, there are discarnate entities in Batforth . . . many of them. I've never heard of activity quite like this before.'

'Discarnate entities,' Tanya said. 'You mean spirits?'

'Yes, I mean spirits. Very, very malevolent spirits . . . and they're being drawn to Batforth by something that's acting as a magnet, drawing them in.'

'Are they dangerous?' Hammond said.

'Oh yes . . . and as I said, I've never heard of so much activity taking place in one area.'

'And the murders? Could these things be responsible?'

'I believe so, yes.'

'Why? What started all this?' Hammond said.

'I don't know,' Stevenson said, collapsing wearily into a chair and drawing heavily on his cigarette.

'Is it something to do with the train crash?' Hammond said. 'It seems to have started then.'

Stevenson nodded. 'Yes, it does. Something about the train crash seems to have released a powerful occult force. If I could visit the scene of the crash, I might come up with something.'

'What could it be?' Tanya said.

'I have no idea,' Stevenson sighed. 'If, for instance, someone on the train . . . someone who was killed . . . was an occult figure of gargantuan proportions, that might explain it. But these earthbound entities aren't being drawn in by a spirit of a dead petty thief or a train guard.'

Hammond sipped some coffee and grimaced when he found

it was cold. 'What are they?' he said, putting the cup down harder than he had intended.

'There's so much activity around Batforth, it's hard to know where to begin,' Stevenson said. 'Some of the things that are here are just weak forces, like chunks of energy, from another time that haven't escaped the earth. They have only a visual existence. They will appear, disappear and drift on. They might even appear to one person and not to another.'

'Like the torchlight procession?' Hammond said slowly.

Stevenson stubbed out his cigarette. 'Yes, like the torchlight procession for instance.'

'And what about my dreams?'

Stevenson shrugged. 'I don't have all the answers, Jon. Nobody does. Most people like to think they understand everything. They like to live their lives within certain defined boundaries. They like to say, this is what we know for sure and that's all there is to it. But really our existence isn't like that. Most people just want to take the easy way out.'

'What about what happened to Tanya?'

'Oh, that's a different thing altogether.' He paused and looked at Tanya. 'I'd like to tell Jon what I think about that later, when you're not here.'

'You will not,' Tanya said angrily. 'I want to know what's going on.'

Stevenson looked at Hammond and Hammond nodded.

'I think you're in very great danger,' he said. 'I think that what you saw at the house and what happened at the hospital are sufficient evidence to suggest you could be being pursued by an entity.'

'Pursued?'

'Stalked might be a better word.'

Hammond leaned forward. 'Is this the same . . . thing that's doing all the killing?'

'I doubt it. There are many, many malevolent spirits here, all very dangerous.'

'But why is the spirit interested in Tanya? Why Tanya and not someone else? Why not William Joss? Why not me?'

Stevenson half smiled, mirthlessly. 'Who can say? In war, not everyone gets hit by the stray bullet. Tomorrow it might be you.'

He dropped his eyes from Hammond's and added, 'Or me. . . .'

'What . . .' Hammond began but Stevenson held up a hand to silence him.

'Let me tell you what I've seen, Jon. I've seen spirits from many eras. Loathsome things that have been earthbound for two hundred years, never able to pass over into the next world for one reason or another . . . but most of what I've seen belongs to one era . . . and it's a modern era. I don't know if this is a clue or not. It certainly doesn't make any sense to me. I've seen column after column of marching soldiers, their uniforms ragged and torn and stiff with the cold, their faces pinched, their eyes vacant. I saw a laughing gang of men in black uniforms hanging a boy of no more than fifteen.' He shuddered, half smiled with embarrassment, then continued: 'A man in uniform with a bullet hole right through his left eyesocket reached for me as we were driving to pick up Tanya. I've seen great ditches and people being forced to stand on the edge and be shot in the back of the neck.'

'Concentration camps,' Hammond whispered, incredulous.

'I think so,' Stevenson said. 'That's the conclusion I've come to.'

'And the soldiers?' Tanya said.

'Soldiers of the Third Reich. Nazi soldiers.'

Hammond breathed: 'And I saw . . . a Nazi torchlight procession. And heard the Horst Wessel song.'

'And Tanya saw an SS officer and the train driver found himself on a train going to a concentration camp with human cargo.'

'I just can't take it in,' Hammond said.

'Of course not. In this existence most of us live on a practical level and that's probably the best way to live. I was trying to do just that when you called me.'

Hammond noticed a note of resentment in Stevenson's voice and bit his lip, waving his hand apologetically through the air.

'The thing is,' Stevenson said, 'we prefer to live a life that we can totally understand. Take the Bible for instance. Most people in this country would say they were Christians, yet I'm sure the vast majority don't believe Christ actually walked on water . . . but that's only because they haven't studied the facts about levitation. Most Christians would say that they didn't believe in the laying on of hands and that's because they haven't studied what faith healers are doing every day. People just close their minds to the mysteries all around them. If they can't understand them, they don't want to talk about them.'

'What can we do?' Tanya said.

'I have no idea,' Stevenson said. 'There's not much we can do until we find out what's causing this. It may go away as suddenly as it began.'

'And it may not,' Hammond said.

'That's right. It may not.'

Stevenson coughed briefly as he spoke the word 'not' then suddenly his body went rigid, his head hanging to one side. He stayed like that for about two seconds then he began to convulse crazily. His eyes were glazed, staring straight in front of him as if in a trance. Tanya drew back, covering her mouth with her hand.

'Is he having a fit?' she said.

Hammond leapt forward, grabbed Stevenson by the shoulders and lowered him to the floor.

Stevenson's face was twitching violently now. It was as if two tiny creatures were trapped under the skin, one on each side of his face, darting about, trying to break through.

Tanya regained her composure and knelt down beside Stevenson, forcing his mouth open.

'I have to make sure he doesn't swallow his tongue,' she told Hammond.

Suddenly Stevenson became quite rigid again and his eyes dropped closed. Hammond noticed the muscles of Stevenson's arms were like steel.

'Roy,' he shouted, 'Roy, wake up.'

Then Stevenson's mouth began to work. A sound came forth, a strangled word, but it wasn't Stevenson's voice. It was husky, somehow distant, like someone whispering a message through an old tin pipe.

Hammond didn't understand the first couple of words, then he heard: 'Hans . . . Worst . . . Totenkopf . . . Battalion. . . .'

'Roy,' Hammond yelled, unable to think of anything else to do.

'Hans . . . Worst . . . Totenkopf . . . Division. . . .' the voice rasped again.

Then Stevenson relaxed and his eyes fluttered open.

'What . . . the hell happened?' he muttered.

'I don't know,' Hammond said, 'I. . . .'

The shrill brnggg-brnggg of the telephone interrupted him. Tanya took up the receiver, said, 'Hello,' then handed it to Hammond.

'It's for you. Ernie Spiers.'

Hammond grabbed the receiver and stood up, leaving Tanya to tend to Stevenson.

'What is it, Ernie?'

Spiers was puffing down the phone, as if he'd been running.

'They've found Bunty,' he said. 'She's in. . . .'

'Alive?' Hammond shouted.

'Yes. . . .'

'Where?'

'She's in the High Street now. . . .'

'What are you talking about?'

'If you'd let me finish a bloody sentence, I'd tell you. She's on the roof of her restaurant and apparently threatening to jump. The police are trying to talk her down.'

Hammond rubbed his eyes. None of it made sense.

'Why would Bunty . . . never mind. Where are you?'

'I'm on my way to the restaurant.'

'Good. I'll see you there.'

TWENTY-TWO

They piled into Hammond's car and he drove crazily towards the High Street.

Stevenson was still feeling disoriented and Tanya sat in the back with him, explaining what had happened.

'I'm receptive,' Stevenson said, 'that's why this Hans Worst chose me.'

'Chose you?' Tanya said, horrified.

'Yes. He's a discarnate entity. He used me like a radio transmitter to get a message back to this world.'

'What's Toten. . . .'

'Totenkopf. They were SS. The Death's Head Division.'

Hammond lost control of the car on a corner, sliding into a four-wheel drift. He steered into it, bumped up over the kerb onto the grassy verge, then managed to control it again and accelerated away, the wheels gouging a muddy trench in the grass.

'Sorry,' he yelled over his shoulder.

Tanya was watching Roy Stevenson. 'What do you mean, he used you like a radio transmitter? Do you mean that you were . . . possessed?'

'No. I was the medium he used. He spoke through me. Maybe he was too weak for possession or maybe he simply didn't want that, or maybe a thousand things.'

Hammond slewed the car into the High Street, braked and dropped into second gear when he saw two police cars, both with their lights on full beam, parked in front of Bunty's restaurant. The second police car had apparently just arrived because Joss and a constable were just getting out.

Hammond parked between the police cars and jumped out.

'What the hell's going on?' he said to Joss.

'I've just got here too, Jon. All I know is that a couple of my lads spotted Bunty on the roof of her restaurant. It seems she's suggested she might jump. That's all I know.'

Joss turned away and Hammond followed him.

'I'm going up too,' Hammond said.

Joss nodded his approval and they went into the restaurant, along a corridor and up a winding, interior staircase to the roof. It was no ordinary roof. It was flat and concreted and Bunty had often entertained the idea of turning it into a beer garden in summer. It was surrounded on three sides by high railings. A low wall, no more than three feet high, ran along the front.

The lights from the police cars below helped to illuminate the scene but it was still very dim on the roof.

What Hammond saw made his stomach churn.

Bunty was standing on the low wall at the front of the roof, facing into the street, her head turned up, staring at the stars.

Two policemen flanked her, about ten feet back. Hammond started forward but Joss caught him by the arm.

'We'll have to be careful, Jon,' he said.

As he spoke, one of the policemen turned, saw them and hurried over.

'What's happening, Ron?' Joss said in a whisper.

'She's been like this for about ten minutes, ever since we spotted her and radioed in.'

'Has she said she's going to jump?'

'She hasn't said anything at all. We tried to get closer once but she leaned forward . . . I thought she was gone. She swayed back and forth on the edge for at least two minutes. We've stayed back since then, just talking to her, trying to calm her . . . but it's as if she doesn't really hear us. And she looks funny.'

'Funny?' Joss said.

'She doesn't look right.'

'What do you mean?'

'I can't explain it. You'll have to see for yourself.'

'Let me talk to her,' Hammond said.

Joss nodded. 'All right, Jon. You know her better than anyone here. But be careful.' Joss emphasized his warning with a wagging finger. 'And don't make any sudden moves towards her.'

Hammond circled Bunty, ending up at a point on the wall about fifteen feet from her.

He was shocked by what he saw. Her hair was matted with earth and leaves, her face grimy, her dress and stockings torn, her shoes covered in mud. The flesh and muscles of her face sagged and her mouth hung open.

'Bunty,' he said quietly. 'Bunty . . . it's me. Jon. Jon Hammond. Come down from there and we'll talk.'

There was no response, not even the tiniest flicker of a facial muscle that might have indicated that she had heard him.

'Bunty,' he said insistently, 'let's go downstairs for a drink.'

He heard a movement away to his left and saw that Roy Stevenson had come up on the roof.

'Bunty, it's me, Jon . . . Why don't you come over to my flat and tell me that story about you and that director up in Liverpool. You remember that one? You always love to tell it.'

He took three very slow steps towards her.

'Bunty, listen to me. I'm here to help you. We're all here to help you. I don't know what happened but whatever it was, it's nothing you can't sort out. You've got friends here.'

He took two more steps towards her then stopped when her head began to turn towards him, her eyes – they seemed drugged to him – seeking him out. When they found him, they seemed to come alive and her face twisted into a lop-sided grin that made her look not at all like Bunty. It wasn't a Bunty grin.

This woman was like Bunty and yet . . . not like Bunty.

Of course it's Bunty, Hammond. What are you thinking about?

'Bunty. . . .'

The grin was sly, mocking.

He took another step towards her and she waved a hand quickly, beckoning him to come forward.

That was when Hammond felt Roy Stevenson's hand on his arm, holding him back.

'Don't go any closer, Jon,' Stevenson whispered.

'What do you mean . . . Why?' Hammond said, his eyes still on Bunty.

'Take a good look at her, Jon. Is that your friend?'

'Of course,' Hammond said uncertainly.

'Are you sure?' Stevenson said. 'Try asking her about something commonplace, personal if you like.'

For a moment Hammond couldn't think of anything, then he said: 'How was business in the restaurant this week?'

146

There was no reply but the leering grin remained fixed on her face, her eyes staring at Hammond.

'All right,' Stevenson said, 'now ask her her name.'

'What. . . .'

'Just ask her who she is.'

Hammond looked down at Stevenson, his brow furrowed.

'Just do it,' Stevenson said.

Hammond raised his eyes to Bunty again and said, 'Who are you?'

Bunty began to laugh. At first it was a low whisper of a laugh, then she threw back her head and a loud bellow of laughter burst out, a rasping man's laugh, a barrack room laugh.

When she looked at Hammond again she spoke in a coarse, harsh, ugly male voice.

'My name is Legion,' she said, 'for we are many.'

'What does she mean?' Hammond said in a whisper to Stevenson as an invisible block of ice slithered down his spine.

'It's mocking you, Jon.'

'What do you mean, *it's* mocking me?'

'Do you really think that's your friend standing there? Just don't go any closer, Jon. You'll be in danger.'

Suddenly Bunty spun around and faced Hammond, teetering on the narrow top of the wall. She bent over, resting her hands on her knees leered at him, and repeated the words.

'My name is Legion: for we are many.'

Then she spun away from him and jumped.

Hammond leapt forward in the same instant, snatching for her but he missed by a long way, his hands grabbing air. He turned his back on the High Street before she hit and closed his eyes tightly but he couldn't shut his ears to the sickening, wet *slap* as her body punched into the pavement.

When he opened his eyes again the policemen were gone, clattering down the stairs. Stevenson was leaning against the wall, studying Hammond.

'What did it mean?' Hammond said. 'What she said . . . what did it mean? And why do you think she was mocking me?'

'It's from the Bible,' Stevenson said slowly. 'The Gospel according to Mark. There was a man who was possessed. Jesus said, "Come out of the man, thou unclean spirit" and asked, "What is thy name", and the answer was, "My name is Legion: for we are many".'

'Right,' Hammond said evenly, bracing his shoulders, 'I'm going to see Inspector Jensen and I'm going to make him understand what's happening.'

'I think you should,' Stevenson said, 'but I'm leaving Batforth right now.'

'Leaving,' Hammond exploded, incredulous.

'Yes . . . I've got to leave Batforth tonight. Right now.'

'I don't understand.'

'I was lucky back at your flat but other entities may come. They know I'm receptive. Everything I told you at your flat is absolutely correct but there's one thing I have to add.'

'What's that?'

'Something has happened in the last couple of hours. Whatever it is that's drawing the spirits in has grown stronger, much stronger.'

Hammond groaned. 'You can't leave. What about Tanya?'

'I won't be much help if I end up like Bunty. I'm going, Jon. You either take me or I walk down that street now and get a taxi . . . but I've got to leave Batforth and every minute counts. Ever since I arrived in Batforth I've been like a man clinging by his fingernails to the sides of a well and in the last couple of hours I've started to slip.'

Hammond put his hand on Stevenson's arm. 'Roy, listen to me . . .'

Stevenson jerked his arm away. 'I won't listen, Jon. I'm not staying.'

Hammond ran the fingers of his right hand through his hair.

'All right, Roy, I have an idea. What if I drive you to Ruttlake tonight. You can stay in the motel there. Would you feel safe there?'

Stevenson looked doubtful, but it was obviously an idea he didn't rule out altogether.

'I could pick you up tomorrow.'

'I don't know.'

'We have to find out what's causing this. You said maybe it started with the train crash. . . . If you came to the crash scene with me . . . maybe . . .'

'No. . . .'

'Come back tomorrow for one hour. That's all.'

Stevenson sighed. 'All right, one hour. Now get me out of Batforth.'

TWENTY-THREE

Tanya was sobbing quietly to herself in the car as they drove out of Batforth, unable to erase the image of Bunty falling from the top of the restaurant from her mind. Stevenson sat stiff and alert in the back seat, like a man expecting an ambush.

'Is the scene of the train crash the best place to start, to try to find out what this thing is?' Hammond asked, about a mile out of Batforth.

'It's as good a place as any,' Stevenson sighed. 'But it's not really me you need for this. You don't need a piddling, tenth-rate psychic like me. What you need is an expert to identify and exorcize this thing.'

'You mean like a priest or . . .'

'No,' Stevenson said firmly. 'Don't get a priest or anyone like that involved. It's too dangerous. The hierarchy of some churches might have men who can tackle this but an ordinary priest or bishop would be destroyed.'

'Who then? Give me some names. Someone I can contact.'

'I'm no expert . . . there are a few I can think of.'

'Just give me three names.'

'There's a professor of parapsychology in London. Oscar Renfrew.'

Hammond took his pad and pen from his inside pocket and handed them back to Stevenson.

'Write them down.'

Stevenson nodded and started writing.

'If you can't get Renfrew, try Alexander Tulley. He's an occult figure.'

'Where does he live?'

'He's based in London as well.'

Stevenson scribbled again.

'And? Give me a third name.'

After a moment's thought Stevenson said, 'The most famous occult figure in the country is a man named David Preece.'

'I've heard of him.'

'I don't know if he'd want to help. . . . You may remember about five years ago the newspapers were calling him The Beast. He's involved in all kinds of things. He's even started his own religion – the Priests of the Aryan Dawn. It's some kind of mixture of old Indian religions and Teutonic myths, although how the two came together I'm not really sure.'

'And where is Preece?'

'County Durham, I believe,' Stevenson said, writing it down. 'He has some kind of big house up there, I think.'

Stevenson became more relaxed as the lights of Ruttlake came into view.

'I'm sorry if you feel I've let you down, Jon,' he said.

'Forget it, Roy, you haven't let anyone down. I shouldn't really have got you involved in this but I didn't know where else to turn.'

'It's just that . . .'

'You don't have to explain anything. I know what you've gone through and I appreciate it. I'll pick you up first thing in the morning.'

Stevenson sighed, still doubtful.

'You'll be there, won't you, Roy? For Tanya's sake.'

'I'll be there.'

When they parked in front of the motel, Stevenson said, 'Don't leave Tanya alone tonight and one of you should be awake all the time. I know this is going to sound crazy but religious objects might help. If you have a Bible, take it out. If you have a crucifix or can make something like a crucifix, wear it or keep it near you.'

He got out of the car and shook Hammond's hand.

'Good luck, Jon.'

He gave Tanya a half-wave, shut the door and disappeared into the motel.

They touched eighty on the way back to Batforth, Tanya's knuckles turning white as she gripped the seatbelt. Hammond drove straight to the police station.

Joss looked up with tired eyes as they entered.

'I've got to see Jensen,' Hammond said. 'Right now.'

'But . . .'

'I'm going to tell him everything, William. Everything. This has got to be tackled now.'

Joss started to protest then stood up, knocked on Jensen's

door and went in. He returned a moment later and said, 'He'll see you.' Jensen greeted them with a curt 'Good evening' and waved them to chairs opposite his desk.

'What can I do for you, Mr Hammond?'

'I've got a story to tell,' Hammond said, 'and you'd better listen because unless you do a lot more people are going to die.'

Jensen fiddled with a pen and said, 'I'll listen, of course.'

Hammond ran through the story in detail, then said, 'So that's what we're really up against and we've got to find a way to fight it.'

Jensen stood up and paced the room with almost military steps.

'Hammond,' he said at last, 'I believe you're well meaning in all that you've said and no doubt think that as a policeman I would laugh at such things, but I don't. I believe there are things in this world that can't be explained, inexplicable things, strange things, unusual phenomena. We don't know what they are now. Maybe we will in fifty years, who knows. Occult people play around with them and perhaps the same can be said of some religious people. It's possible some of these things are happening in Batforth right now. I've read that this type of thing can happen in the presence of extreme violence. But as for the murders themselves. . . .' He gave Hammond a brief, knowing smile. 'No, they were committed by a man, an extremely violent and dangerous man and we intend to catch him very soon.'

Hammond slammed the heel of his hand onto the desk and jumped to his feet.

'You're wrong,' he shouted.

Jensen remained calm.

'You're overwrought, Mr Hammond. You look very tired. Why don't you go home and get some sleep and leave the police to do the job they're paid for?'

'What can I say to convince you?'

'Nothing.'

Hammond's face twisted in fury but he swallowed the words he was about to speak when he felt Tanya take his arm.

'He's not going to listen, Jon,' she said.

He let her lead him to the door then turned as if to make a final appeal to Jensen.

He decided it was useless and waved a hand at the inspector in a dismissive, contemptuous gesture.

They drove across Batforth without speaking. Back in the flat, Hammond said to Tanya, 'Bring me a can of beer. No. Bring me half a dozen cans of beer.'

He sat down at the telephone and flipped open his pad at the entries Stevenson had made.

He rang the operator and got the numbers of Oscar Renfrew and Alexander Tulley. 'Could you be more specific than County Durham for the other person?' the operator asked him and he said he couldn't.

'Well, I . . .'

'It's all right, forget it,' he said and hung up.

He dialled Renfrew's number first. There was no answer so he hung up and tried again. This time he let the phone ring for a long time but still there was no answer.

Then he rang Tulley's number.

'Yes,' a female voice said.

'I'd like to speak to Mr Tulley please.'

'I'm sorry, he's away on holiday.'

'It's very important. I must speak to him.'

'I'm sorry, he's in the Caribbean. He won't be back for at least a month.'

Hammond ground his teeth, then said, 'Look, I wonder if you could help me. If I can't get Mr Tulley, I have to get in touch with a David Preece. Would you have his number? I believe he lives in. . . .'

'Yes, I think we may have Mr Preece's number. Just a moment.'

Hammond drummed his fingers on the table as he waited. Then a voice said, 'Yes, we do have that number.'

He took it down, muttered his thanks and hung up. He thumbed through the telephone book, searching for the Durham dialling code. When he found it he dialled Preece's number.

The Tall Man stood in the centre of the room before the stone altar, his arms raised high in prayer, his eyes closed. He was flanked by two naked novitiates, girls still in their teens. The first was tall and slender, with pale skin and fair hair. The second was black, Nigerian black, dark as a seam of coal. She was several inches shorter than the first girl, broad-shouldered, with full breasts and heavy buttocks.

The Tall Man stood in the centre of a vast, circular, golden carpet, patterned with a series of ever-diminishing circles, thirteen in all, with one foot placed on each side of the centre circle in which was woven the hideous face of Hatta-Matu, tongue protruding, eyes bulging.

When he lowered his arms and opened his eyes, the novitiates approached, unfastened the cords at the front of his full-length red robe and lifted it from his shoulders.

His eyes travelled along the altar to the bronze statue of Hatta-Matu then across her bulging thighs, thrusting belly, huge breasts cupped obscenely in five hands and came to rest on the staring eyes.

'Hatta-Matu,' he intoned.

'Hatta-Matu,' the novitiates repeated.

'Hatta-Matu,' he said louder.

Again they repeated his words.

He turned to the fair-haired novitiate.

'Are you prepared?' he said.

'Yes, Magus.'

He assumed the lotus position as the girl knelt down beside him and performed the Ritual of the Thirteen Zones, biting him, licking him and rubbing her body against him. When she had finished he sprang to his feet, lifted her in his arms and carried her to the altar. He laid her on her back, spread her legs apart and entered her, holding one of her ankles in each hand. He drove his flesh into hers fiercely, violently, cruelly until she gasped and screamed. Instantly he withdrew, without climaxing and walked over to where the black girl knelt.

'Are you prepared?' he said.

She nodded.

This time he remained standing while she performed the ritual.

Then he carried her to the altar, bent her head between the feet of Hattu-Matu and entered her, thrusting savagely. When she too had climaxed, her body convulsing, tiny screams coming from her throat, he strode to the centre of the floor and knelt above the woven face of Hatta-Matu, facing the statue.

'Hatta-Matu,' he intoned.

'Hatta-Matu,' the girls repeated.

'Hatta-Ma . . .'

He stopped abruptly then fell onto his back. As the girls watched he rolled and convulsed on the floor. A great red weal appeared on his back then another on his inner thigh. His flesh was pushed and twisted and obscenely kneaded by invisible hands. He was dragged from a squatting position to a kneeling position then thrown onto his back and dragged to the front of the altar. A scratch appeared across his chest and blood ran down over his belly.

Suddenly he stood up, climaxed, then collapsed on all fours, gasping for breath. The novitiates waited, watching him as if in a trance. The room was hushed, a silence beyond silence. At last he stood up and motioned to the girls. They brought oil and ointment and gently tended to his cuts and weals. When they had finished they brought the red robe and he shrugged his shoulders into it and stood silently while they tied the cords at the front.

He left the altar room without another word and went upstairs and sat at a window in his study which looked down over the dark shapes of his vast garden and the black lake beyond which was splashed in the centre with shimmering yellow moonlight.

The sense of power was overwhelming. It seemed to rush through his body like a very potent drug. The superficial pain of the cuts was nothing.

Power.

He had the power to *know* what other men did not *know*, to reach where other men could not.

Then he thought of what he had bought from Erwin Kininsky and of the moment the box had slipped from his hands as the train crashed at Batforth. But for the intervention of fate what powers would he have had now? Hardly a day passed that was not marred by that thought.

At that moment the phone rang and he crossed to his desk and picked up the receiver.

'Yes,' he said.

'Mr Preece?' a man's voice said at the other end of the line. 'Mr David Preece?'

'That's correct. Who's calling?'

'Jon Hammond's my name. You don't know me but your

name was given to me by a friend who said you might be able to help. You've probably seen something of my problem on television and in the newspapers lately . . .'

'I neither read newspapers nor watch television nor concern myself with worldly things,' Preece said.

'I'm calling from Batforth,' Hammond told him. 'Please hear what I've got to say.'

'What is it?'

Preece stiffened and began to play with one of the cords on the red robe as Hammond related the story of the train crash and all that had happened at Batforth.

The box was intact. It was still there.

'This friend of mine who gave me your name says we have to identify the source of the problem. He says you might be able to help, to suggest something, or . . .'

The powers that fate had snatched away might still be his.

'I'm sorry, I can't help you,' Preece said, cutting him off.

'But . . .'

'I'm sorry, it's out of the question.'

Then he hung up and stared out into the night.

It was out there. It was alive. It was waiting for him.

TWENTY-FOUR

'Any luck?' said Tanya, coming into the room as Hammond slammed down the telephone.

He shook his head. 'One doesn't answer, one's away and one doesn't want to help.'

Then he noticed the black, leather-bound Bible she was holding.

'Where did you find that? I haven't seen it for years.'

'On your bookshelves in the bedroom.'

'Let me see it.'

She handed it to him and he flicked open the front cover and read the inscription: 'To Jonathan, from Mum, Christmas 1959'.

He leaned back and let the book close gently in his hand.

'What do we do with it?' he said.

She shrugged and put it down on the table.

'I've made this too,' she said, turning back into the kitchen.

She returned a moment later, holding a cross she had made out of two plastic rulers she had found in a drawer.

He rubbed his temples with both hands.

'This can't be happening to me,' he said. 'It's all so bloody absurd.'

He snapped open a beer can and took a long drink as Tanya went to the front door and propped the makeshift cross against it.

The night was comparatively uneventful. They spent it on the settee, watching video tapes and drinking coffee to keep them awake. Tanya dropped off into a light sleep three times but each time she woke with a start after a few minutes, disgusted at the dreams she had had. He didn't ask her about them. He reckoned that would only make it worse. Instead he just held her tightly, tucking in the rug she had wrapped around herself. He dozed off only once and instantly the song began – the Horst Wessel song. It started immediately, loud and clear, not distant as it had been at the beginning of all his dreams during the past few days.

At nine a.m. they drove to Ruttlake to pick up Stevenson. On the way back to Batforth, Stevenson asked about the three people he had suggested Hammond contact and when Hammond told him what had happened he said, 'It's a pity you didn't get through to Oscar Renfrew – he was your best bet.'

They drove on in silence for about ten minutes then Hammond said, 'Roy, this is totally outside my experience. I'm one of those people you described as wanting to live a practical life inside boundaries I can understand. You said on the phone when I called you that you'd had a bad experience just before you left Ruttlake. You said you might tell me about it one day. How about now? It might help me to understand.'

Stevenson considered Hammond's request for a moment, then said: 'All right. What happened was this. After I came back from having all those tests done at the university, I started reading everything I could about psychic phenomena, the paranormal, occult, and stupidly, I started dabbling in a few things. Then it happened. One day I was sitting at work writing out the rough draft of a business letter. When I finished it, I discovered I hadn't written what I thought I'd written. It was *my* letter, in *my* handwriting but it was written in what I can only describe as old English. It was addressed to a woman called Rachel and signed Anonymous and was the most foul, disgusting letter I've ever read in my life, pure pornography plus. I tore it up and threw it away. That was on a Friday. That night I had the most awful dreams about life in what seemed to be some kind of manor house a long time ago. There were orgies in the dreams and torture and I was taking part in the torture and enjoying it. The next morning I caught a bus to London. I don't know why I did it, I just did it. I remember getting on the bus and the next thing I knew I woke up on the Thames Embankment late on the Sunday night. I'd lost about forty hours. I was pretty dirty . . . pretty drunk too. I tidied myself up and came home.'

He paused, wincing at the memory, then continued:

'For about a week, strange things kept happening. I'd find myself writing odd things I hadn't meant to write. I'd lose an hour here and there, remembering nothing about what had

158

happened. Then one day I had this overpowering urge to rape
my secretary – well, more than rape actually. I couldn't believe
I was thinking such things. I knew then I had to get some
help. I didn't know what to do. I started to ring the professor
who had conducted all the tests on me but then I thought that
all he'd want to do was rush me into his lab and start a new
series of tests that he could write a booklet on. Anyway, I don't
know where I got the idea from but I was due a week's holiday
so I went to France. Why France? Don't ask me. I took a train
to Lourdes. Again, I don't know why. I spent a week there,
taking the waters. On the Thursday I took some kind of fit
and was admitted to hospital with convulsions. They couldn't
find anything wrong with me and I left two days later.
After that, I was fine, but I never dabbled with anything to
do with psychic phenomena from that day until your call,
Jon.'

'Jesus,' was all Hammond could say when Stevenson con-
cluded his story as they passed through the outskirts of Batforth.

He took a short cut to the crash scene, along Horatio Street
and the narrow, rutted Moulson's Lane.

He parked the car across the field from Moulson's Pond,
and, as he got out, he heard a voice say, 'Good morning, Mr
Hammond.'

A short, chubby, elderly woman was standing in her garden,
holding the collar of a snarling Labrador. Hammond knew the
woman by sight but not her name.

'Morning,' he said.

'What brings you down here, Mr Hammond? Not another
story about the crash, is it?'

'Something like that.'

'Nobody seems to be coming down here since the night of
the crash. There used to be kids playing here all the time, or
men fishing, or young couples. It's almost as if the crash has
scared them off.'

'Must be the weather,' Hammond said.

'Never bothered people before. I've never seen it so deserted.
Do you know, since they cleared up the mess after the crash
the only people I've seen on that field are Back and Shoulder
– you know, George Murdoch and that Henry Somebody –
and they didn't stay long. Looked to me like they found

something in the pond. They'd scavenge anything, those two. Amazing what you find in ponds. Tyres, bikes . . .'

'Yes, that's true,' Hammond said. 'Well, good morning Mrs. . . . um. Good morning.'

As he turned away from the woman, it started to rain, as suddenly as if a tap had been turned on. Hammond, Stevenson and Tanya trudged around the pond in a steady drizzle and climbed the railway embankment.

'That's where it left the rails,' Hammond said, 'and you can see where it went.'

Stevenson's eyes followed Hammond's pointing finger, his eyes picking out the ragged, rain-filled trenches which had been gouged out by the train's wheels.

'Well?' said Hammond. 'What do we do?'

'There you go again,' Stevenson said, 'thinking I know all the answers.' He looked around and screwed up his face against the rain. 'I think my guess might have been wrong,' he said. 'If there is a centre of the psychic activity in Batforth, it's not here. I'd feel it.' He turned to Hammond. 'I'll tell you one thing, between last night and now the activity through the town as a whole has increased.'

He looked away down the slope, then said, 'Let's take a look down there, where the train must have overturned.'

Hammond nodded.

'I'm going back to the car,' Tanya said, pushing a fringe of wet hair back from her forehead. 'I'm getting soaked. In fact, I've just realized I'm starving. We didn't have any breakfast this morning, Jon. Give me the car keys and I'll drive over and get something from that shop over there.'

She nodded to the small grocer's store at the far side of the field, about three hundred yards away.

Hammond was doubtful, 'I don't . . .'

'I won't be out of sight of either of you,' she said.

'O.K.'

He handed her the keys and he and Stevenson half walked, half slid down the slope, heading towards the pond.

'Probably just as well the train didn't end up in that lake,' Stevenson said.

'Moulson's Pond? It isn't all that deep.'

As they reached the edge of the pond, Hammond heard the car's engine start and looked up, raising his hand in a wave.

But Tanya had already set the car in motion and was watching the road in front of her.

It was as he was about to turn back towards Stevenson that something in the back seat of the car caught his attention.

A shape, a dark form.

He blinked, wiped the water from his upper face in two quick gestures and looked again. This time he saw it more clearly. It was about the size of a man yet with no distinct outline, like a black smudge on a film.

'What's wrong?' Stevenson said, seeing the look of horror on Hammond's face.

Then the black form seemed to shift and Hammond thought he saw two eyes watching him and a grinning mouth about three inches lower down.

'Tanya!' he shouted. 'Tanya!'

Then he broke into a stumbling run.

TWENTY-FIVE

Within seconds Hammond had found his rhythm and he ran as he had never run before, his feet punching dark holes into the rain-sodden earth.

'Tanyaaaaa,' he shouted and he felt cold spots of rain in his mouth, pricking him like tiny needles.

She was only two hundred yards from him now, but drawing away all the time, and at such an angle that he couldn't clearly make out anything in the back seat.

'Tanyaaaaa.'

What the hell was that thing? What did it want? What would it do?

Suddenly the drizzle became a downpour and he heard a clap of thunder far, far away.

Stevenson was a long way behind him when he cleared the drainage ditch in the centre of the field as if it didn't exist and sprinted on, his fists pounding the air, his eyes slitted against the lashing rain.

'Tanyaaaaaaa.'

She was turning into the narrow street on which the grocer's shop stood but still he couldn't clearly see into the back seat.

The field was bordered by rows of bushes and regimented copses of trees which blocked his view of the shop. He hurdled the first row of bushes and kicked his way through the rest. As he skirted the last group of trees he saw that Tanya had parked the car and was entering the shop. He scanned the back seat with rain-blurred eyes.

Was it still there?

He couldn't see.

'Taaaanyaaaaaaa.'

The shop door fell shut behind her as he left the field, his feet slap-slapping their way up the street.

He drew nearer to the car, peering into it, shielding his eyes with his hand. The thing wasn't there. The back seat was empty. No smudge. No shape. A surge of relief flooded through him. Had it been his imagination? Had it been . . .

He was no more than fifteen feet from the shop when the window exploded outwards. Jagged chunks of glass scythed through the air and a hailstorm of tiny glass fragments peppered the pavement and the road. Instinctively Hammond threw himself against a wall, turning his face away and ducking. An instant later he spun around and sprinted towards the shop, the glass crunching under his feet.

A large packet of soap powder flew from the window now, as if thrown violently. It struck the bonnet of his car and split open, spewing its pale blue contents across the road. As he reached the door, three cans shot through the window. Two flew high in the air and the third punched into the door of his car.

He threw open the shop door and stood frozen with horror on the threshold for what was only a millisecond but seemed like an eternity. It was as if the world stood still, as if the past and the future had collided violently in that instant.

Tanya was lying on her back in the centre of the shop. Her coat had been tugged almost from her shoulders, her blouse ripped, her skirt thrown up. Her clothing danced and jerked about as if she was lying in the middle of a hurricane. Or as if a score of hands was trying to strip her naked. As he watched, her tights were tugged down. They caught on her thighs and another savage jerk ripped them in two. A red weal appeared, running from her shoulder to the valley between her breasts and some force pulled on her bra with such savagery that her head slapped back against the floor. The features of her face were sculpted into a tortured scream but no sound came.

All around her was a maelstrom of tumbling boxes, collapsing pyramids of tins, violently trembling shelves, bottles and cans flying haphazardly across the room.

At the far side of the shop, behind the counter, the shopkeeper was pressed into a corner in a half-crouch, his hands gripping the wall on each side of him as if seeking to escape into it.

Hammond jumped forward but felt a powerful force trying to push him back. It was not solid like a man, but yielded like taut rubber or elastic. He swung two round-house punches through the air and felt them strike something. Again it was not like striking a man, nor was it like striking air. It was as if he had punched his hand through a silent waterfall or a dangling pillowcase. He threw his weight against the force and moved forward like a man wading through treacle. He reached Tanya and flung himself down beside her, dragging her to him.

'Tanya, we've got to get out of here,' he yelled.

Her head swung round and she looked at him as if she had never seen him before.

'Tanya, we've got to . . .'

Suddenly a hush fell over the room. The cans and boxes and shelves lay still. It was as if it had all been a nightmare and they had just woken up.

Hammond jumped to his feet and dragged Tanya up, pulling her coat back over her shoulders.

'I couldn't get through the door,' Hammond heard Stevenson saying behind him. 'Something was holding me back.'

Hammond cupped Tanya's face in his hands.

'Are you all right?' he said quietly.

Her eyes darted about, then found his.

'Jon . . .' she breathed.

'It's all right now,' he said, holding her close.

'Jon, they tried to rape me. There were a lot of them. I couldn't see them but . . .'

'Don't talk about it now.'

'They were pushing things into me, like fingers or . . .' She shuddered with horror. 'They were pushing them into my ears and my mouth and every place, Jon.'

A voice away to Jon's left said, 'You're H-Hammond of the *Courier*, aren't you?'

Hammond turned his head to the storekeeper and nodded.

'Wh-what's going on here? What happened?'

'We don't know,' Hammond said.

'I s-suppose I should call the police.'

'You do that,' Hammond told him. 'And be sure to tell Inspector Jensen, Jon Hammond said, "I told you so".'

Hammond led Tanya from the shop and helped her into the back seat of the car. Stevenson climbed in after her and put his arm around her shoulders.

'I'm taking you to the hospital,' Hammond said, sliding into the driver's seat.

'No,' Tanya said firmly.

'Why not?'

'They can't do anything for me, Jon . . . and I don't want to be left alone there. Just take me back to the flat.'

He nodded and started the engine.

'Why did it stop?' he said, looking at Stevenson in the rear-view mirror.

'I don't know, Jon, maybe it's playing some kind of game. I told you, these are malevolent spirits, you never know what they'll do.'

Hammond set the car in motion, drove slowly around the field, then turned up Moulson's Lane. Suddenly he braked so hard that Stevenson had to grab Tanya to prevent her being thrown into the back of the front seat.

'What the hell are you doing?' Stevenson demanded.

The gearbox crunched in protest as Hammond snapped the gearstick into reverse. He sent the car shooting back down Moulson's Lane, braked at the bottom, snatched on the hand-brake then turned in his seat and pointed through the window.

A very tall, dark-haired man in a trenchcoat was striding along the far side of the pond, heading for a white Mercedes, his head bent forward against the rain.

'He was on the train with me on the night of the crash,' Hammond said. 'He doesn't come from around here. I wonder what brought him back?'

Stevenson wound down the window and pushed his head out.

Hammond said, 'I wonder what he wants in Batforth. He's hardly out for a Sunday stroll on a day like this. I . . .'

Stevenson turned and stared at Hammond. 'Do you know who that is, Jon?'

'No, who?'

'That's David Preece.'

Hammond stared back into Stevenson's eyes, their gaze filled with a thousand questions.

'The occultist?' Hammond said. 'The man who started the Priests of whatever it was?'

'The Priests of the Aryan Dawn. Yes.'

TWENTY-SIX

Hammond sent the car roaring forward then did a shuddering U-turn and shot back to the bottom of Moulson's Lane.

'He's gone,' Stevenson said, jerking a thumb at the spot where the Mercedes had been parked.

'There's only one direction he could have taken,' Hammond said.

The rain began to ease as he sent the car hurtling around the road that circled the pond and had stopped by the time he turned up the narrow lane opposite the point where the Mercedes had been parked.

There were long stretches of dimness in the lane, where the dripping trees which touched high above them cast giant shadows. They plunged from blackness to bright sunlight, exploded from deep shadows into sectors where the wet road glistened so brightly that it hurt Hammond's eyes. Darkness, light, darkness, light. It was as if someone was flicking a switch off and on.

They turned the third corner but still there was no sign of the Mercedes.

'Where the hell is he?' Hammond said.

'He must be travelling,' Stevenson said. 'Is this the only way he could have come?'

Hammond nodded. 'Yes, we'd have seen him if he'd headed back towards Batforth.'

The trees and bushes which crowded against the lane were a blur as Hammond pushed his foot all the way to the floor.

'It can't be just a coincidence that he was on the train,' Stevenson said in such a way that Hammond was uncertain if it was a statement or a question.

Hammond braked hard and wrestled the snaking car around another bend.

'There it is,' Tanya said, just as Hammond saw the back of the Mercedes disappear around a corner up ahead.

He accelerated, caressed the brake and wrenched the car

around the corner. The Mercedes was only two hundred yards ahead of them now, on a long straight section of the lane.

Hammond began to sound his horn in long sporadic blasts.

They were gaining on the Mercedes. Two hundred yards became one hundred and fifty, then one hundred.

Suddenly the Mercedes accelerated, drawing rapidly away from them.

Hammond left his hand on the horn for a full ten seconds.

'It must be obvious we're signalling him to stop,' Stevenson said.

'Damn him,' Hammond yelled.

The Mercedes was three hundred yards ahead of them now and still pulling away.

It swept around another bend and Hammond followed, puffing out his lips as the car bucked then straightened out.

'Why is he running away?' Stevenson said.

They hurtled up a hill and down the other side, sweeping through the green fields now.

'There's a junction up ahead,' Hammond said, 'where this lane crosses the Hampton road. He'll have to slow down there.'

'How fast are we going?' Tanya said, gripping the back of Hammond's seat.

Hammond glanced at the speedometer and said, 'Don't ask.'

A few seconds later, he saw the Mercedes' brake lights winking.

'Here comes the junction,' he said.

The Mercedes slowed almost to a halt then took a sharp left into the Hampton road.

'Say a prayer,' said Hammond.

He didn't brake until the last minute. The car shot into the junction, slewed into a four-wheel drift, scythed down twenty feet of grass on the verge on the right-hand side of the road then straightened out.

'You made up some ground on that corner,' Stevenson said in a shaking voice.

'Why the hell won't he stop?' Hammond shouted, blasting on the horn.

Then he realized he was gaining on the Mercedes. One hundred yards, fifty, twenty, ten. He pulled into the outside lane and put his foot flat to the boards.

The front of his car was almost level with the tail of the

Mercedes when it began to pull away again. That was when Hammond saw the lorry roaring towards him.

He jerked his car back in behind the Mercedes, his heart thumping wildly, as the lorry driver gave him a loud blast on his horn. The lorry thundered past, its bulk making Hammond's car shake, and Hammond pulled out again, drawing level with the Mercedes.

'Pull over,' he yelled, sounding his horn.

There was a right-hand bend up ahead and Hammond knew that this would give him the edge. He started to ease towards the Mercedes, his nose just in front.

Twenty yards from the bend, the Tall Man eased back, seeing the danger if he tried to take it at speed with Hammond outside him.

Hammond saw his chance. He veered in front of the Mercedes and brushed his brake, easing his speed back. He slowed to thirty, watching the Mercedes in his rear-view mirror.

'He's stopping,' Stevenson said as the Mercedes slowed right down and bumped onto the verge.

Hammond puffed out his cheeks with relief, braked and reversed onto the verge, parking in front of the Mercedes.

He climbed out, sprinted back to the Mercedes and jerked the door open.

'Get out,' he rasped.

'What is this? Who are you?'

'You're David Preece. I'm Jon Hammond. I called you last night. Introduction over, now *get out*.'

He grabbed Preece by the collar and dragged him from the car.

'Why were you so anxious to get away from us?' Hammond said, still holding the Tall Man's collar.

'I didn't know who you were. I saw you watching me. You could have been thugs for all I knew. Or people who knew my face. I don't like publicity. I haven't for many years now. The Press aren't very sympathetic to me . . . Will you let me go?'

Hammond let his hand drop to his side and the Tall Man straightened his coat with a jerk.

'What are you doing here? You said last night that you didn't want to help.'

'I was curious. I'm interested in any unusual phenomena.'

'What do you know about what's going on in Batforth?'

'What do I know? Nothing.'

'You were on the train the night it crashed in Batforth and that's when all this started.'

'I've never been in Batforth before in my life.'

'You were on the train,' Hammond insisted, a note of exasperation in his voice. 'I saw you . . . People are being killed in this town. Why are you denying you were on the train? You know you're lying.'

Stevenson had come up behind Hammond and now he touched his arm. 'It's too much of a coincidence,' he said. 'David Preece on the train, the train crashes, strange things start to happen. There has to be a connection.'

Preece held up a hand to silence Stevenson. 'All right,' he said, 'this has gone on long enough. You've forced me off the road and manhandled me. I intend to inform the police at the next town. I am leaving *now*.'

As Preece turned and started to get back into his car, Stevenson said, 'He knows something, Jon.'

Hammond looked down at the small man, then his eyes shifted to his own car. He could see the back of Tanya's head through the car window. She was bent forward, her face in her hands, sobbing quietly.

Suddenly all the fears, frustrations, worries and horrors of the past few days vanished from Hammond as if plucked away by pincers. They were replaced by a single emotion, a depth of intense, burning anger like nothing he had ever felt before.

As Preece's fingers plucked at the ignition key, Hammond's right hand folded around his throat, cutting off his air. He dragged Preece from his seat and slammed him against the side of the car.

'You'll talk,' he said in a low growl. 'You'll tell me everything you know.'

The Tall Man was hunched forward, holding his neck, struggling for breath. He spun away from Hammond and stumbled around the car.

There was a copse of trees beside the road and just inside the treeline a shallow stream gurgled its way towards Batforth. Preece bumped into a tree and turned to face Hammond, panting for breath.

'You're in deep . . . trouble . . . now. I'll see . . . you get . . . five years for this.'

As Hammond started forward, Stevenson grabbed at his sleeve. 'Don't do that to his neck again, Jon. You don't know your own strength. You might . . .'

Hammond swept him aside and broke into a half run to where Preece stood. He seized Preece by the lapels and lifted him off the ground.

'Talk. Tell me what you know.'

'I don't . . . know anything. I wasn't on the train . . . you're mistaken.'

Hammond lowered the man onto his feet again and hooked an awesome punch into his solar plexus. Preece staggered back, tripped and splashed into the edge of the stream. Hammond was after him immediately. As Preece tried to rise, Hammond slapped him on the face and he fell on his side into the water. He rolled onto his back, coughing and spluttering, propped on his elbows in about a foot of water.

Hammond dropped on Preece, straddling his chest, his seventeen-stone bulk driving the wind out of him.

'Talk,' he yelled. 'Tell me what's going on.'

'I . . . don't know . . .' Preece panted.

Hammond put both hands under Preece's chin and forced his head back under the water. He held it there for a long time, grimly watching the Tall Man's face whipping backwards and forwards, his lips pressed tightly together.

Stevenson splashed into the stream and grabbed Hammond's arm.

'You'll kill him, Jon. For God's sake!'

Hammond lashed out with his left hand and struck Stevenson on the chest, sending him sprawling back onto the bank.

Suddenly Preece's mouth burst wide open in a silent cry. Instantly Hammond grabbed a handful of his hair and roughly pulled his head out of the water.

'Your choice,' he yelled. 'Your choice. Next time you go under, you stay under for good.'

'You'd never know then,' Preece said. 'If you kill me you'll never know.'

Hammond bent his head forward until his nose almost touched Preece's.

'Listen carefully,' he rasped. 'I said it's your choice. Next time I put your head under the water it stays there until you're dead.'

Preece hesitated, staring into Hammond's eyes. Hammond let three seconds pass, then let go of the Tall Man's hair and clamped both hands over his face, pushing him back again.

Preece screamed, 'All right', just as the water closed over his face.

Hammond pulled him up again.

'I want to know everything, from start to finish. I want to know what's going on.'

'All right,' Preece shivered. 'All right, I will tell you everything.' He shivered again, then said. 'Is there somewhere we can talk? I have to get out of these wet clothes before I catch pneumonia.'

'Let's take him back to the flat,' Stevenson said.

'O.K.' Hammond nodded, dragging Preece to his feet. 'You ask Tanya if she's able to drive my car back to the flat. You can drive the Mercedes. I'll get in the back seat with . . .' He gave Preece a contemptuous look. 'With this.'

Preece had a small overnight bag in the boot of the Mercedes and Hammond let him carry it up to the flat after unzipping it and giving it a quick search. Hammond changed into dry clothes and let Preece do the same. Preece slipped on a black polo-neck pullover and black trousers.

'I don't have a spare pair of shoes,' he told Hammond, holding up the saturated pair he had been wearing.

'That's O.K.' Hammond said. 'You're not going anywhere.'

He threw Preece's shoes down in front of the central heating outlet, then took him by the arm and led him into the lounge. There he whipped a hard-backed chair from the dining-table and set it down in the middle of the room.

'You sit there,' he said, flopping onto the settee beside Tanya. Stevenson stood in one corner, sipping a whisky.

Preece smirked. 'What is this? Some kind of Lubyanka interrogation?'

'If that's the way you want it,' Hammond said as Preece sat in the chair. He could see that some of Preece's confidence was returning.

'O.K.,' said Hammond. 'Let's start at the beginning. What the hell is this all about?'

Preece waved a finger at Hammond. 'I *may* tell you everything,' he said, 'but before I do, I want some guarantees.'

Hammond looked at Stevenson, then back at Preece again. 'Guarantees,' he breathed.

'I'll tell you what you want to know, provided it's kept in the strictest confidence and you help me to recover something that I have lost.'

'No guarantees,' Hammond said quietly. He paused, then added, 'You don't understand yet, do you? The message hasn't got through. People are being murdered here. My girlfriend is in extreme danger.'

Preece smirked again. 'There are some things that are far more important than a few lives,' he said. 'Besides, how can you take up a moral stance when you've just kidnapped me?'

Hammond launched himself across the room, his face contorted with rage. He struck Preece with the back of his hand with such force that his lip split open, spattering blood over his pullover. Preece toppled sideways off the chair. Hammond dragged him to his feet by the neck of the pullover and slammed him back into the chair.

'I don't give a damn if this is kidnapping,' Hammond growled, enunciating every word clearly as if he wanted to be certain that Preece was in no doubt about the position he was in. His eyes burned into Preece as he added, 'This is going to be murder if you don't tell me what I want to know.'

There was a long silence. Preece, Stevenson and Tanya all stared at Hammond. No one in the room doubted that he meant what he said.

When Preece spoke again it was as if he was talking in the quiet of a cathedral. 'All right,' he said. 'All right, let me go.'

Hammond let his hands fall back to his sides.

'Now talk.'

'It's something I had on the train with me,' Preece said. 'I lost it in the crash. I thought it had been smashed to pieces or maybe stolen . . . but it must have survived.'

'What is it?'

'It's a . . . a relic.'

'A relic,' Hammond said, puzzled. 'You mean all this has something to do with an object, something tangible?'

Preece nodded. 'I should never have taken it on the train. I just didn't realize how powerful it was. I've never seen anything like it. It's capable of giving off great heat and then creating its own cold spot. It's capable of . . . so much.'

Preece paused and wiped the blood from his mouth. He glanced at Stevenson then turned back to Hammond. 'Do you think I could have one of those drinks?' Hammond nodded to Stevenson and the little man poured a whisky and handed it to Preece.

Hammond was looking quizzically at Stevenson. 'Yes,' said Stevenson, as if Hammond had asked him a question. 'Relics can have awesome occult powers. Something like that could act as a magnet to discarnate entities.'

'What kind of thing are we talking about here?' Hammond said, looking from Stevenson to Preece and back again.

Stevenson shrugged. 'One example is the spear which pierced the side of Christ. It's believed to have tremendous occult powers . . . it's supposed to be around somewhere even today.'

Stevenson drained his glass, splashed another large whisky into it, then added, 'But I've never even read about the kind of things that are happening here.' He paused and looked deep into Hammond's eyes. 'It keeps on getting stronger, Jon. Whatever it is, it's twice as strong today as it was yesterday. I noticed it immediately when I came back to Batforth today.'

He took another sip of his whisky and Hammond noticed his hand was shaking.

Hammond dropped his eyes back to Preece again and Preece said: 'I'll begin at the beginning. That's in April, nineteen forty-five, when Adolf Hitler and Eva Braun committed suicide in the bunker in Berlin. The bodies were doused with petrol and burned but they weren't totally destroyed. They were still there when the Russians overran that sector. An order was issued to take the bodies back to Moscow. They were taken there and various tests were carried out on them.'

Hammond stepped back quietly as if he didn't want to interrupt the flow of Preece's story and flopped into the settee next to Tanya.

'The man in charge of the examinations,' Preece continued, 'was a Doctor Noblachev. He disposed of Eva Braun's body fairly quickly but continued to make tests on Hitler for a long time, particularly his brain, before disposing of the various specimens of bone and tissue in nineteen forty-eight. There was only one thing he kept. Why he kept it I don't know. A keepsake perhaps or a medical curiosity? We can only guess at his motivation.'

Everyone in the room seemed to tense as if they knew that here at last was the answer to the mystery. It was about to be presented to them as if by a magician snatching back a black curtain and shouting 'Hey Presto'. The final piece of the jigsaw which had tormented them was about to be slotted into place.

'What he kept,' Preece said, 'was the skull.'

There was a pause as if all of them had been rendered incapable of communication by some electric charge running through their bodies. Then Stevenson said in a high-pitched voice: 'Is that what you've brought to Batforth?'

'Yes,' Preece said.

Hammond leaned back, hooked his hands behind his head and stared at the ceiling.

'Adolf Hitler's skull,' he breathed.

PART THREE

The Skull

TWENTY-SEVEN

'I read somewhere that there's a group in England today who still have the skull of Oliver Cromwell,' Stevenson said.

He had walked to the window and was staring down into the street.

'Yes,' Preece said, 'I believe so.'

'So far, your story only goes up to nineteen-forty-eight,' Hammond said. 'That's nearly forty years ago. Has the skull been in a Moscow laboratory since then?'

'Oh no,' Preece said, 'a lot's happened since nineteen-forty-eight.'

'You'd better tell us everything.'

Preece paused a moment as if assembling all the facts in his mind, then said. 'In December nineteen-forty-eight Doctor Noblachev hanged himself in his lab with piano wire. Apparently he had always been a cheerful, thoroughly professional man. He had no family problems, he was well respected and had a future that promised a great deal. There was no obvious reason for him to kill himself. His son, Josef, cleared out his Moscow apartment and took everything to his home near a small village called Sombirsk where he was the local doctor. Shortly afterwards, Josef's wife and children were murdered, horribly mutilated. Josef was missing and wasn't found until a week later wandering in the countryside, out of his mind. He was placed in a mental institution where he died three years later. I'm not sure about the circumstances of his death. At about the same time that Josef's wife and children were killed and he was committed, unusual phenomena began to take place in and around Sombirsk. The activity was so intense and people began to leave in such numbers that the authorities became alarmed. They wanted to know what was going on and launched an investigation. The findings were kept secret of course, but the reports are still in the archives of the Moscow Institute of Parapsychology.'

Preece finished his whisky and put the glass down on an

occasional table, waving aside Stevenson's offer of another.

'What the investigators didn't know,' Preece continued, 'was that Josef had taken the skull from his father's Moscow apartment back to his home. They didn't know anything about the skull at all. Today Sombirsk is a ghost town. No one will live there. Quite how the next connection is made, I don't know, but a Professor Wallenski found himself in possession of a lot of bits and pieces that had belonged to the Noblachev family. Most of it was Noblachev senior's notes and papers but there were some personal papers too. One of the letters he found was from Doctor Noblachev to his son, telling him about the skull. There was also Josef's diary, which for some reason we can only guess at, he had written in code. Breaking the code became a hobby with the professor. When he had, he discovered not only the story of the skull but where Josef had buried it after the paranormal activity had begun. The professor was aware that he had discovered something of considerable value. He also believed it might be his ticket to a new life in the west. The rest is straightforward. He had read about me and knew I was a rich man. He contacted me through a friend and said if I got him out to the west and gave him a certain sum of money he would hand over the papers and the diary and I could then take steps to find the skull.'

Preece smiled and Hammond found it intensely annoying.

'I agreed, of course,' Preece said. 'I promptly arranged for a man called Erwin Kininsky to get the professor out of Russia and three months later gave Kininsky a small fortune to arrange to have the skull dug up and smuggled to the west. I picked it up in West Berlin last week.'

'Why the hell couldn't you have left it where it was?' Hammond said.

'Left it,' Preece laughed. 'How could I leave it there when I knew the power it could have, the power that I could harness?'

'Harness it,' Stevenson groaned. 'You bloody fool.'

'O.K., so it's the skull of Hitler,' Hammond said thoughtfully. 'But . . . how . . . why . . .'

'I believe Hitler was possessed,' Preece said simply.

'By what?' Hammond asked.

Preece shrugged and sighed as if to say he wished he knew the answer.

'Something as old as time,' he said at last. 'Ultimate evil, give it whatever name you like. We'll never know when he became possessed. Perhaps in his days as a down-and-out in Vienna. Perhaps he exchanged his soul for power. But I believe the fact that he was possessed is beyond doubt. He told a story about something that happened to him in World War One. He was eating a meal in a trench when voices told him to move away. He did so and a few moments later a shell killed everyone in the trench. There were two Hitlers. There was the Austrian filled with doubts and uncertainties, unsure about himself and his future; the one who talked of suicide in the twenties. And there was the other one, the forceful, vicious, cunning dictator and manipulator of people's lives. If you watch Hitler speaking, you can even *see* the transformation coming over him, from one Hitler to the other, from the uncertain almost withdrawn Hitler to the ranting, raving, violent Hitler. In the bunker towards the end, he told Albert Speer, his armaments minister, of his intention to commit suicide. Yet a few minutes later the other Hitler emerged and he was telling General Krebs, his army chief of staff, how the situation could be saved. He was *optimistic*. Hitler and the Nazis dabbled with everything from astrology to ancient myths, quack medicines to weird theories about the creation of world chaos and they were obsessed by omens. The real Hitler knew long before Berlin fell that the war was lost, but the possessed Hitler kept the carnage going, even when victory was out of the question.'

Preece was silent for a moment, thinking, then he said: 'It was as if he was honouring his side of some kind of pact, paying off his debt in blood and suffering.'

He paused and glanced at Stevenson. 'You mentioned the spear which pierced the side of Christ, the Spear of Destiny. Hitler possessed the spear and he no doubt had heard the stories that the deaths of many of the monarchs who had had it over the years were apparently related to the spear. I've heard that as the Germans retreated, Hitler had it sealed into a vault. The Americans broke into the vault and found it. That day Hitler committed suicide. It was April thirtieth. Does that mean anything to you?'

He looked over at Stevenson then his eyes jumped to Tanya and finally settled on Hammond again.

'No,' Hammond said. 'Should it?'

'April thirtieth is Walpurgisnacht . . . the night on which all the evil forces of the world consort with the devil. I believe Hitler simply chose to return to his master.'

'I've heard enough,' Hammond said. 'Tell me what happened during the train crash.'

'The skull was in a metal box and it had become so disturbingly active that I decided to get off in Batforth and catch a taxi the rest of the way home. It was starting to arouse suspicion on the train. I was standing by the door when the train crashed. The box went flying out through the window. After the crash I searched everywhere for it. Then I assumed it must have been smashed. Somebody said some boys had been stealing luggage from the wreckage. I thought there was a chance one of them might have found it. I searched the area again in the morning but it wasn't there.'

Hammond frowned. 'There was a crew clearing up luggage after the crash. The luggage was taken . . .'

Preece shook his head. 'No, I checked all that luggage. It wasn't there.'

'We can assume it wasn't smashed,' Hammond said, 'not after all that's happened. So it must be somewhere in Batforth.'

'It's definitely in Batforth,' Stevenson said.

'It was either stolen by one of those kids you mentioned or . . . it's still where it fell after the crash. Somewhere that the clearing-up team wouldn't have looked. Under a tree or a bush . . .'

'No,' Preece said positively. 'I searched thoroughly.'

'Maybe it's in the pond,' Tanya said and the three men turned and looked at her.

In the lounge room of the last terraced house at the northernmost edge of Batforth, Miss Agnes Davenport looked up from her romantic novel at the light above her head. It had started to sway to and fro as if caressed by a gentle breeze. Miss Davenport looked around the room, searching for the source of the draught. But there was none. Her eyes returned to the light and she saw it was swaying violently now, bumping the ceiling at the end of each arc.

Then a movement in the dim bedroom away to her right caught her eye. She stood up and walked slowly into the bedroom. In the meagre light which filtered through her curtains, she saw the bedroom light had begun to sway too, the metal frame of the lamp tap-tapping against the ceiling.

Her mind struggled to find an answer but couldn't come up with one and she began to feel frightened. She went into the kitchen to make a cup of tea, her solution to most problems, and saw that the kitchen light was also thudding backwards and forwards on the ceiling.

She hurried to her telephone, picked up the receiver and cradled it on her shoulder while she leafed through the telephone book, looking for the number of the police station. She found the number and had dialled the first digit when it occurred to her how foolish she would look trying to explain swaying lights to the police. What could they do about it?

She hung up. Horror began to seep into her bloodstream like a strange drug as she became aware of a feeling that there were people in the room, standing behind her, watching her. She spun around. The room was empty.

With an outward show of calm, as if she *knew* she had an audience, she picked up her handbag, went into the hall, kicked off her slippers and stepped into a pair of shoes. As she shrugged her shoulders into her coat, she saw that the hall light was thrashing about as if at the mercy of a gale.

She was closing the door behind her when the bulb in the hall exploded with a hollow *plop*, showering the floor with tiny fragments of glass. She hurried down her garden path and started up the street at a half run.

The street was empty and yet she had the strangest sensation that there were people all around her, turning their heads to watch her go by. She had an intense feeling of relief when she saw the taxi at the corner. She waved it down and climbed in.

'The High Street, please,' she said to the driver.

She had an overwhelming desire to lose herself among the crowds of shoppers, to be one face among many.

TWENTY-EIGHT

'The box couldn't have rolled as far as the pond,' Preece said doubtfully, in a tone that suggested he wanted somebody to contradict him.

Hammond didn't answer immediately but after a moment he said, 'It could have.'

Stevenson put down his glass, strode into the centre of the room and stabbed a finger at Preece.

'Your search was very thorough?'

Preece nodded and Stevenson said, 'All right, let's assume that it's not tucked away under a bush somewhere. If a child had taken it, he would have been in the most danger; yet no child has been injured to our knowledge. So, if the three possibilities are bush, child or pond there is only one we haven't eliminated.'

'The pond,' Hammond said, standing up.

On their way back to Moulson's Pond, Hammond parked in the High Street and borrowed three pairs of waders from Tom Albertson in the fishing tackle shop.

'Three sets?' said Albertson.

'That's right . . . three.'

'Just a sudden urge to go fishing?' Albertson asked.

Hammond opened his mouth to reply, then found himself laughing. He hadn't intended to laugh and it came out very loud with a crazy edge to it.

He clamped his mouth shut and took the waders from Tom Albertson, avoiding his eyes.

'I'll explain it all to you one day, Tom,' he said.

As he got back into the car, Stevenson said, 'Preece wants to know what you intend to do with the skull if you find it.'

'Destroy it,' Hammond said without hesitation.

'You can't,' Preece protested, putting a hand on Hammond's shoulder. 'It's my property. I . . .'

'I'm going to destroy it,' Hammond said, shrugging the hand away.

'I could do so much with it. Don't you understand the power it has?'

'I don't give a damn,' Hammond said, sending the car gliding into the High Street traffic.

Preece sat back in his seat and puffed out his cheeks. 'I don't know that you can destroy it.'

'I'm going to smash it to a pulp.'

'I'm not sure that would destroy its powers. You don't know what you're up against.'

Stevenson rubbed the stubble on his chin thoughtfully, then said, 'Yes, it would. If you broke it in two, you'd cut its power in two, if you quartered it, you'd divide its power into four . . . if you smashed it into tiny pieces and scattered it about, almost all its powers would disappear.'

'But . . .'

Hammond cut Preece off. 'If I can do it, I'm going to make sure you never get your hands on that skull again.'

Ten minutes later, Tanya was seated alone in the car beside the pond, watching the three men starting their search from the northernmost bank. Once she glanced into the rear-view mirror but snatched her eyes away immediately. The face that had looked back was like a stranger's face. It was her and yet it was not her. Her hair was dishevelled, her face puffy, her eyes sunken. There was a bruise on her forehead and a red weal across her left cheek.

It's a nightmare, she thought, and that comforted her. *Nightmares were finite. People always woke up from nightmares. Didn't they?*

Billy Semple was doing eighty miles an hour on his motorbike along the Ruttlake road when he felt as if two hands were clasping his waist. It was as if he had a pillion passenger who was holding on to him. At first he thought it was just the wind, a movement of his leather jacket. But the grip grew tighter. . . . and tighter. It was like a pair of pincers now, digging into his flesh.

He looked over his shoulder but there was nothing there. His mind sprinted through a minefield of possibilities. Was it some kind of illness? A muscular spasm brought on by sitting too long on his bike? The effects of the punch in the kidneys he had received during a fight outside the Blue Boar three nights before?

Fear began to dismantle the studied arrogance in his nineteen-year-old face. He tried to decelerate but the bike kept on at the same speed no matter what he did.

Just as he saw the Batforth bridge, he felt a hand clamp over his mouth with something that felt like a thumb and finger pinching his nostrils closed.

He tried to pull away but found he didn't have the strength. The panic of suffocation exploded through him and he let go of the handlebars, his hands leaping up to his face.

The bike bucked, jerked to its right and hit the retaining fence at the end of the bridge. The fence whipped the bike from under him and he flew over the edge and plummeted to the muddy riverbank one-hundred-and-fifty feet below.

TWENTY-NINE

Ernie Spiers drummed his pencil irritably on his desk, pursed his lips and glared at the telephone with exaggerated anger.

'You're not looking very happy, Ernie,' Jemma said.

'There's a reason for that,' he said. 'I'm *not* very happy. I'm wondering who's going to call next. Everybody's called but the Pope. I just had an American newspaper on the phone wanting to know if it's true that mass hysteria has seized this town. What am I supposed to say. . . . "No, it's always like this." And where's our illustrious editor? Disappeared.'

Irritability was a frequent state of mind for Ernie and Jemma knew that. She put it down to age. Generally it seemed to inject him with a slightly caustic but very funny sense of humour.

He had been calling Hammond's flat and Tanya's cottage off and on all day without success. It seemed absurd to him that Hammond should disappear in the middle of the biggest story in the history of the *Courier*.

'You look like you're ready to do someone an injury,' Jemma said. 'It's just as well you've never been a boxer or studied karate.'

'Never studied karate,' Spiers said, 'shows how little you know. They used to call me the man with the iron fists and the flying feet.' He held up a nicotine-stained right hand. 'See those knuckles. I used to pound gravel with those. There was a time when there wasn't a piece of gravel in Batforth that was safe when I was around.'

He snatched up the telephone and rang Hammond's flat again but there was no answer. He brushed his chair back, stood up and pulled on his jacket.

'Do you know where I'm going?' he said.

'The pub?'

'Correct.'

He stamped down the stairs and crossed the road to the narrow, enclosed lane which led to the shopping mall.

185

I should have stayed in retirement, he told himself. I should never have made a comeback. I should have bought myself a little cottage in the country and spent the remaining years of my life contemplating nature or even painting watercolours or gardening . . .

Then he remembered the devastating boredom of the three years of retirement he had managed to survive and that made him more irritable than ever.

Halfway up the lane, something away to his right caught his eye and he swung his head around. He saw a window there which one of the big stores had once used to advertise women's fashions. It was dark and disused now. His eyes swept through the dimness beyond the smeared, dirty window, picking out a poster for a long-forgotten sale, a couple of wooden crates and two shop-window dummies.

Dummies.

His eyes had moved on past the window when it occurred to him with a chilling certainty that one of the dummies had moved. Surely it was an optical illusion.

He looked again.

He saw now that they weren't dummies at all. They were . . . men? Both were of medium height, thick-set and the features of their faces seemed to be lost in a kind of puffiness as if plasticine had been inserted under the skin. They were peering at him now like men who were lost and confused and had suddenly found themselves in a strange place.

It was as they began to shuffle towards him that fear seemed to clamp a tiny, frozen fist over every pore in his body. The one nearest him opened his mouth as if to speak but no sound came and the mouth continued to open, wider and wider, until it was like a huge hole. The second one raised an arm and Spiers watched as the plump fingers reached out towards him, the arm extending, growing longer and longer as if it was made of elastic.

Spiers faltered in his stride, stumbled, then began to run, ripping his eyes away from the window.

Had the fingers pushed their way through the glass? That had to be an illusion. Didn't it?

He burst into the sunlight of the mall, bumped into a woman with a shopping trolley, shoved her aside and continued to run, elbowing his way through the crowd.

186

A voice away to his left shouted, 'Hello, Ernie,' but Spiers didn't look round. He just kept running, oblivious to his shortage of breath, the ache in his chest and the pain in his knees and ankles. One thought dominated his mind – escape, flight, to put as much distance between himself and the lane as possible.

Hammond, Stevenson and Preece waded in a line through the shallows at the northernmost end of the pond. They swept backwards and forwards through the water, working their way deeper and deeper with each sweep, searching every inch of the bottom, leaving nothing to chance.

Preece didn't speak at all and Hammond knew he was trying to think of a way of saving the skull if they should find it.

When they were halfway through a sweep that was carrying them fifteen feet from the bank, Hammond glanced over at Stevenson and said in an exasperated tone, 'I'm not sure it could have gone this far in. The train was going very fast when it crashed and the box would have come flying down here . . . but I'm not sure it could have come this far into the pond.'

Stevenson shook his head slowly. 'I don't think it's here at all, Jon. If it was here, I'd feel it. But I'll tell you one thing I do know . . . wherever it is, we've got to find it soon. There's a kind of charge running through Batforth and it's getting stronger all the time.'

Hammond stood for a long time with his hands on his hips, looking out across the pond, then he said, 'Let's try a sweep along the west bank.'

Stevenson nodded doubtfully and they waded on as dark clouds began to gather above them, threatening more rain, dimming the sunlight.

THIRTY

Spiers returned to the office an hour after he left with a smell of whisky about him that Jemma noticed immediately because Spiers was a beer drinker who usually drank spirits only on special occasions. He hurried into the office, made himself some coffee and sat at his desk, leafing through a newspaper, not looking at her.

Jemma thought he looked odd, worried, but she put it down to whisky and pressure . . . and he wasn't getting any younger either, was he?

She looked out of the window and saw that the rain which had been on and off all day had stopped again.

'I think I'll get over to the railway station now, while the rain's off,' she said, standing up and putting on her raincoat. 'I've got some stationery to collect.'

Spiers nodded without looking up.

The door was closing behind her when the telephone rang. She swung it open again as Spiers grabbed the receiver and said, '*Courier.*' He listened for a moment, then said, 'Jon isn't here . . . yes . . . yeah' and began to scribble in his pad. 'Yes . . . I've got that . . . yes.' When he had finished taking notes he read the facts back to William Joss, double checking that he had got everything right.

Jemma turned away and let the door close slowly behind her. Deep in thought, she walked down the stairs to her car, climbed in and headed for the station. As she turned off the High Street into Trafalgar Avenue she saw Hammond's car coming towards her. At first, he didn't seem to see her and she sounded her horn and waved frantically. He drew into the side and she pulled up with her window next to his.

'Hello Jemma, what's up?'

Jemma gave Tanya a quick smile then switched her attention back to Hammond. There were two other men in the car but she didn't know them.

'Ernie's in quite a state. I think the pressure's getting to him. He's been trying to get you all day, phoning your flat and the cottage. Did you know there'd been another murder?'

The two men in the back seat leaned forward to listen.

'Murder?' said Hammond. 'Today?'

'Yes. Ernie got a phone call from Sergeant Joss just as I was leaving the office.'

'Who was it?'

'I can't remember the name now. It didn't ring a bell with me. The body was found along the track that leads up the hill on the other side of Batforth.'

'O.K. thanks Jemma,' Hammond said, noisily engaging his car into first gear.

'Will you call Ernie?' she said as he began to ease the car forward.

'Yeah, as soon as I get back to the flat. See you, Jemma.'

As she drew away, she noticed the dark clouds which had populated the sky for hours had multiplied and thickened, blotting out almost all the sunlight. She flicked on her headlights and kept them on for the rest of the journey to the station.

As she turned into the dim station car park, thunder exploded in the heavens and rain began to teem down, drumming on the roof of the car, lancing through the funnel of light from her headlamps like rods of steel. A streak of lightning slashed across the sky like a razor slicing through a black curtain, letting in a flash of brilliant light that lasted no longer than the pop of a flashbulb.

She pulled up on the double yellow line at the station entrance, tugged up the hood of her coat and slipped out of the car, leaving the engine running. Her high-heeled boots slithered on the wet asphalt as she ran around the car and into the station entrance. Under cover, she paused and shook her coat. The front of her jeans were wet and water trickled down into her boots as she hurried into the parcels office.

'Mark,' she called, rapping on the counter. 'Mark, are you there?'

There was no answer. The only sound was the distant drumming of the rain.

'Mark!'

She raised her voice to a shout.

'Charlie . . . Charlie McMurty, what kind of station are you running here?'

Still there was no answer. She looked over her shoulder, across the station entrance into the ticket office. It was empty.

'Dammit,' she muttered. 'I'm not going back empty-handed.'

She unbolted the door at the end of the counter.

'Charlie,' she shouted, walking along past the roof-high racks of parcels and luggage.

Ten feet from the back wall, she faltered as she heard a brushing, swishing sound, very soft, very gentle. She listened intently and noticed it was accompanied by a gentle creaking.

'Charlie.'

She was becoming a little afraid now and that annoyed her. Her eyes searched the luggage racks, seeking the source of the sound.

It was when she reached the last aisle and glanced up between the grey wall and the pile of orange-stickered suitcases that she saw Charlie McMurty and a sensation like an electric shock ran through her.

The stationmaster was suspended about ten feet from the ground, swaying gently backwards and forwards, stark naked. Doubled-up string was looped around his neck with the other end knotted around a beam high above him. The body was mangled and covered in bruises. Shattered bones thrust through the skin and blood ran across the torso, down the legs and dripped from the toes onto the floor. The bulging eyes seemed to seek her out, plead with her.

The tingling electric shock sensation lasted for perhaps five seconds then was replaced abruptly by a numbness that encased her from head to foot. She turned and stumbled back towards the front door. At the counter, she hesitated, gagging.

It was when she saw blood running under the ticket office door and forming a pool that she started to run.

THIRTY-ONE

When they entered the flat Stevenson went straight to the window and looked out. 'You'd think that night had fallen already,' he said as battalions of raindrops battered against the window pane inches from his face.

He turned slowly and studied Preece, who was helping himself to a whisky.

'You feel it too, don't you?' he said.

'What do you mean?'

'A current in the air ... like an electric current that's getting stronger and stronger.'

Preece smiled a smile that could have meant anything.

'The skull is acting as a magnet, isn't it? Drawing in discarnate entities ... Just like at that place in Russia. What was it called?'

'Sombirsk.'

'No wonder it became a ghost town.'

Hammond sat down on the settee beside Tanya and ran his fingers through her hair.

'Are you all right, Tanya?' he asked.

She nodded, invaded by an odd feeling that she was a ten-year-old girl again and this was her father talking to her. She felt so childlike, so vulnerable, so unlike the woman she had thought she was a week before.

'Do you want to lie down for a while?' he said.

'No,' she sighed, then looked deep into his eyes. 'How are we going to find it now?'

'The skull? We'll find it,' he said and his tone was so positive that she felt a warm glow of reassurance begin to form inside her.

'How?'

'We'll find it,' he repeated.

His gaze slipped past her, brushed the telephone, then returned to her face.

'I'd better call Ernie,' he said, standing up.

As he dialled the numbers, he thought about the fruitless search of the pond.

Stevenson had kept insisting the skull wasn't there. 'I'd feel it if it was here,' he had stated over and over again. But Hammond had been stubborn. 'We'll keep looking until we're sure it's not here,' he had said. And they had. When they had left the pond Hammond had been certain beyond any shadow of a doubt that the skull was not in the water.

The phone rang for about half a minute before Spiers answered.

'*Courier.*'

'Hello, Ernie, it's Jon here.'

'Oh, nice to hear from you,' Spiers said acidly. 'I've been trying to get a hold of you all day. It's pandemonium in here. The phone never stops ringing.'

'I'm sorry for leaving you on your own, Ernie, but I'm tied up on . . .'

'Tied up,' Spiers exploded.

'Yes. As I said, I can't explain all this now . . .'

'Can't explain.'

'Stop repeating everything I say, Ernie.'

'Can't explain why you've disappeared right in the middle of the biggest story ever to hit Batforth.'

'There's nothing I can do about this, believe me,' Hammond said with as much patience as he could muster. 'Just tell me about the latest murder. Who was it?'

'Henry Low. He's the . . .'

'Yes, I know Henry Low. Was he killed just the same way as the others?'

'Exactly the same. Joss said it was like he went through a mincing machine. Do you know, they can't even find one of his legs?'

'Where was he found?'

'You know that track that leads off North Street and goes up Lincoln Hill. It leads to George Murdoch's cottage.'

'Yes, I know it.'

'He was found a couple of hundred yards along the track.'

Tanya had stood up and was tugging at Hammond's elbow now. He gave her a quick frown that told her he didn't want to be interrupted and slipped his arm over her shoulders.

'What are the police saying about Bunty?' he asked Spiers.

'Suicide, of course. She was in shock after the death of . . .'

Tanya snatched the receiver away from his ear.

'Jon, listen to me . . . just listen . . .'

'What is it?' he said. He brought the receiver back to his ear and said to Spiers, 'Hold on a minute, Ernie.'

'Is it Henry Low that's dead?' Tanya asked.

'Yes.'

'Don't you remember what that woman said when we arrived at the field this morning . . . the woman with the dog?'

'What did she say . . . What about?'

'She said no one had been near that pond since the accident. Except George Murdoch and Henry Low.'

'That's right. I remember now. And she said . . .'

Tanya nodded excitedly and cut him off. 'Yes, she said they had taken something from the pond.'

'Good God,' Hammond breathed, thumping his forehead with the heel of his hand as if to emphasize his own stupidity.

He put the receiver back to his ear. 'I've got to go, Ernie.'

'But . . .'

'Sorry, Ernie. I've got to go. Goodbye.'

He slammed the receiver back in its cradle.

'If Henry and George found the box in the pond, what's the first thing they'd do?' Hammond said, thinking out loud.

'Try to open it,' Tanya said.

'But it was securely locked,' Hammond said looking at Preece who confirmed his statement with a single nod.

'Then they'd have taken it somewhere to try to force it open,' Tanya reasoned.

'Murdoch's cottage?' Hammond said quietly.

'Possibly,' Tanya said.

'Only one way to find out,' Hammond shrugged.

They all went downstairs again and ran across the car park through the pelting rain to Hammond's car.

They were still puffing from their exertion when Tanya said, 'Jon, maybe we should go to the police.'

'No,' he said in a tone that dared anyone to argue. 'They wouldn't listen and they wouldn't help us. We'll get the skull and then we'll go to the police.'

No one spoke for several minutes as Hammond swung the car through the dim, rain-drenched streets, the windscreen wipers slashing tirelessly at the torrent of water that sluiced over the car. As they turned into North Street, Hammond looked at Stevenson in the rear-view mirror and jerked a thumb to his right.

'There's Lincoln Hill,' he said.

Stevenson hunched forward and looked up over the roofs of the last line of houses in Batforth. Through the rain-smeared window and the driving rain beyond, he could make out a low, dark, tree-covered hill with haphazard lighter patches where there were clearings.

After a moment, he leaned back with a sigh, stared at Preece and said, 'The box has been opened. I know it has.'

When the rain eased to a drizzle then stopped, the policemen got out of their cars and resumed their search of the cordoned-off area around the spot where Henry Low had been found.

Sergeant Joss stretched, flexed the stiffness out of his muscles, then stood absently watching Inspector Jensen who was standing about a hundred yards up the narrow, rutted track talking animatedly to a detective from the Scotland Yard task force.

Low had been found at a point in the track where it turned through a clearing in the trees. When the rain had started the blood-spattered spot had been marked by the chalk outline of a man. Now the blood had been washed into a pothole, staining the puddle of rainwater the colour of red wine, and the chalk outline had almost disappeared under the force of the pelting rain.

There was a thick, leaden, after-rain atmosphere in the clearing, a heaviness about the air that Joss had noticed on other occasions after thunderstorms, and it contained a pungent wet-vegetation smell. It was as if the rain had stripped the vegetation naked and washed away all the impurities, leaving only the essence of the trees and bushes and grass. A constable strode up the track towards Jensen and the clunk of his shoes was dull and almost inaudible, as if the heaviness of the air was forcing the sound back into itself.

Joss turned his attention to the row of policemen who were bent double and moving across the clearing in an uneven line, searching every inch of the ground.

As he started towards them, a flash of light blue against the greens and browns of the hillside caught the corner of his eye and he looked around.

A woman's dress?

His eyes searched through the dripping trees but found nothing. He dismissed it as a trick of the light and the atmosphere and was about to talk to the constable nearest him when he saw it again.

This time he stopped and hunched forward, peering into the gloom.

It *had been* a woman's dress. There *was* a woman out there among the trees.

He could see her clearly now.

As he watched, she walked a distance of about twenty feet and disappeared behind a clump of bushes.

He strolled over to the treeline and stood there with his hands in his pockets for a minute, waiting.

Then he saw a flash of blue again and the woman reappeared. This time she saw him and stopped, smiling and waving, and he recognized her. He waved back and felt a sudden urge to join her out there in the woods. She was beckoning to him now and he felt a strange compulsion to go over and talk to her.

He pushed his way through the bushes at the treeline and started towards her, an odd feeling of elation running through him. She was still waving, beckoning him to come forward, but she seemed further away now. He hurried to catch up with her.

Then he realized a distant voice in his brain was trying to tell him something.

Bunty Robinson, he heard it say at last. *That's Bunty Robinson.*

Well, of course it was Bunty Robinson. He knew that. She had lived in Batforth long enough. She was an attractive, vivacious woman. What did it matter if she was wandering about in the trees on Lincoln Hill? What was wrong with that?

He had an overwhelming desire to hear her voice, her laughter, to run through the woods with her.

Then an irritating thought began to prod its way into his brain. It was trying to tell him something but he wasn't getting the message. It was as if his brain was clogged with a sticky substance, which was preventing him from thinking properly.

She isn't walking, he thought suddenly, *yet she still seems to be getting further and further away*. He increased his pace.

The irritating thought was still there but he couldn't make it out.

Something's wrong . . .

Then the thought burst into his consciousness, elbowing everything else aside.

Bunty Robinson is dead.

The words filled his mind like a huge neon sign.

He tried to stop but his legs just kept stumbling forward.

He looked over his shoulder and found he had gone much deeper into the woods than he had realized.

Bunty Robinson is dead.

The words flashed in his brain again and urgently added: *Go back. Now.*

The urge to talk to Bunty, to run with her through the forest was still there but gradually he managed to slow to a halt.

As he turned to head back for the clearing he felt a physical force restraining him, drawing him back into the forest. Like an invisible web wrapped around him.

He leaned all his weight against it and broke into a stumbling run, throwing a quick glance over his shoulder.

Bunty was suddenly much closer now, coming slowly towards him as if she was gliding over the ground. He felt that strange compulsion again.

Go back and talk to her. Run through the forest and be free.

But he was sprinting now, his size-twelve shoes crunching through the leaves. He shrugged away the strange thoughts like a drowning man shrugging off a heavy overcoat.

Go back into the forest.

He kept running.

A moment later he burst through the treeline into the clearing. He had been gone less than a minute yet it felt like a long, long time. He straightened his coat and composed himself.

One of the constables searching the ground stood upright, stretched his back and looked over at Joss quizzically.

'Call of nature,' he said with a shaky grin, by way of explanation.

THIRTY-TWO

Hammond slowed and dropped the car down a gear when he reached the clearing where the police were gathered. He saw Jensen standing to the left of the track and the inspector turned as if expecting Hammond to stop. Hammond gave him a wave of recognition and saw the inspector frown as he motored around a bend and out of sight.

Beyond the clearing the track became quite steep and the car wobbled and bumped in and out of potholes and ruts.

Stevenson and Preece sat silently in the back seat; Stevenson sitting rigid with tension, his arms folded; Preece leaning forward, his elbows on his knees, watching the forest roll slowly by, deep in thought.

'I've never been up here before,' Tanya said to Hammond.

'There isn't much up here except Murdoch's cottage,' Hammond said. 'I've only been up here once myself when I was doing the story about George Murdoch trying to get the council to seal this road properly.'

'How much further?'

'Half a mile maybe. There's an area near the top of the hill which has been cleared and fenced. Murdoch's cottage is in one corner. I think he used to work the land but I don't think he bothers now.'

The bushes, trees and long grass crowded close to the edge of the track now, whipping at both sides of the car, and the tree branches joined above them, allowing only occasional glimpses of the dark, cloud-laden sky.

They swung around a bend and Hammond braked sharply as the furthest limits of his headlights picked out a figure on the track up ahead.

'Good God,' Tanya whispered and gripped Hammond's arm.

'It's Mrs Lord,' Hammond said as the figure in the white dress stumbled towards them. She held her arms out in front of her, feeling the air with her fingers as if she was blind.

Hammond changed into second gear and rolled forward.

'She's dead,' he said. 'I saw her buried.'

Mrs Lord stepped into a rut, tripped and almost fell. Then she moved away to her right, her fingers finding the bushes. After a moment's hesitation, she parted them and pushed her way through, staggering out of sight.

Hammond accelerated and drew up at the point where she had disappeared.

'Don't stop,' Stevenson yelled as Hammond reached for his handbrake.

'What . . . why . . .'

'Drive on.'

'It's Mrs Lord,' Tanya said with an edge of hysteria in her voice.

'It's not,' Stevenson said evenly. 'At least not the Mrs Lord you knew. It's something else altogether.'

Tanya wound down her window.

'Mrs Lord!' she shouted. 'Mrs Lord.'

In the leaden atmosphere, her words seemed to come back at her off the wall of trees, flat and hollow-sounding.

Hammond jerked open his door and Stevenson grabbed his shoulder.

'Don't get out of the car. Please listen to me, Jon. You can't help her and it's very dangerous. Drive on. Right now.'

Hammond turned and looked into Stevenson's eyes for a moment. Then he slammed the door closed with a reluctant sigh.

'Believe me, Jon, I'm right,' Stevenson said.

Hammond sent the car shooting forward, bumping and thudding through the ruts.

After a moment he said: 'There's a corner about two hundred yards straight ahead. Around that corner, on the left-hand side, are Murdoch's fields. The house is about four hundred yards further on.'

A new tension seemed to fill the car, a tension that made them silent and watchful.

The car hit a pothole as it rounded the last corner, jarring them.

Then the headlights picked out a barbed-wire fence and a field overgrown with tussocky grass.

'That's the cottage up there,' Hammond said, nodding

towards a whitewashed cottage across the field. A single light burned in one of the windows.

'He's home,' Tanya said.

Stevenson breathed: 'Kill the lights.'

'What for?' said Hammond.

'Just do it,' Stevenson insisted.

Hammond stabbed a finger at the light switch and the yellow beams of light withdrew, plunging the track ahead into darkness.

'Stop the car,' Stevenson said and when Hammond drew the car to a halt, he added, 'Turn off the engine.'

The rhythmic grumbling under the bonnet ceased and the night was invaded by an awesome silence, punctuated only by the sound of their breathing, which seemed loud and harsh now. It was the first time in Hammond's life he had ever been aware of the sound of air moving in and out of his lungs and he self-consciously tried to breathe more quietly.

'It's here,' Stevenson whispered after a moment and everyone knew what he meant.

Then the silence folded over them again, like the silence of a sealed crypt or the interior of an undisturbed pyramid. A sharp metallic *click* came from the cooling engine, startling Tanya. She turned to Hammond as if to say something but Stevenson touched her shoulder and held a finger up to his lips. She slumped back in her seat again, gripping Hammond's hand.

Then they saw the shape detach itself from the cottage like a small pocket of mist wafting up out of a hollow. It was about the size of a man and it glided across the field at the speed of a man walking quickly. Hammond stared at it, too fascinated to be frightened, and thought he could make out the indistinct outline of legs in the lower half and facial features near the top.

'Lights?' he whispered to Stevenson, reaching for the dashboard.

'No,' Stevenson rasped abruptly. 'No lights.'

The shape reached the woods, seemed to hesitate, then disappeared among the trees.

Preece glanced from one face to another, his mouth twisted into a smug, self-satisfied grin. He chuckled quietly to himself as if he knew something the rest of them didn't.

Stevenson raised a hand in a gesture of silence then pointed through the front window. 'Look,' he whispered.

A figure had appeared on the road in front of them. It was a man – Hammond could see that much – and he was wearing a tattered uniform. A steel helmet was pushed to the back of his head and there was a rifle slung over his shoulder. His collar was turned up as if against a cold wind and his eyes stared despairingly at the ground as he crossed the track, walking in a relentless, exhausted rhythm.

'A soldier,' said Tanya.

It was when the figure reached the far side of the track where the ground fell away to the woods that Hammond realized this was no man. When the soldier left the track, his feet did not follow the sloping ground but shuffled on in mid-air as if following an invisible road. At that instant Hammond discovered he could see through the soldier. The ragged uniform and the body beneath were filmy, flimsy things, as insubstantial as an image on the surface of a still pond.

As the soldier disappeared among the trees another appeared, then a group of three, then more and more, all travelling the same road, all on the same journey, all with their heads bowed, eyes staring dully at the ground. One had a bandage around his head, stained red with blood. Another had an injured foot and limped along, his arm slung around a comrade's shoulders.

'Das Reich,' Preece said in an almost inaudible whisper and the others looked at him.

Preece was still wearing the mocking smile. 'They're soldiers of the Das Reich Division,' he said. 'The SS. Hitler's élite.'

Perhaps a hundred soldiers passed by, the pad of their feet muffled, as if heard from a long way off, the mugs and cans on their packs clanking softly.

The last figure was smaller than the others and wore a different uniform. He was a boy of no more than fifteen, with a thin, drawn face and huge bulging eyes. He seemed to be hurrying to try to catch up with the others. His head was thrown back, his face anxious.

As the boy disappeared among the trees a movement away to their left drew their eyes back to the cottage. They saw a shape like the one they had seen drifting across the field a few moments before slip away from a wall, glide towards the barbed wire fence and hover there like a puff of steam emitted from a factory. As they stared it began to divide into two and both halves took on the rough outline of men and flitted across the field as if searching for something. Near the centre of the field the shapes became more discernible as men and began to move with a walking motion.

Hammond concentrated all his attention on the one nearest him. He could make out the figure of a man, hatless, with iron-grey hair, a black, half-unbuttoned tunic and black trousers. The man *seemed* to be walking but in an instant had covered twenty feet or more.

'There's more of them,' Tanya said in a very faint whisper that seemed almost like a shout to Hammond and startled him.

More figures had entered the field at the far corner and were moving in all directions, some fast and purposefully, some slowly, aimlessly.

A moment later, Hammond saw a figure coming towards them along the barbed-wire fence. It was a man and Hammond could see his head was held at a strange angle, tilted back as if staring up at the dark, cloud-filled sky. Once he brushed the barbed-wire fence and the strands jangled against their wooden posts.

That means he's tangible. That means he's flesh and blood. Doesn't it?

Tanya whispered, 'It's George Murdoch,' at the same instant as Hammond saw the crowbar which had been thrust into the man's throat and protruded six inches from the back of his neck.

Hammond sighed, 'Yeah, it's George.'

Murdoch bumped into a tree stump near the corner of the field, paused, then turned and started back towards the cottage.

The field was crowded with shapes and figures now. The shapes were white and translucent and shimmered and quivered like slightly disturbed water. The figures were quite distinct and clearly men and women but they were surrounded by a white outline or aura like people seen at a distance encapsulated in a jacket of early-morning mist.

'What do we do?' Hammond said to Stevenson. 'Where . . .'

At that instant Preece jerked at his door handle, shouldered the door open and leapt out. Hammond lunged across the back of his seat and made a grab for him but Preece slapped his groping hand aside.

As the door swung shut behind Preece, Hammond reached for the handle on his door.

It was Stevenson's voice which froze his hand in mid-air.

'No,' the smaller man said. 'Just wait. They haven't seen us yet.'

His voice was as sharp and cold as a sliver of ice.

They watched as Preece jumped over a drainage ditch that ran down one side of the track, placed his hand on a fence post and vaulted the barbed wire. As he strode into the field, the figures froze, watching him.

'I think he's miscalculated,' Stevenson said. 'I think he has underestimated them.'

Preece was approaching a hillock near the centre of the field now, gesticulating to the shapes all about him. Hammond could hear him shouting what sounded like commands but he couldn't make out the words. As Preece lengthened his stride to climb the hillock a thunderclap from far away rumbled across the sky.

Then the shapes and figures began to converge on him, moving at speeds which astonished Hammond.

That was when Hammond saw something in the field he hadn't noticed before. Floating dark forms, almost invisible in the dimness, black smudges hovering in the waving grass of the field.

Like the thing he had seen in the car with Tanya.

Preece was near the top of the hillock when he fell forward. He rolled over and appeared to be struggling with something. Then they heard a terrible cry of pain.

A pale shape folded over him and disappeared. Two dark forms moved in front of him, hiding his face from their view for an instant. Then they too disappeared.

'Oh God,' Stevenson murmured and his voice broke.

'What's happening?' Hammond said.

'They're entering him,' Stevenson rasped, shuddering. 'I knew he had overestimated his own powers.'

THIRTY-THREE

Preece was on all fours now, scrambling back down the hillock. Another dark shape blurred across him and disappeared. Then a figure kicked at him, knocking him onto his back. As Preece struggled on the ground, the figure seemed to stand on Preece's face, then begin to diminish, like a rapidly deflating rubber doll collapsing into Preece's mouth.

More figures gathered around him, punching and kicking at him, squatting on him. Pale shapes shot into him then bits of them reappeared, licking around his body like tongues of fire.

'We've got to do something,' Tanya breathed.

'Nothing we can do,' said Stevenson.

With a superhuman effort Preece dragged himself onto his knees, flailing his fists through the air. Then he pushed himself upright and began to stagger back towards the car.

He opened his mouth to yell and it opened so widely that it looked as if his jaw had been unhinged.

'Heeeeelp me,' they heard him shout and something that looked like a great white flame hissed six feet from his mouth and returned instantly.

He reached the bottom of the hillock and staggered on a few yards before falling again.

Hammond watched in horror as the figures crowded around Preece, attacking him with the ferocity of a pack of ravenous dogs. Old men in tattered clothes and uniformed men and women with witches' hair kicked and punched him. As his screams rang through the air, Tanya dug her nails into the palm of Hammond's hand without realizing she was doing it. Pale shapes convulsed, diminished abruptly and speared into Preece.

A moment after he fell the second time, he was on his feet again but this time he was not trying to get away.

He stood quite still, staring up at the sky, his hands raised high above his head. The figures and shapes moved back from him and stood watching. A hideous yell of pain and anguish came from deep inside him, reaching an intensity that made Hammond want to cover his ears.

Stevenson blinked. It seemed to him that Preece was *expanding*, as if an unbelievable intensity of pressure was building up inside him, trying to force its way out at a thousand points. His face seemed to grow bigger, swelling alarmingly, the features puffing and spreading. The fabric of his coat was drawn tighter and tighter over his chest until two buttons popped.

There was a terrible, flesh-ripping, bone-snapping sound and Preece grew an inch taller . . . then two. His head began to thrash wildly about then gyrate slowly on his shoulders.

'What's happening to him?' Tanya said too loudly and Stevenson clamped a hand over her mouth.

'Be quiet,' he whispered. 'Don't let them hear you.'

Then Preece exploded.

It was as if a hundred grenades had been inserted into his body with time fuses which had slowly tick-tocked his life away. But the sound was not that of a mechanical explosion. There was no *carump* of a bomb or the dull, hollow *bam* of a hand grenade. Instead there was a wet *scheeplattt* as if a thousand butchers had driven their axes simultaneously into a freshly killed beast.

There was nothing left of Preece. It was as if he had been atomized. All that was left in his place was a grey, cloudy substance which immediately began to divide and reform into the figures and shapes which had entered him.

Tanya pulled her eyes away from the scene and buried her head in Hammond's chest. Hammond held her close and looked at Stevenson. The smaller man shook his head and dropped his face into his hands with a heavy sigh.

'We've got to go for the police now, Jon,' Tanya said, lifting her head. 'We don't have any choice.'

'No,' Stevenson said abruptly.

'What do you suggest?' Hammond asked.

'We've got to destroy the skull now. It's growing in strength all the time, probably tripling or quadrupling every hour or so.'

'You saw what happened to Preece,' Tanya said, sitting up.

'What can we do? You were the one who didn't even want to come back to Batforth today.'

'We've got to destroy the skull,' Stevenson said firmly. 'Now.'

'We don't even know where it is,' Hammond said.

'Then we have to find it.'

'And what do we do then?'

'We smash it. We smash it into tiny pieces. We smash it so this can never happen again.'

'The police would . . .' Tanya began, but Stevenson interrupted.

'I have an idea. I won't pretend it's not dangerous because there will be a lot of activity around the skull. It will be guarded, if you like. I won't pretend it's sure to work . . . but I think it's worth a try. All of us have to play a part. If we don't do it now, right now . . . half an hour or an hour from now might be too late.'

Tanya shook her head violently. 'But . . .'

'No buts. If we leave here now, when we come back with the police the skull might not be here.'

'You mean, it could be shifted by . . .' She pointed a finger at the field.

'I don't know. I just don't know. All I'm sure of is that we have to destroy it.'

'All right,' Hammond said, 'I'll go along with you, whatever you decide. What do we do?'

'First we've got to find out exactly where it is. We're in a dark part of the road, hidden by the fence and the foliage and we haven't been spotted yet. I suggest you and I climb down into that drainage ditch and go along it. We'll get as close to the cottage as we can . . . and see what we can see.'

Hammond thought a moment, then nodded.

'O.K. I got you into this, so I'll go along with whatever you say. What about Tanya?'

'Tanya will be safer in the car than she will be with us,' Stevenson said. 'We'll only be gone for a few minutes. At the moment all I want to do is to see if we can pinpoint where the skull is.'

Hammond looked at Tanya. 'Will you be all right?'

She nodded uncertainly.

'I'll leave the keys in the ignition. If anything does happen just drive like hell.'

'We won't be too long,' Stevenson said. He intended to be reassuring but Tanya did not feel reassured.

'What is this idea of yours, anyway?' Hammond said to Stevenson.

'First we have to find the skull. Then I'll know if it'll work or not.'

Hammond bit his lower lip thoughtfully, a mannerism he thought he had left behind at school almost twenty years before.

'All right, let's go,' he said

He kissed Tanya on the forehead, flicked off the interior light switch so that it couldn't flash on when he opened the door and eased down the handle beside him.

A moment later they were wading uphill, against the current, in the six inches of muddy water in the bottom of the drainage ditch, hunched over, keeping their heads below the line of the field. Hammond stood upright once and peered over the edge. He saw that the figures and shapes were mostly around the hillock where Preece had died, at the far side of the field and up ahead of them, around the cottage. He bent forward and moved on, pushing his legs soundlessly against the water.

Finally Stevenson stopped and took his arm. 'We should be level with the cottage by now. Let's take a look.'

They flattened themselves against the soaking wet grass of the slope and gazed under the lowest strand of barbed wire.

Hammond began by surveying the area at the front of the cottage. There was nothing there and he had just shifted his attention to the front door as Stevenson tensed and whispered, 'Jon . . . it's in there.'

Hammond glanced at Stevenson then followed the direction of his eyes.

'Where?' he said.

'There . . . in that shed.'

About a hundred feet away to their right, there were two huge, overgrown bushes, their branches and leaves dancing crazily in the evening breeze. The first thing Hammond saw in the area of garden framed by the bushes was a tall, uniformed man with a steel helmet set on his head at an odd angle. There was a hole in his greatcoat and it seemed to Hammond that the hole went right through the man, and if he looked into the hole he could see the dark trees of the woods beyond. As the man staggered out of sight, stiff-limbed, Hammond saw the shed.

It was similar in construction to a thousand other garden sheds, planks overlapping other planks, a tin roof, a small door – which was slightly ajar – with a heavy bolt on it. There were no windows he could see but he guessed there would be one at the back.

For a moment he didn't see anything to distinguish it from any other garden shed in Batforth. He assumed Stevenson had located the skull intuitively.

He turned his head and was about to say something like, 'Do you think it's in there?'

Then he jerked his head back and froze, cold horror dancing up his spine.

The shed had glowed. For an instant. Just for the merest fraction of a second. *But it had glowed.* Dull reddish rays of light like nothing Hammond had ever seen before had streamed from the partly-open door into the garden, streaked down from the tiny slit between the tops of the planks and the roof and oozed between the planks themselves.

Hammond grabbed Stevenson's arm, seeking human contact, needing to be reminded that this was real and not a nightmare.

Then the tall soldier moved back into the section of the garden Hammond could see. He was leading a man in ragged clothes and a cloth cap who had his hands tied behind his back. A quivering white shape came up behind them and in its depths Hammond could make out a face which seemed to be looking directly at him with malevolent, animal eyes.

Stevenson put his hand on Hammond's head and pushed him down.

'O.K.,' Hammond whispered, 'What now?'

'There's one chance,' Stevenson said. He paused, then added, 'I think my plan can work. Come on.'

He started back down the drainage ditch towards the car and Hammond followed.

Hammond and Stevenson were away from the car for no more than five minutes but that five minutes took its toll on Tanya's nerves. She sat in the driver's seat, staring around the treeline, across the field at the shapes and figures moving about. Then she shifted her attention to her hand, which rested on the ignition key, and it seemed a strange alien thing. She began to worry that it might twitch around of its own accord and the engine would growl and bring all those *things* rushing towards the car. She was thinking about what she would do if that happened, imagining the pursuit down the hill, the car hurtling along the dim track, when she sensed there was something in the car with her.

She spun around quickly but the back seat was empty. *Best to be sure.* She bent forward and searched the space between the seats with her hand.

Nothing. It had been her imagination.

But what if there was something outside the car watching her?

She had started a methodical search of the foliage at the edge of the track when she heard a *splosh* sound and saw Hammond and Stevenson climbing out of the drainage ditch.

'Did you find it?' she said as they both slipped into the back seat.

'Yes,' Hammond said.

'And?'

'I think my plan has a good chance of working,' Stevenson said, 'but it won't be easy. All three of us will have to play our part.'

'I'd rather Tanya was left out of this,' Hammond said. 'I wish . . .'

'No. We need Tanya. We need three people to have any chance.' He turned to Tanya. 'But it's up to you . . .'

'I'll do what I can.'

'O.K. Just tell us what to do,' Hammond said.

'Right. First of all it's going to be dangerous, very, very, dangerous, but it has to be done.' He hunched forward, resting his elbows on his knees. 'Let's start with you, Jon. You cross the track into the woods, circle round and come up as close behind the shed as you can. It's your job to get the skull and destroy it.'

'But how . . .'

'How can you get past those entities in the garden? That's where Tanya and I come in. Everything that each one of us does depends on the other one doing everything absolutely correctly. When you're in position behind the shed, I'll make my move. I'll go out into the field and draw them away.'

'But . . .'

'No buts. It's the only way.'

He looked at Tanya now. 'When I draw them towards me, I'll leave it till the last minute then I'll signal you with a wave of my hand. When you see that, you turn on the car lights and keep flashing them, turn on the radio as loud as you can and keep sounding the horn. The noise and the lights will confuse them and give me a chance of making it back to the car. In the meantime, with any luck, Jon will have got inside the shed and smashed the skull to pieces. Remember, all these entities are here because of the skull. Their power depends on the skull. When it's smashed, they may not disappear immediately but their power will be diminished. Clear?'

He looked from Tanya to Hammond and back again.

'I don't know,' Hammond said. 'You going out into that field . . . I just don't know . . .'

'It's got to be done. It's dangerous for all of us. You just wait till you think the moment is right . . . then go for that skull and don't let anything stop you.' He glanced at his watch. 'I'll give you ten minutes before I move . . . oh, and you had better take something as a weapon . . .'

'I'll get the tyre lever from the boot, that's solid steel.'

'Fine. Let's do it then.'

Hammond leaned forward, wrapped his arms around Tanya and held her tightly. After a moment, he leaned back, gently opened the car door and stepped out without another word.

Stevenson and Tanya watched him going to the boot for the tyre lever and heard the metallic whispering of the boot's hinges. Then they saw him jogging across the track and down the slope into the trees.

To Hammond it seemed as if the forest was breathing but he told himself as he jogged through the wet leaves and dodged dark trees that it was just a combination of natural things: wet vegetation expanding after the rain, wind murmuring in the foliage, raindrops dribbling from the treetops and hitting the fallen leaves with a whispered plop.

He headed north, running parallel to the track for several

minutes, then turned west, re-crossed the track and entered the woods behind the cottage.

Beyond the fence at the bottom of George Murdoch's garden, a brief, bare slope rose gently to the forest. When Hammond reached the treeline, he threw himself forward onto his belly.

From this position, he could see clearly into the garden and what he saw chilled his blood.

THIRTY-FOUR

Below Hammond, the garden was a mass of activity. As he stared down, his body pressed into the carpet of damp leaves, he realized for the first time that he and Stevenson had seen only a small corner of the garden from their position in the drainage ditch.

What he saw was overpowering; it overwhelmed his emotions. Somehow he couldn't take it all in. It was one thing to listen to Stevenson talk about discarnate entities and the paranormal but this was *real*, he was witnessing this with his own eyes.

Or was it real? He wasn't sure any more.

Three glowing shapes, in the folds of which Hammond thought he could make out men, flitted across the garden, hesitating by the shed then moving on.

By the cottage wall, a makeshift gallows had been set up. As Hammond watched, a soldier dragged a woman roughly up onto a stool, adjusted the noose around her neck then kicked the stool away. Hammond closed his eyes for a moment, shutting out the sight of the jumping, jerking body.

Several soldiers guarded the shed, shuffling aimlessly about, grotesque, mis-shapen, gaunt figures in the black uniform of the SS. Hammond selected one man and studied him – a thick-set figure of medium height in an officer's uniform. The man was bent and twisted, one shoulder held much higher than the other, and his uniform hung on him as if it had been made for a much bigger man, the sleeves almost hiding the skeletal hands. The skin of his face was as thin as tissue paper and drawn tightly over the jutting cheekbones and the eyes were so deeply sunken in their sockets that Hammond couldn't see them. The soldiers were like corpses, Hammond thought. Corpses who had lain a long time in their graves then been brought out, resurrected to follow their master, to be his honour guard through the centuries.

Away to his right, a group of naked men and women of all

ages jogged to the edge of a pit which Hammond could see was already half-filled with bodies. They lined up facing the pit, their faces drained of emotion. A line of soldiers behind them raised their rifles listlessly, bored by their endless task. There was a ragged volley of fire and the men and women toppled forward into the pit.

But why had the shooting sound seemed so far away, Hammond wondered.

The execution squad was no more than fifty yards from where he lay and yet the rifle fire had seemed to come from miles away, sighing through the trees.

In the centre of the garden stood two men in suits, gesticulating as if they were arguing but Hammond could hear no words. *They* looked real enough, he thought, but then noticed there was a strangeness about them too, an awkwardness in their movements, a puffed, twisted look about their faces. Then one of them turned and Hammond saw the right side of his face was putrid, swollen obscenely.

Hammond was dazed by all he saw, a reclining frozen statue in the damp leaves. It was the glow from the shed which snapped him out of it, reminding him of who he was, where he was and what he was meant to be doing. It was the same dull, reddish glow as before and again it lasted for only a fraction of a second but this time he saw it more clearly because there was a tiny window at the back of the shed and the glow funnelled out, illuminating a long narrow section of the grassy slope.

He edged forward and slithered diagonally down the slope to a bush no more than twenty feet from the shed. His eyes darted across the garden, trying to see if he had been spotted. The thought of what had happened to Preece lanced into his mind and made him shiver.

Another volley of distant rifle fire sighed over him and he saw a second row of bodies topple forward into the pit. Then the soldiers and the pit and the area around them seemed to shimmer, the outlines growing fainter and he realized this was just an image, like a picture on a television screen, as insubstantial as a puff of smoke.

That was when he heard the scream, a terrible shriek that made his spine bristle and instantly stepped up the beating of his heart to a wild *thud-thud-thud-thud-thud*.

* * *

'It's time,' Stevenson said, switching his gaze from the field to Tanya and she looked into his eyes and saw resignation and a heavy sadness there.

'Roy, be . . .'

'Be careful. I will. Funny thing, my mother always said that to me.' His laugh came out as a sigh. 'Now, listen, Tanya,' he said, his face hardening. 'That man of yours is big and tough and he's a survivor . . . You have to think of yourself. Just do what I've told you but . . . if anything goes wrong, if they enter me, I want you to get away from here as fast as you can. Drive like hell and don't stop for anything. You'll have a good chance. Remember, they'll be attracted to me.'

'Oh, Roy,' she sobbed. She threw her arms around his neck and held his face against hers, feeling the tears running down her cheeks. After a moment he lifted her arms away and stepped out of the car.

'What are our chances?' she whispered.

He shrugged. 'Who knows. But we have to try.'

He turned away, jumped the drainage ditch, lowered the top strand of barbed wire and stepped over the fence into the field. As he started forward he didn't look back towards Tanya because he feared that if he did he might lose his nerve and let everybody down. He was in no doubt about what he was up against.

If he had looked back he would have seen the dark form behind the car which was growing and spreading, taking on the shape of a man, a tall man in a black uniform with fair hair and cruel, blue eyes.

Hammond spun his head around, his eyes zipping across the garden, searching for the source of the scream. It had seemed so near. But where . . .

Then the scream came again, this time dissolving into hysterical laughter.

His eyes focused on the cottage window where a weak yellow light fell into the garden and he was transfixed by what he saw.

The dim, shadowy figures of twenty or so men and women were crowded into the room, some half dressed, most naked. There were thin, gaunt young men, fat old women, middle-aged men with protruding bellies and young girls whose faces seemed to have rotted away. They were piled on the floor in the centre of the room, lying on the table and heaped across a large, easy chair. They were swigging wine from tall, green bottles and indulging in every sexual perversion Hammond had ever heard of and many he had not. He saw whips, canes, chains and steaming pokers thrust into yielding, putrid flesh.

Hammond stared at the scene for a long time until he felt he was actually among them, one of them, touching and being touched, licking, biting, drinking.

He dragged his eyes away and looked down at the shed and that was when he saw the dark form behind it, hovering behind a pile of wood. A pair of white eyes seemed to be looking up towards the trees. Hammond moved deeper into the bush behind which he hid. As his eyes drifted away he caught sight of another dark shape, by the bottom of a rusted drainpipe at the back of the house. Then he saw another and another and wondered why he hadn't seen them before. They were everywhere, loitering in the darkest places.

It's not possible, a voice in his head said. *You're never going to get at the skull.*

Surely Stevenson had never envisaged anything like this? A wave of panic broke over him. *The plan could never work. It had no chance.*

He had to get back to the car. He had to tell Stevenson what he had seen. He had to get Tanya away from all this.

He swung his head around and looked up the slope, gauging how long it would take him to scramble back to the treeline.

Then he heard Stevenson shouting.

Tanya watched Stevenson walking purposefully into the field, her left hand on the radio knob, her right hand on the light switch, waiting for his signal.

Four pale shapes on the hillock ahead of Stevenson seemed to freeze and half turn, suddenly aware of Stevenson's presence. An electric charge filled the air. Then the shapes began to glide rapidly towards Stevenson. The other shapes and figures had seen him now too and it was as if he was a magnet, as if everything in the field was shooting towards him.

Tension pain began to gnaw at Tanya's wrists.

Make the signal, a tiny voice inside her head pleaded with Stevenson. *Make the signal now and run.*

When the shapes from the field drew to within twenty feet of him she saw Stevenson begin to turn.

She never saw if he made the signal or not. She did not flash the lights or turn on the radio or sound the horn as she was supposed to because at that moment a black-uniformed man with cruel, blue eyes pulled open the car door and lunged at her.

Stevenson's yelling jerked Hammond's eyes up and he looked over the cottage roof. He could see Stevenson running across the field, shouting something indistinguishable at the top of his voice, surrounded by figures and glowing shapes which pulled and snatched at him.

A surge of emotion seized at Hammond's throat. He had to help his friend. He had to do something.

Abruptly he switched his gaze to the far corner of the field, to the section of the track where the car was parked.

Where were the lights? Tanya was supposed to be flashing the lights and sounding the horn and yet there was only silence and dimness in that corner of the field.

Something was wrong. Something had happened to Tanya.

He began to stand up, his mind racing.

He had to do something for Stevenson. He had to get to Tanya. They had to get away from all this. . . .

Suddenly he realized the garden below was emptying. Glowing shapes whipped around the cottage towards the front. Soldiers unslung their rifles and lurched out of the garden into the field. The image of the gallows disappeared.

Then his mind cleared. He knew what he had to do. Stevenson had been right. This was his chance.

The dark form he had seen at the back of the shed was gone now. The last soldier was hurrying across the garden, heading away from him.

He started to run down the slope now, jerking the tyre lever out of his pocket.

Tanya tried to fight but it was useless. The man's strength was awesome. He yanked her coat down from her shoulders, trapping her arms. Her blouse was ripped open, her bra dragged down and the cold, dead-man's hands cupped her breasts. His wide mouth folded over hers, his tongue thrust into her and she gagged at the fetid smell of his breath and the rotting taste of him. Her head was swimming when he pulled his mouth away and began to fumble with the belt on her skirt.

Just before he pushed her into a reclining position across the seats she looked through the window for an instant and saw that Stevenson had fallen down. All the shapes and figures in the field were gathered around him.

Hammond hurdled the fence and swung left, sprinting for the shed door.

It was going to be easy. So easy. He couldn't believe his luck.

The garden was empty now, just like any other garden.

Stevenson's plan had worked. As he kicked his way past overgrown bushes and shrubs, something in his brain began to laugh and the laugh rose to a hysterical giggle.

His mind raced ahead of him. What would it look like? Just like any other skull, he supposed. Perhaps slightly smaller, its owner hadn't been a very big man.

Then the shed glowed and in the narrow beam of red light which spilled from the slightly open door, he saw a pale shape away to his right, near the cottage wall.

He was not alone.

He kicked harder, concentrating on the shed door, aware that the shape had started to glide towards him.

He raised a hand, ready to shove the door open and plunge into the dim interior.

What if he couldn't see it straight away? What if he couldn't find it? Tanya? Roy? Were they all right. Their lives might depend on him, hang on what he did. He was five feet from the shed when the door slammed shut. A surge of anger rushed through him. He swung his hand in front of him and dropped his shoulder. Nothing was going to stop him now.

He was running at full speed when his seventeen-stone bulk hit the wooden door, shattering it, sending jagged splinters flying through the air, wrenching the hinges from their sockets.

The bulk of the door thudded to the floor of the shed, sending up a cloud of dust.

Through the dust he saw the skull. It was a frail, white thing lying on its side on the floor.

As he tried to step into the shed, he felt hands gripping his arm. The shape had reached him and folded all around him and a hideous, putrid, old man's face was thrust close up to his.

He heard himself roar with anger and swung the tyre lever through the air, hacking and stabbing at the face, which twisted into a silent scream.

The grip on his arm weakened and with one huge effort he snatched it free and leapt into the shed.

The instant he crossed the threshold everything changed. It was as if he was not in the shed at all but trapped in a capsule filled with colours and images and noises which were so loud they threatened to drive him crazy.

Before his eyes, columns of Panzer tanks raised dust clouds as they clattered and clanked through desolated cities, vast crowds stood with their right arms extended in the Nazi salute, corpses swayed on barely visible gallows, shells whined through the air and exploded in great white clouds where people huddled in the remains of tenements. The noise was so piercing that he felt his eardrums might burst. Machine guns rattled, bombs exploded, thousands of voices shouted '*Sieg heil*' over and over and over. *Sieg heil. Sieg heil. Sieg heil.* Rough soldiers' voices sang the song he had come to know so well – the Horst Wessel song.

It's not real, not real, not real, a voice echoed in his mind. *Get the skull!*

Through the whirlpool of images, Hammond saw the skull and it seemed to be emanating all the colours of the rainbow in quivering shafts. As he stared at it, it seemed to him that two piercing, malevolent eyes were glaring back at him, but the sockets were empty.

He started to move forward but it was like walking against the current in a rain-swollen river.

He had gone only two paces when he felt hands grabbing at his waist, pulling him back. He turned awkwardly and lashed out again with the tyre lever. He saw that the figure holding him was not the one he had struggled with in the garden. It was one of the soldiers who had been guarding the shed and his skeletal fingers bit through Hammond's flesh.

Beyond him, other shapes and figures were funnelling in through the door of the shed now, reaching for Hammond. He thrust and hacked all about him, the tyre lever dancing through the air like a sword. Fists punched into him, boots kicked at his legs trying to trip him up and remorselessly he was being drawn away from the skull, out of the shed.

Suddenly he felt his grip on the tyre lever loosen. A punch on the arm sent it spinning from his grasp. He snatched for it but missed, hitting the metal bar with the side of his hand, sending it flying across the shed.

The weight of the bodies clawing at him now forced him to one knee. Something that could have been a fist or a boot crunched into his lower side and he winced at the new surge of pain as two ribs cracked

Now or never, Hammond. Now or never.

Powerful, cold bony hands began to twist his right arm up behind his back.

He took a deep breath, gathered all his awesome strength, kicked himself to his feet and leapt backwards, diving for the skull.

The skull's the thing, Hammond, Stevenson's voice said in his head. *Their power comes from the skull.*

He landed with a thud on the floor of the shed, his fingers stretching for the pale white skull. Hands grabbed at his feet, pulling him away but he jerked himself forward again.

It was there, within his grasp now. He could see the small hole in the top where the suicide bullet had exited and the thin threads of fractures running away from it.

Take it, Hammond. Take it.

He thrust his right hand forward and looped a finger through the eye socket.

It was cold. So cold.

He raised the skull high in the air and crashed it to the floor. Two fragments broke away from around the bullet hole. An astonishing weight dropped onto his back and he felt as if his spine might snap. But he raised the skull again and punched it onto the floor for a second time. More fragments flew away, scattering around the shed.

He felt himself being lifted aloft but he held the skull to his chest and rolled his body around it. Hands punched and scratched at him but he was beyond pain now, his body numb.

He jammed his fingers into the hole in the top of the skull now and worked away at it, tearing out chunk after chunk, some coming away like chalk in his hands, some so hard it ripped his nails back.

He was being carried roughly out of the shed now, shoulder-high. He tugged at the widening hole again and this time a large lump of bone fell away and a cry rose up from the figures around him, a cry of pain and intense anguish.

He was thrown down outside the shed and something stamped fiercely on his leg, snapping the bone. He rolled over, his mind wavering on the slender borderline between consciousness and unconsciousness. There was a tap beside him with a concrete slab underneath and a drainage grill. He hammered the skull into the metal tap and a great section fell away.

Desperate hands tried to drag him across the garden but he kicked with his good leg and banged the skull into the tap again. Fingers scrambled over him, grabbing at his hair, thrusting into his eyes. But. . . .

Were they getting weaker? Was their strength ebbing?

He raised the skull high into the air and smashed it into the concrete slab with both hands.

It broke into half a dozen pieces.

Instantly the hands around his head and shoulders disappeared. Two hands still tugged at his ankle and he rolled onto his back and lashed out with his good leg. The SS officer with the sunken eyes took the full brunt of the kick in the face and fell back. Weakly he propped himself up on one elbow and looked at Hammond, his eyes pleading, his face filled with melancholy.

Hammond swung himself into a seated position and began to stamp on the skull fragments, crunching them to dust.

When he had finished he turned on the tap and watched as a great gush of water washed the white substance away.

The garden was almost empty now. Far away to his right, two pale shapes seemed to be embracing each other, whimpering strangely. The SS officer's outline began to waver and he started to disappear, shrivelling up before Hammond's eyes.

Hammond didn't know if he passed out or not but he could never recall crawling out of the garden. It took him twenty minutes to drag himself across the field and in that time the pain returned, a thousand stabbing pinpoints of torture.

He found Stevenson hanging on the barbed wire fence, his head twisted round, eyes sightless. He searched for a pulse but of course there was none.

He pulled himself upright with the help of a fence post and managed to get through the barbed wire.

'Tanya,' he rasped and realized his teeth were broken and his mouth was full of blood.

He flopped into the drainage ditch and dragged himself up onto the track.

'Tanya.'

The car door was open. It creaked in a gentle wind. He grabbed it and pulled his body into the car.

'Tanya?' he whispered.

She was in the back seat, her knees drawn tightly up under her chin, her fingers clutching her coat tightly around her.

Her eyes were strange, distant and filled with pain.

'It's me, Tanya,' he said quietly. 'It's Jon.'

He reached over and touched her and she drew back with a gasp as if someone had flicked a hot poker across her skin.

'Tanya, can you drive? My leg's broken.'

After a moment she said, 'I can drive,' and great tears filled her eyes and tumbled down her cheeks.

As they drove back towards Batforth, Hammond saw several white shapes moving about in the foliage near the track. They seemed confused, lost, insignificant.

Once he heard a sound far away to his left like someone wailing deep in the forest, crying for help.

EPILOGUE

Hammond had worked out a system in which he could rest his plastered leg on a stool under his desk and type quite comfortably.

He was seated in this position now, three weeks after the events at Murdoch's farm, writing a story about a missing Batforth boy.

It was quarter to twelve when Ernie Spiers said, 'Nearly the big moment.'

Hammond nodded. 'Yes, the taxi should be here any minute. Tanya will be so glad to get out of hospital, so glad to be in her own house again.'

'Did you see her last night?' Jemma asked.

Hammond nodded.

'How was she?'

'Fine. She's been much better this last week. They've cut right back on her sedatives.'

He stood up, hopped round the desk and jammed his metal crutch under his armpit.

'I ordered the taxi for ten to twelve,' he said. 'It'll probably take me at least five minutes to get down the stairs.'

It had been a hectic three weeks for Hammond.

He had sold several variations of the skull story to newspapers and magazines all over the world. At first, editors had been loath to buy the story. It seemed too way-out, too improbable, too far-fetched. But then a police sergeant called William Joss had told about his experience and Jemma and Ernie Spiers told what had happened to them and Hammond had become something of an international figure.

He had been interviewed by all the television networks, the subject of a thirty-minute documentary and had been invited to Edinburgh to describe his experience at length to a professor who specialized in the paranormal. In the past week he had been offered a handful of jobs, all of which paid more than double what he earned at the *Courier* but he hadn't made any decisions yet.

Stevenson's funeral at the Ruttlake cemetery had been a harrowing experience on two counts. It was bad enough to have lost a good friend but he also had to contend with a heavy burden of guilt too; the knowledge that if not for him Stevenson would never have come to Batforth and would be alive today. He found it hard to face Stevenson's sister and aunt and the cousins who had gathered from around the country. Immediately after the graveside service he had asked William Joss to drive him back to Batforth.

The taxi was waiting for him now as he emerged from the *Courier* building and he slid into the back seat and managed to shut the door behind him.

'Hospital is it, Jon?' the cabbie said and Hammond nodded.

The houses and shops of Batforth went past in a blur.

The first week had been hell for Tanya. Her sleep racked with dreams, she had spent most of her time heavily sedated. But there had been a dramatic improvement in the past few days and she was virtually back to her normal self now.

When they drew up at the hospital, Hammond said, 'Wait for me, will you, Tom?'

He edged himself out of the car and swung his way along the pathway to the main entrance, surprisingly good on his crutch now.

Tanya was waiting for him, fully dressed, her bags packed. He was surprised at how good she looked. The colour had come back to her cheeks and the heavy-lidded, sedated look she had had in her eyes was gone.

'Ready to go home?' he said and she nodded. 'I'm ready.'

One of the other nurses carried Tanya's bag to the taxi and kissed and hugged Tanya before she got in.

She and Hammond didn't talk much on the way to Tanya's cottage. They just sat wrapped in each other's arms.

At the cottage she poured him a beer and sat on his good knee and he said, 'How do you feel? Really?'

'Fit as a fiddle,' she said and smiled her old smile. 'Did you miss me?'

He nodded then grinned wryly and said, 'Haven't had a good meal in three weeks.'

She smacked him playfully on the cheek. 'Feel like a good steak?' she said.

'No, you don't feel up to cooking right now. I was only joking.'

'No . . . really . . . I'd like to cook you a meal.'

'All right.'

He relaxed in the easy chair, sipping his beer and watching television as the steaks sizzled and the potatoes fried.

It was about ten minutes later when she started singing and he recognized the song immediately and stiffened. He pulled himself to his feet, snatched up the crutch and hobbled along the hall.

'Tanya,' he shouted.

Then he noticed her voice had grown deeper, rasping and throaty.

'Tanya,' he said going into the kitchen. 'Why are you singing that song? I didn't know you could speak German.'

She was bent over the sink, resting on her elbows, looking out into the night as if searching for somebody.

She continued to sing, in a man's voice now. The words of the Horst Wessel song rang harshly through the house.

'Tanya,' he yelled and she spun around and faced him. He saw that her eyes had changed. They were no longer brown. Now they were a piercing blue, cold and malevolent.